TWICE THE HOT LEAD, TWICE THE HOT LOVIN' IN A GIANT SPECIAL EDITION!

AMBUSH!

Buckskin looked around the store at the various implements and tools of the mining trade, then checked out the window. The man was still there, only Black Hat had moved to the other side of the storefront. Buckskin left the store and walked quickly to a 40-foot-wide slot between the buildings, where nothing had been built yet. He stepped just around the corner, drew his six-gun, and pressed against the wall.

The man came around the corner of the store walking fast. He had no chance to stop when he saw Buckskin.

"That's it, friend, just keep coming. You and me gonna have ourselves a nice chat back here in the alley. No! Keep your hand away from that iron unless you want to get planted out on the hill. No man can beat an already drawn hogleg. Easy now. Fold your arms on your chest and walk up here."

They were in the space between the buildings but only 20 feet from the street when a second man in a black hat jumped into the void and lifted a shotgun aimed directly at Buckskin. The detective from Denver knew the shotgunner was going to pull the trigger. He shifted his sights to the right and fired....

The *Buckskin* Series from *Leisure Books:*
#42: MORGAN'S SQUAW
#41: GOLD TOWN GAL
#40: SIX-GUN KILL
#39: BLAZING SIX-GUNS
#38: DERRINGER DANGER

Double Editions:
RETURN FIRE/RIMFIRE REVENGE
SCATTERGUN/APACHE RIFLES
LARAMIE SHOWDOWN/DOUBLE ACTION
COLT CROSSING/POWDER CHARGE

Giant Editions:
SHOTGUN!
BAWDY HOUSE
MUZZLE BLAST

GIANT SPECIAL EDITION

BUCKSKIN

CRIPPLE CREEK SONGBIRD

— Kit Dalton —

LEISURE BOOKS **NEW YORK CITY**

A LEISURE BOOK®

November 1995

Published by

Dorchester Publishing Co., Inc.
276 Fifth Avenue
New York, NY 10001

BUCKSKIN
CRIPPLE CREEK SONGBIRD

Chapter One

The rifle shot slammed over the loaded freight wagon like a whisper of death, and Buckskin Lee Morgan crouched lower on top of a long cardboard box where he had been catching a quick nap. The four-horse team pulling the rig slowed as the man in the driver's seat jerked back on the reins.

Buckskin pressed tightly against the freight where he was hidden from the gunman, who must be in front of the rig.

"Hands in the air, teamster, and I won't gut-shoot ya," a loud voice called.

Buckskin had drawn his six-gun at the first sound of the rifle shot, and now held it ready as he tried to see around or over the freight without giving himself away. He peered through a space between a box of apples and a bolt of cloth. On the near side of the big wagon he spotted one man who wore a kerchief mask pulled up over his nose and rode a roan.

Figuring the range automatically, Buckskin decided the target was no more than 30 feet away. He sighted in and fired between the freight. Immediately Buckskin jolted upright, cocked the hammer again and swung his six-gun to cover a second rider he found gawking at his partner. The first robber had slammed out of his saddle and lay groaning on the ground.

The second masked man held a rifle, but before he could lift it to aim, he took Buckskin's .44 round in his shoulder. He dropped the rifle but held his saddle.

"That all of them?" Buckskin asked the teamster.

The driver still held the reins in his hands, but they were frozen in place. Buckskin had to shake him to bring him out of his dazed condition.

Shorty Nelson, the driver, bellowed in surprise. "Land a' Goshen! I never done been robbed before. Them nasty varmints actually shot at me. Did you hear that rifle round part my hair?"

Buckskin had dropped down from the wagon, taken the six-guns away from both masked men and pushed the rifleman down in the dirt beside his partner. The first man Buckskin had shot yelled in pain and stared at the others. The bloodstain on his chest kept growing and he had turned pale.

"You done killed me. That's what you done. Just a little robbery. Nothing to kill a man over." He stared at Buckskin, shook his head and then wailed in pain. He tried to lift up from where he lay at the side of the trail, but couldn't. He blinked, tried to say something, then flopped down, his head whacking the ground hard. A long sigh gushed from the robber's dead lungs.

Buckskin knelt in front of the dead man, reached over and closed his eyelids. "Robbery's a hanging offense in this county," he said to the other man. "You ever thought about stretching a rope?"

The man looked up, terror staining his face. He shook his head. Buckskin backhanded him across the face. The man barked in pain, then glared at Buckskin.

"What the hell you do that for?"

"You just tried to rob the supply wagon, remember? Somebody put you up to this?"

"Put us up?" the man snorted. He looked to Buckskin to be about 20, no older. "Naw, we just ran out of money and out of food, so we figured we'd relieve the wagon of a couple of sacks of grub and head out for Denver."

Buckskin looked at Shorty, the driver. "What do you want to do with them?"

"Hell, you shot the guy, Buckskin. Ain't much law yet in Cripple Creek. I don't want to bother with them. Take his rifle and his six-gun and make him bury his friend there. Then send him scampering for Denver. You take the dead man's horse and saddle. He sure as hell won't be needing it."

They did it that way.

The rest of the way into Cripple Creek, Colorado, home of the latest gold strike in the West,

Buckskin talked to the driver, trying to learn all he could about the new little town.

"Cripple Creek's grown a bunch since a year ago, I've heard," Buckskin said.

Shorty Nelson sent a long squirt of brown juice off the side of the wagon with the wind. He wiped the sides of his mustache and nodded. "Damn well better believe it. When old Alonzo Welty started this hauling operation just a little over a year ago, we didn't do much business t'all. Now we could use two wagons and sometimes three just hauling food into town. The closest railroad to here is at Florissant. Roads is terrible going the other way into Colorado Springs."

"You said there's not much law in town?"

"Not much, not much of any. County sheriff is over in the Springs. We supposed to have a deputy sheriff here sometimes, but now he's here and then he ain't."

"Is there a town marshal?"

"I guess so. Don't rightly know because I don't get me into no trouble."

"So when did they hit the first strike here?" Buckskin asked.

"That one's easy, October 20, 1890. Bob Womack done it. Got the whole shebang started. Warn't till the next May that the first mining district was formed. Hell, I was in on that. Then two months later we had a townsite plotted with the county and things began to take off.

"Hail, by November of 1891 we had the Count here with money, and he paid eighty thousand dollars for a claim. After that the rush was really on. Takes money to dig gold out of the rocks, lots of money."

"How many people in Cripple Creek now, Shorty?"

"Hail, I'd say nigh on to two thousand souls. Women and kids all over the place. Getting to be a regular city, by damn."

They rode along in silence for a ways. Then Shorty sent another squirt of tobacco juice over the side and stared at Buckskin.

"You ain't coming here for gold, plain to see. Way you used that six-gun, I'd figure you might be a lawman, but don't ken no badge. You on the trail of some wanted?"

"In a way, Shorty. Actually I'm searching for a runaway, a girl about eighteen. You didn't give her a ride into the camp three or four days ago, did you?"

Shorty chuckled and shook his head. "You ain't married, are you, son? Not likely I'd give a pretty like that a ride. My old woman would have my hide. Got a stage that makes a round trip a day now from Florissant, or at least it does sometimes. You said it was all busted down today."

"Think back, you might have seen her. She's about five-two, long blond hair, eighteen years old, pretty little thing."

Shorty chuckled. "If I'd seen a pretty like her I'd have remembered. Don't cost nothing to look at them, just don't touch."

They ground around the side of a slope and then angled up a gentle rise. They could see some buildings in the distance.

"There she is, Cripple Creek," Shorty said. "Unlikely place for a town, so after the mines close, probably won't be nothing here but ghosts of these former good times."

"You're a philosopher, Shorty. How did you get so smart?"

"Living fifty-one damned years, body's got to smarten up a little along the way."

"Any one man or group of men in town who control things?"

"Hail, not yet. No time for that. Every man is for hisself; out to get rich quick while the gold is still here. Oh, we have a few merchants who are doing fine. Honest, hardworking types. But there ain't no king of Cripple Creek, if'n that's what you're askin'."

"That was it. I like to know what I'm up against when I come into a new town."

"This girl, she a whore?"

"Her father hopes not. He's one of the richest men in Denver and he wants her back safe, sound and undamaged. She told her friends that she was fascinated with the gold rush and she was furious that just because she was a girl she couldn't go."

"Not many ways for a woman alone to make a living in Cripple Creek. She couldn't hire out as a maid like she could in Colorado Springs, or as a girl in an office. Here whoring and singing like a bird are about the only two things a woman can do."

"Doesn't help me much. How many hotels in town?"

"No problem there, just one. Miners who have

hit it big have built houses of their own. The ones with an unproductive claim can't afford a hotel or a boardinghouse so they use a tent. Lots of tents around. Only two boardinghouses. Be your best bet to find the young lady. A pretty like that shouldn't be hard to find. Not many in Cripple Creek yet."

Soon they were in town, rolling down a main street that had no sign on it. Shorty cut into an alley and stopped in back of a store with a sign for Alexander's Hardware and General Store.

"End of the line. Thanks for stopping that robbery. They might have decided to take the whole damn wagon and shot me full of holes. I 'preciate it."

Buckskin shook his hand and looked at the freight. "Want me to help unload?"

"Hail, no. You got important things to do. Besides, Abe has a kid to help him now. He ain't too big, but a gutsy little guy. There he comes."

A slender boy looked out the back door of the frame store, then pushed the door open and blocked it with a nail keg. He was short, maybe 16, Buckskin figured, with close-cut dark hair and a grin.

"Shorty, you made it again," the kid said. Buckskin waved at the boy and Shorty and took off down the alley. After talking to a lot of people in Denver, he'd at last found a ticket agent who remembered Harriet Braithwaite. She had purchased a ticket to Colorado Springs. He was six days behind her and had no idea where he was going to start looking.

There was no law in town to help him, he had learned. So first he'd check a couple of saloons. The fancy ladies often knew more in a town like this than anybody else. He'd start with the Cripple Emporium.

It wasn't hard to find. A two-story false front blared the name in rich red and yellow paint. Inside he found the usual stand-up bar along one side. There was poker, faro, blackjack, seven-up and even a roulette wheel. Toward the back he saw dozens of chairs, and then a small stage at the far end of the 100-foot-long building. A stairway went up the near side to some rooms over the back one-third of the building.

The barkeep drew him a beer but said they didn't have any fancy women in the place.

"Bossman's wife won't allow it," the apron said. "She and the kids live upstairs. Built it like a house up there."

At the next saloon he found half-a-dozen girls and he asked them what they knew about a small blond girl, new to town within the last two or three days.

"Hey, we got enough competition now," one said.

"Darling, you have a name?" Buckskin asked.

"They call me Chunk, just cause I have a few pounds on me. I'm good at poking. Give you a nice soft ride, better than them skinny bitches."

"I bet you could, Chunk. I don't have the time right now. Have you heard anything about a Harriet new to town?"

"Not a word. Course I don't get out much." All the girls laughed.

"We don't get many new girls here nowadays. For a time we got a new one every day or so, but things slowed down just a hair."

Buckskin thanked them and moved on to the next saloon. After talking to girls at the eight big saloons in town, he hadn't turned up any hint of a new girl among the whores. Good news.

He checked out the two boardinghouses next. Each was run by a widow of a man killed recently in the mines. Neither woman said she'd rented a room to a small, pretty blond lady within the past year. He thanked them and tried the hotel next. He took a room for the night and talked to the desk clerk. They looked back in the register for the past six days: no Harriet.

"Sir, I'm a single man," said the clerk "and if a delightful little lady like this came in here, I'd be sure to remember her." The clerk gave the picture back to Buckskin and nodded. "Oh, yes, I'd remember a remarkable little woman like that one."

"Watch out for her for me, would you?" Buckskin slipped the man two one-dollar greenbacks.

"Yes, sir, Mr. Morgan, I surely will. I've put you in Room 212 in front the way you asked. Can I help you with your bag?"

A few minutes later, Buckskin dropped on the lumpy bed and looked at the wallpapered ceiling. So far he'd found absolutely nothing. He'd stopped in Colorado Springs only long enough to get a ticket on the spur line running to Florissant. That was exactly what he'd figured Harriet had done.

She must have wanted to get to the gold fields as quickly as possible.

Now he was having his doubts. Where could a pretty 18-year-old blonde hide in this town? It wasn't that big. There were few things she could work at. She had some spending money and a bank draft with her, but her money wouldn't last long. What in the world would a pampered girl do in Colorado Springs or in Cripple Creek? He shook his head in dismay.

The job had started out easily enough. Twice he'd received envelopes, hand-delivered, at his small office on Prescott Street in San Francisco. He went there only occasionally, and the last time he found both envelopes, both with the engraved return of Hercules Braithwaite.

The Braithwaite name was one to reckon with in Denver in 1892. He opened one of the envelopes first and read the terse note.

Seeing you haven't responded to my previous invitation, I'll extend it again. I need to see you in my office here on Cherry Street as soon as possible. It concerns one of my family and is of utmost importance to me. H. Braithwaite.

Morgan tore open the other envelope and found an earlier date and much the same message. That afternoon he caught a train to Denver, went to 476 Cherry Street and found himself hurried up in the elevator. The private office of Hercules Braithwaite was on the tenth floor of the Braithwaite Building.

All he saw at first was a luxurious office, a huge cherry-wood desk without a thing on it, and a high leather chair with the back toward the desk. Over the top of the chair hung a considerable cloud of blue smoke. A quick sniff confirmed that it was cigar smoke.

Buckskin didn't cough or clear his throat. He simply stood and waited. All of the patience that he possessed he had learned from an Indian friend. He had no doubt he could outwait the millionaire.

After a two-minute stall, the chair turned slowly and Buckskin had his first look at the self-styled Demon of Denver.

Braithwaite stood from the chair to his full six-foot, six-inch height and leaned on the desk. His face showed anger in a frame of white hair, mustache and beard.

"Morgan, where the hell have you been? My daughter is missing. Has been missing for four days now, and I want you to find her."

Buckskin watched the other man. Braithwaite relaxed a little and sat down. His shoulders slumped, and his face lost its anger and softened into pain, frustration and worry.

He quickly explained the situation. "The school wired me the day she was due in and said she didn't arrive. I alerted my people all along the line, but my guess is she never intended to go to Chicago. For weeks she's been asking me to take her to the gold fields down in Cripple Creek. I've declined, saying it's no place for a woman. I worked the gold fields. I know.

"My people have talked with the trainmen who took her away that first day. She had a compartment. The porter said he never saw her after the Fort Morgan stop eastbound. That's about seventy miles east of here. My guess is that she doubled back to Denver, disguised herself somehow and got a ticket south toward Cripple Creek.

"I want you to find Harriet. I have a packet of pictures, what she likes to do, what foods she likes, everything I think that might help you. My people are not detectives. They try, but they aren't as good as you are.

"I'll pay you fifteen dollars a day, and any expenses you think are prudent, until you find her and bring her home safely. I want her undamaged, do I make myself clear?"

Buckskin nodded.

"When she's home safe, you'll get a five-thousand-dollar bonus. Any questions?"

"I'm working on a case."

"Cancel it."

"I don't do that to a client."

"I'll hire your client another detective."

"You take care of my client, then pay me twenty dollars a day and expenses, a thousand in advance and a ten-thousand-dollar bonus for Harriet Braithwaite's safe return."

"Done." Braithwaite held out his hand. The story was that he almost never signed contracts. If a handshake wasn't good enough, he didn't do business with you. He'd never been taken advantage of that way yet.

Ten minutes later, Buckskin had a thousand

dollars in cash in his pocket, and headed for his hotel, where he had a permanent room. He packed a carpet bag and caught the 9:15 out of Union Station south to Colorado Springs.

Chapter Two

Five days before Buckskin arrived in Cripple Creek, Harriet Braithwaite watched out the window on the train heading for Chicago. The scenery was the same. She'd seen it twice a year for forever. She had told her father that she didn't want to go back to the Continental Finishing School for Young Ladies. She wouldn't. She was all grown up. Why, she'd heard of girls of 15 who were married and had babies already. Here she was more than 18 and still in some stupid school.

Harriet flipped long blond hair back over her shoulder and pinched in her pretty face. She was 18 and a woman; she should be able to do what she wanted. So she would. She felt the reticule she carried. Deep inside were two 100-dollar bills. She also had a bank draft her father had given her to use only in case of an emergency. She had seen the figure: 500 dollars.

It was a great deal of money. She might have been raised in a rich household, but she knew a lot about the ordinary people. Mary was her best friend; Mary's father worked as a bank teller. Harriet knew that he made just under 500 dollars for a whole year.

She had started planning two months ago. It had to work.

She knew about money and how to save and spend it. That was how she had saved the two 100-dollar bills. She had spent only half of her allowance and saved the rest.

She frowned a moment. It was for sure that her father would send someone to bring her back. For a year she had wanted to go to the gold strike at Cripple Creek. How exciting! How thrilling to be in on the latest big gold strike. And it was due south of Denver. She could think of nothing else that could get her bubbling with wonder and enchantment. Just to think of finding gold in the ground and digging it out and becoming rich set her imagination on fire. It was a fantastic adventure that she had to be a part of.

First she had to get there.

She listened to the wheels of the railroad car clicking along on the joints between the sections of the tracks under the car. She smiled, thinking how she would fool her parents. Yes, she had planned it all out carefully two weeks ago when her father had shaken his head and given her his final and unchangeable decision. She couldn't go to Cripple Creek. She would go back for her last year at the finishing school.

She had protested. He would have wondered if she hadn't. But she'd given him no clue what she would do. Now it was all in motion. She had kissed her mother and father good-bye, boarded the eastbound train at 7.30 A.M. and settled down in the compartment. She had not unpacked. Up the Union Pacific Railroad line 70 miles the train would stop at the small town of Fort Morgan. It was large enough so enough people would be getting on and off that she wouldn't be noticed. She had carefully packed before she left home. All of her fancy dresses and silk underthings she had put in the trunk the porter had put in the baggage car. She had two leather valises she could carry easily with her. In them she had her everyday clothes and some personal things she didn't want to be without.

She looked out the window of the compartment and saw the landscape flying past. The train reached speeds of 40 miles an hour on this section, the steward had told her. He had checked with her before they left the station and twice after that. She was certain that her father had given him a ten-dollar tip so he would be sure to take good care of her all the way to Chicago.

For just a moment she grinned, thinking how angry her father would be when he found out she wasn't in Chicago. He would know where she was. She'd have to figure out something to keep him from finding her.

For just a moment, Harriet felt wetness touch

her eyes. She blinked it back. Her mother had not been a lot of help to her. She had always given in to her husband's will. Well, Harriet had been away from both of them for the best part of three years at the boarding school. Now she was ready to make the break complete.

She could read and write and do sums and had a high school diploma. She had thought about going to the university and becoming a teacher, but the idea of the gold fields had drawn her like a beautiful moth to a candle burning outside at midnight. Three young men she knew in Denver had thrown aside everything and hurried to the gold rush. She would do the same!

An hour later she watched the train come to a halt in the station at Fort Morgan. She'd had her valises ready, and had left her compartment and mingled with the other passengers in the car behind hers. She waited patiently with them to get off the train.

It was simple. She walked off with no one paying any attention to her. She had hidden her long blond hair under a brown and exceedingly unattractive hat. Now she kept her glance down and walked into the station and to the ticket window.

An hour later she sat on the coach car of a Union Pacific train heading west again. She would get off at the Union Station and go to the ticket counter for a ride to Colorado Springs. The Springs were only 70 miles due south of Denver. It was the closest stop to Cripple Creek. There she would take a room in a small hotel and find out all she could about the gold rush country. She would need to make some adjustments, she realized, or her father would send someone and find her a day after Miss Marstad wired him from the finishing school in Chicago informing him that little Harriet had not arrived on schedule.

Later, on the run to Colorado Springs, Harriet sat next to the window and watched the countryside. It was higher country and more colorful than the run out into the high plains to the east. Mountains soared everywhere. She had a touch of a thrill as she wondered just how exciting this adventure would be.

Someone sat down beside her and his leg brushed hers. She moved toward the window more and frowned at the man who looked straight ahead. He was in his 30s, with dark, straight hair and a black mustache. His gray suit was not of the best cut.

He looked over at her a moment later and nodded. She frowned again. Five minutes later the train jolted to the side as it went round a curve and he fell toward her, his hand falling on her thigh. He moved his hand and apologized.

She frowned again, watching him. She had heard of men like him, had seen one on the train on another trip bothering a young girl. If he tried it again, she knew what to do.

Ten minutes later, the man looked at her, slid his hand onto her thigh and pressed it toward her crotch. She gasped, then smashed her balled-up fist into the bridge of his nose. He bleated in pain and pulled his hand away from her legs. In the same instant she slammed her fist downward at his crotch where his legs lay spread and hit his private parts.

The man bellowed in pain this time and bent over. She pulled her hand back and her frown turned to a small smile as she stared out the window. She heard movement beside her and a moment later when she looked around, the man in the cheap suit had moved up the aisle.

Her two valises lay at her feet and she rode the rest of the way to Colorado Springs with the same small smile. She felt as if she had passed the first test of taking care of herself.

When the conductor called out, "Colorado Springs!" Harriet had already taken her two bags to the end of the car and waited near the steps that led down. She had hidden her long blond hair inside her hat again. She carried her bags outside the station and looked up and down the street. It wasn't a large town. She had known that. She could see two hotels from the station. Automatically she chose the smaller of the two. It was also the closest one. She walked there not feeling the weight of the two bags at all.

Inside the hotel, she put her bags down at the clerk's desk and looked at him.

"I want a room for two nights," she said in what she considered to be a businesslike tone.

"Will your parents be with you, miss?" the clerk asked, his forehead wrinkling slightly.

"No. I'd like something in front on the second floor so I can see the street." She'd heard her father say that once. The clerk nodded, made a notation and turned a large book around for her to sign.

She picked up the pen, dipped it in the inkwell and signed the name she had decided on two weeks ago, Ruth Carson. Once she was out of Colorado Springs she'd change it again.

"That'll be two dollars in advance, miss," the clerk said.

She took out her reticule and handed the man a five-dollar greenback. His brows went up and he made change for her.

"Up the steps and second door to the left," he said. He hesitated. "I can get some help with your bags."

She ignored his offer, picked up her bags and carried then up the stairs. She didn't look back.

Inside the room, she closed and locked the door, then fell on the bed and shrilled in delight.

"I did it! I got away! I'm free!" She sat up and stared out the window. Free, but for how long? How could she escape the detectives she was sure her father would send looking for her? She furrowed her brow a moment and walked over and looked out the window. This room was no more than a third of the size of her bedroom at home. She shrugged and stared out through the thin curtain.

Colorado Springs was still a frontier kind of town without the refinements or facilities that Denver had. It would grow. She looked across the street and saw two women leaning over a second-story balcony. Both wore some kind of robes and called to the men on the street below. One man looked up and evidently called back. The woman opened her robe and revealed her breasts.

Harriet's mouth fell open in surprise. The man called something and ran into the building. The woman on the balcony grinned, and closed her robe and went inside.

Harriet smiled. Fancy women. She'd heard about them. They took off their clothes and let men do it to them for money. That was one way to make a living she wasn't going to stoop to, no matter what.

She tightened her mouth and pinched in her green eyes making her face frown. So how was she going to make a living in Cripple Creek? How was she going to stay hidden from her father and his bloodhounds? She didn't have the slightest idea. She couldn't be a seamstress. She couldn't really clean people's houses, since she had never tried that in her whole life at home. What could she do?

She could do sums. She could greet people and listen to them talk. Maybe she could be a clerk at some fancy store there in Colorado Springs. Maybe. She was sure they wouldn't have any fancy stores in Cripple Creek. She would think about her plight. She had known it would be a problem, but from a practical standpoint, she couldn't spend a lot of time on that before she knew if she could get away from her parents. Now she had. Now she would worry about it.

That evening she ate her dinner in the hotel. The dining room was small, the menu even smaller, but she settled for a beef stew that was surprisingly good. At the next table she noticed a man and two boys who she guessed were 16 or 17. They were excited, and she could overhear their talk about the gold fields.

The father cut into their chatter. "Now, enough about Cripple Creek. I keep telling you we get there tomorrow, then we try to find our gold mine. It ain't gonna be easy. Gold is in shafts—upthrusts they call them, pillars of rock that rise up through the ground."

"So we just run round until we find ourselves one of them upthrusts," the older boy said.

The father chuckled. "Wish it was that easy, boy. Trouble is, them upthrusts gonna be ten, twelve, maybe fifteen feet underground. Been covered up for ten thousand years. We got to dig down to find them."

"How we know where to dig, Pa?"

"That's why they is three of us. We can dig three holes time I could dig one. You boys gonna get blisters on them hands of your'n afore you knows it."

The idea in Harriet Braithwaite's brain germinated and took root and she smiled as she finished the stew. It could work. She went to the general store and bought some items, then hurried back to her hotel. She still had her long hair under the hat. No use advertising her appearance here. Make the detectives earn their pay.

Harriet sat on her bed in the small hotel room and looked at the items that lay beside her. She had a pair of long thin, barber shears, a package of hair dye and a comb. She looked at them for several minutes, then stared into the cracked mirror on top of the cheap dresser.

"It will work, scaredy-cat. You know that it will work. No chance that anyone would recognize you again." She lifted her brows and sighed. It was the only idea she'd had all day that might work. Harriet picked up the scissors and put one of the long strands of blond hair inside the blades. For a moment she shivered. Then she set her jaw and cut.

Ten inches of blond hair fell on the bed beside her. A slow smile worked its way around her eyes and then her mouth until she had a full grin. She looked back at the mirror and her smile went wider.

A half hour later, she had cut off most of her long hair. It was jagged and ragged in back, and still too long on top. She mixed up the dark brown hair dye in the bowl with water from the pitcher in the room. Harriet shivered. Lose her blond hair? It was mostly gone anyway. Yes. She daubed some of the dye on hair over her forehead, and cocked her head. Maybe. Then she bent her head and got busy. It took her three tries to get her hair the dark brown she wanted. She threw the dye out the window when things below on the street quieted down after dark.

She looked in the mirror and gasped. No longer a blonde, she had short brown hair. It would need to be shorter and better-cut. She would go to the barber tomorrow. But first she needed some clothes. Harriet Braithwaite went to bed that night grinning. She could do it. She would do it.

The next day she put on her oldest dress and the same brown hat and went to the smallest general store.

"Ma'am, my ma told me to buy some britches and shirts for my brother. He's a little taller than me, maybe an inch. Can you show me what I need, right size and all?"

The woman clerk nodded. "Probably headed for the mines. We've got just what you need. Ain't too pretty, but they wear like iron."

Harriet bought two pairs of denim and two pairs of another tough weave, blue and brown. She got four matching shirts and hurried back to the hotel. Later she'd get a pair of boots and some stockings. When she dressed in the pants and shirt and took off her hat in the hotel room, she was surprised. She could do it. She looked like a boy. She could pass for a young boy.

The barber never lifted more than one brow as she sat in his chair wearing her new clothes.

"Regular haircut, my pa said. He tried. Didn't work."

The barber grunted and finished the cut in ten minutes. Harriet gave him a quarter and hurried out. Back at the large general store, she bought underwear, a pair of boots and six pairs of socks. She found two hats she liked. One had a bill and looked like a boy's hat. The other was straight all the way around to ward off a rainstorm. She bought both of them. She'd need more things, but she could get them in Cripple Creek.

It was too late that day. She put her dress and hat back on and paid for another night's lodging at the clerk's desk, then went upstairs and checked her haircut. It was a boy's haircut, short on the sides, no part and hair two inches long on top. She fashioned a part on the right side and put on her cap hoping to train her new dark brown hair.

She took another look in the cracked mirror. Yes, she was a boy. No one should have any doubts about her. She had never had a big bosom, so that would help. Maybe she'd use a wrapper to keep herself from bouncing. She'd try to keep her voice as low as she could. It should work. In the morning she would buy a ticket on the branch rail line that went to Florissant, around the mountain. From there it was only 18 miles or so to Cripple Creek. She hoped there was a stagecoach to take her the last leg of her journey.

Chapter Three

It was near the end of his first day in Cripple Creek and Buckskin had absolutely nothing to show for his efforts to find Harriet Braithwaite. Yes, he knew she wasn't a whore working the town and that she hadn't checked in at any of the village's boardinghouses or the hotel. That amounted to almost nothing. He had to find a trail quickly or he'd have one hell of a time locating the girl. The more time she had to hide herself, to establish an identity here, the tougher it would be.

The knock came on his door a moment later, and he drew his Colt from the gunbelt that lay on the bed beside him, cocked it, turning the cylinder to a live round, and hurried to the wall side of the door.

"Who is it?" he asked.

"A friend," a muffled voice answered. He

couldn't tell if it was a man or a woman. He turned the key in the lock and edged the door open staying by the protection of the wall.

A girl pushed the door open, stepped out of the dimness of the coal-oil lamplight of the hallway into the closer glow of his own lamp. She was maybe 25, with coppery red hair and a big grin. She held two soft white towels.

"Figured that maybe you could use some fresh towels. That is, if'n you was going to have a bath."

He took the towels. "Thanks. I didn't expect such good service." He noticed that her white blouse had three buttons open at the top and a line of cleavage showed between heavy breasts.

The girl stepped inside the room further and closed the door. Her hands moved to her blouse, the other buttons came open and she spread the cloth to each side.

Nothing else covered her breasts. The large orbs swung out with their thumb-size red nipples and three-inch-wide pink areolas.

"That is, if'n you're not busy." She said it with a husky sound that stirred Buckskin. He reached out and petted her breasts, feeling the heat of them, watching the nipples rise to his touch. She sighed.

"Oh, but that feels fine." She stepped closer and lifted her face to his to be kissed. When he didn't move, she reached up and kissed his lips, then opened her mouth and kissed him again and his arms came around her.

Her hands went to the back of his neck and held his lips tightly to hers. Then she gently broke away and turned so she could lock the door. When she looked back at him she had dropped her blouse and held out her arms.

Buckskin scooped her up in his arms, carried her to the bed and put her down gently. Then he lay on top of her and kissed her again. When they came apart she smiled.

"Saw you in the lobby talking to Bert at the counter. Figured you was a gent who could use some relaxation. My, but you are a pretty man, rugged but cut from an old oak tree and solid and just right. Your hips in them tight pants really got me thinking about what's underneath."

Buckskin rolled over. "Take a look."

She sat up and stared at him, then nodded, her grin growing wider. "Oh, I'm Lois. I work here at the hotel making up beds and cleaning."

"Call me Buckskin." He laced his fingers together in back of his head and watched her. She unbuttoned his shirt and flipped the sides back, playing with his chest hair. She kissed his nipples, then worked down to his belt. After some trouble with the buckle, she got his belt unfastened and then labored with the buttons on his fly.

She flashed him a grin. "Damn lot of work undressing a man, but I don't mind. Kind of like it." She dropped down and fed one of her big breasts into his mouth.

"You have a bite of me and then later on, I'll have a long chew on something of yours." She laughed softly. "Damn, but I love it when a man's chewing on my titties. Feels so good, kind of warm and gooey, and wanting to tear my clothes off and lay on my back with my legs pointing at the sky and just hoping that I can get my cunnie all filled up and get me a good poking."

Buckskin slipped away from the orb and laughed. "Lois, I'd say there's a good chance something like that could happen."

She slid down and pulled at his boots, tugging them off, then working his town pants down until she could pull them over his toes. She stared at the short underwear he wore.

"What the hell is this, some of them French underclothes things?"

Buckskin lifted his hips and slid down the cotton underpants. "What they call briefs in New York. Just short underwear. Then we don't have to cut off our long jake underwear from the winter."

"Glory be. What won't they do next?" She stared at his crotch and reached over and petted the limp snake that lay there. "This guy ever get excited?"

"Convince him."

She bent and used her tongue working over the length, paying special heed to the pointed head, and slowly the worm turned into a lance and she yelped with delight.

"Figured you could do it," Buckskin said. He sat up and helped her pull her skirt and two petticoats down. She was a little more heavily built than he figured at first, with strong thighs that tapered quickly and hips that made for easy childbirth. She wiggled out of a pair of drawers that came to her knees and threw them against the far wall. Then she went on her hands and knees, pushed him flat on the bed and dropped on top of him.

"Always wanted to do that. How about the first time with me on top?"

Buckskin nodded and she pushed up and felt below, then positioned herself and his erection and sank downward with a screech of delight as he penetrated her and then slid in until their pelvic bones ground against one another.

"Marvelous! So fine, so fine. I love it. This is worth all the bad ones I've ever had. You wouldn't believe the pawing and groping and downright fights I had when I was younger. The boys told me how good it would be, but until I was fourteen I didn't let anybody get his hands on me. Then one night I felt just right and I helped and it was good. The next time was better. You remember your first fuck?"

Buckskin chuckled. He ground slowly against her and she moaned in delight."

"Oh, damn, yes" she said. "Do that again, That is fine, fine."

"Move around a little more," he said. "Don't make me do all the work."

"First damn time I've been up here. Let me enjoy it."

Buckskin caught her breasts with his hands and began pumping upward hard with his hips. A minute later she trilled a high note and then panted as her whole body shook with a giant spasm, then shook again and again until he thought she would shake herself into pieces. She sighed and went limp a moment, then went into the same series of spasms and contractions and tightened every muscle in her body before she exploded with a scream of delight and then dropped on him spent, panting and limp as yesterday's noodle.

He let her recover, then pumped upward gently, increasing the speed and depth. She roused and worked against him, and in two minutes he bellowed in delight and sprayed his seed upward in a dozen hard thrusts, then let out a long sigh and collapsed. He lay there panting hard, trying to get enough air into his lungs so he could go on breathing and living.

They lay there pinned together for another five minutes before Lois sighed and rolled off him.

"So damn good," she said. "Just so fucking good. I may keep you until tomorrow night. Can I come back tomorrow night? You might need another clean towel."

She looked over at him. "Just hope you don't think I'm a whore the way I busted in here and all. I just saw you and wanted you and I sometimes kind of take matters into my own hands." She made some motions with her hands at the ceiling. "Hell, I ain't all that smart, went through the fourth grade. I can read and write some and do some sums. I guess what I do best is fuck." She looked over at him. "No, really. I'm good at it. I never had me a man who couldn't get his load dumped with me. One said he never had been able to, but I got him off four times that night. But I ain't no whore. I don't never take no money. Just pleased to have the partner."

"Then you don't have to rub yourself off at night in a lonely bed."

She sat up and frowned. "How the hell you know that?" She lifted her brows. "Oh, God, another man smarter than me. Hell, might as well get my clothes on and go home."

"Welcome to stay the rest of the night."

She brightened, and Buckskin thought of a little puppy wagging its tail.

"Yeah, like to. Then we can fuck some more, right?"

She was right.

The next morning, Lois had already left when Buckskin slid out of bed at 6 a.m. It was his usual getting-up time. Today he would work the merchants. If Harriet Braithwaite wasn't at a boardinghouse or in a hotel, that meant she had a place of her own, probably a tent, and that meant she would have to buy food. She couldn't just hide in a tent all the time.

He had breakfast and then walked through the town watching the people. There were quite a number of women up and around. One woman delivered fresh-baked loaves of bread to the two stores that sold food. He stopped her and talked, but she hadn't seen any young blond girl in town during the past month. He thanked her and moved on.

The first store he went into was the Cripple Creek Grocery and General Merchandise. It had a section for canned and dried food and fresh fruit. Ten loaves of bread were being placed on a table by the bakery woman and three men stood in line waiting for her. Each one snatched two loaves and hurried to the wooden counter built across the back of the store.

When the last customer left, Buckskin asked the proprietor about Harriet and showed him a picture.

"Nope, can't say as I've seen her. Not many girls up here that pretty. Sure that I'd remember her if I'd waited on her. Course I'm not here all the time. Got me a claim I like to dig in about half the time. When I'm gone my son works the store."

The boy wasn't there, so Buckskin said he'd stop back later.

The next store was Alexander's Hardware and General Store. It looked to be the largest in town, with an original section and then a second room built on the side. The store was packed with all kind of goods including a big section for food. Here there was twice as much food and twice as much variety as at the other store.

A man came forward to meet Buckskin. He held out his hand.

"Morning. I'm Abe Alexander. You must be new in town."

Buckskin smiled. "Must be a hundred new people pouring in here every day. How can you remember everyone?"

Alexander chuckled. "Hell, I can't. I saw you when you came in with the supply wagon yesterday. Shorty told me how you saved our bacon and beans and all the rest of the supplies out there on the trail. He says you saved his life and he might be right. I want to thank you as well. Would you like a gratis box of cigars? I just got some in from

Atlanta that look to be some of the best around."

Buckskin nodded. "I could use five or six. Not a box, I'd just lose them. Also I'd like to ask you some questions."

"Shorty said you were hunting a young girl. I worked over my brain for an hour or so, and couldn't think of anybody in town recent who she could be."

A young boy came in from the back room with a stack of men's pants. He walked past and put them on a display table with the other clothes, then came back and hesitated. Alexander held out his hand.

"This young lad is Harry. He might know about a pretty girl in town. Harry, have you seen a pretty young girl, maybe eighteen, with long blond hair, who came in less than a week ago?"

The boy thought a moment, then shook his head. "Nope, can't think of one." He waved and walked back to the rear of the store.

Buckskin frowned. "How did you know she had long blond hair and was eighteen?"

"Shorty told me. You asked about the girl on your ride in from Florrisant."

"True. I'd appreciate it if you'd keep a lookout for me. If she's in town she isn't at a boarding-house or the hotel. So she has to eat something somewhere."

"I'll do that. Here are ten of those cigars. My pleasure."

From the store, Buckskin checked in at every one of the eating establishments in town. There weren't many, and they were small and on the crude side, as were most of the new stores in a town that might not be around long.

The last place he stopped at had a wooden counter covered with oilcloth, three tables with chairs and a cook who looked through a long high window from the rear. After the man said he hadn't seen a pretty like Harriet, Buckskin ordered a big bowl of chili con carne and three thick slabs of bread and coffee.

That afternoon he toured the bars again. In the Cripple Creek Emporium he saw a picture of a singer who would be working there that night. She was pretty and had long blond hair, but she wasn't Harriet Braithwaite.

Somebody yelled at him from a poker game.

"Hey, you with the brown hat. Wanta play some poker? We only got three. Can't play poker with three hands. Cost you ten dollars to get in, fifty-cent limit on bets."

Buckskin shrugged. He didn't have any good ideas to run down. He liked the looks of the talker, a sunburned older man in his fifties with a full white beard that had tobacco stains down one side. The man squinted at Buckskin as Buckskin flipped a ten-dollar gold piece on the table.

"Ain't I seed you somewhere before, cowboy?"

"Might. I been somewhere more than once."

The older man laughed. "Just a wonderment. Maybe Cheyenne?"

"Maybe. Deal me in."

The poker wasn't prime, but neither were the pots. Buckskin lost the first two hands, as was his poker etiquette, then won the next two and was five dollars ahead. One man seemed to be losing all the time.

The loser was in his thirties, tanned, with a working man's scarred and grubby fingers. The others called him Douglas. He drew two cards in the next hand of five-card draw and Buckskin saw the delight that broke through the man's poor poker face. Douglas checked his chips. He was down to three dollars. On the last round of betting by the older man, who had drawn two cards, Douglas couldn't meet the three 50-cent raises.

"I'm light a dollar," Douglas said.

"No light, damn it. You meet the bet or you fold," the fourth man at the table snapped. He wore a black suit, and Buckskin figured him as a merchant.

Douglas scribbled something on a piece of paper and threw it in the pot. "A one-eighth interest in my claim, the Lucky Lady. It's gonna hit big, I'm sure."

The merchant scowled, started to shake his head, then shrugged. "Might as well let him do it. He just might win the pot, who knows."

Buckskin won it with three queens. Douglas swore, kicked over his chair and stormed out of the saloon. Buckskin looked at the scrawled note.

I, Larry Douglas, hereby sell one eighth of my claim, the Lucky Lady, to the bearer of this note for a proper exchange of goods or services.

Buckskin frowned at the writing. "His claim any good?"

"Could be, but he don't have the cash money to hire a monkey to go down and tunnel six ways to Sunday hunting an upthrust."

Buckskin tossed the note on the table. "Anyone want to buy this eighth share for fifty bucks? I'll take one gold slug if anybody has one."

The merchant frowned. "What the hell is a gold slug?"

The older man snorted. "You call yourself a store owner and you don't know what a gold slug is? Government minted them for two years, back in '51 and '52. A gold coin worth fifty dollars. About two and a half ounces of gold. Heavy little bastards."

"Any takers?" Buckskin asked. The three men shook their heads. "Looks like the game is over," he said. He raked the greenbacks and silver coins across the table and added them to what he had there. When he had stacked the money, he found he had earned over 30 dollars. Not a bad afternoon's work.

He headed for the door. Next he'd try to find the sheriff's branch office and see if anyone was there. If not, he'd check for a town marshal. There had to be some law here somewhere who would give him some help.

He left by the front door, and had just adjusted his brown Stetson when a shot jolted through the air a half inch from his head. He dove sideways, drew his six-gun and tried to figure out who was trying to kill him.

Chapter Four

Two days before buckskin arrived in Cripple Creek, Harriet Braithwaite had decided on her new name before she arrived in Florisant. She had discarded one of her valises in the hotel in Colorado Springs and packed all of her boy's clothes in the other one. She had taken only a few of her treasures with her when she walked out the back door of the hotel that morning.

She caught the 8:14 for the hour-long trip to Florisant. She wore her jeans and a blue shirt that was a little large for her so it bagged nicely over her chest concealing her breasts. She had used a wrapper that morning and fastened it tight to bind down her breasts even more. It hurt a little, but she'd get used to it.

Her name. She had picked out Harry as an obvious choice for her first name and Carson, like in

Kit Carson, for her last name. Harry Carson. She said it over and over again and wrote it down in a small notebook she carried with her. Yes, it would work. If someone yelled, "Harry," it was close enough to Harriet to bring her up listening and moving.

At Florissant she inquired about the stage to Cripple Creek. It had met the train and there were six people for the 18-mile trip. Plenty of room in the small stagecoach. The bumpy ride was as bad as she had heard, and there was a thin, misty rain when the stage came to Cripple Creek.

At first glance she was disappointed. The town was mostly white tents set up everywhere. One main street led down a long line of clapboard buildings—some finished, some only started, others half-done and abandoned, weathering in the summer sun. No streets, no sidewalks. There was a boardwalk along the best street, but she didn't know what to call the street since it had no sign.

The misty rain blew away and the sun came out bright and warm and inviting. It lifted her spirits. She had begged to come here for a year. Now that she was here, what in the world was she going to do? She had her money safely sewn into her shirts, in back, where it wouldn't show and where usually it would be tucked inside her britches.

The boy's clothes were strange, but they did give her so much freedom. No longer did she have to worry about keeping her knees properly together, and she could sit spraddle-legged anytime she wanted to.

For a half hour she wandered up and down the

street, gawking at the stores, moving quickly past the saloons. She had never been in one, not even the fancy ones in Denver. She'd have to try to take a look inside one of these days.

After passing four places to eat, she suddenly realized that she was hungry. She had money. Before she cut off her hair, she had gone to the bank in Colorado Springs and changed one of the $100 bills into tens. The teller had looked at her closely, then had examined the bill critically and at last had shown it to two other employees. They'd approved and he'd given her the tens.

After that she didn't have the nerve to try to cash the $500 draft. Then too, if she cashed it, her father would know precisely where to look for her. She had the draft stitched into the lining of her valise.

At last she picked out what looked like the best of the small cafes and went in. She sat at small counter with her valise at her feet and ordered a sandwich. She loved coffee, but from one look in the mirror she knew the waitress would think she was too young a boy for coffee.

She ate the sandwich, drank a glass of milk and resumed her walk. She made the trip up and down the four-block-long main street and then realized it was starting to get dark. She had just about decided that she should find a hotel room when she walked into one of the stores. It was the biggest one on the long street, Alexander's Hardware and General Store.

She looked around a moment. Then a man

came to wait on her. He held out his hand and smiled.

"Hello, I'm Abe Alexander. You must be new in town."

She shook his hand gently, then nodded. "Yes, sir, I am. I wondered how much a loaf of bread is?"

"Fifteen cents. I know that's a lot, but it's baked right here in Cripple Creek by Mrs. Musgrove."

"I'll take one."

"Not much for your supper," Alexander said. "How about some cheese?"

"Yes, please."

Alexander watched the boy a moment, then nodded. "Let me cut some slices of that bread for you. Then I'll get the cheese. It's some that broke off the wheel and I can't sell it. No charge."

Alexander watched the lad eat and smiled. "Now, that's better, but you should have some milk to go with that. I've got some that was fresh milked this morning. Do you want some? No charge."

"That would be good." Harry tried not to let her voice go too high, but she was hungry again.

About 20 minutes later, Harry had eaten three slices of the thick bread, with cheese, and downed two glasses of milk. She couldn't remember ever eating so much at once.

Abe Alexander pulled a chair up beside the small table in the back of the store where he had set out the milk and cheese for the young lad.

"Now, I have a question for you. I've seen a lot of people come to Cripple Creek this past year, but none of them have been like you. My guess is that you ran away from home so you could come to the gold rush. Am I right."

"No, no. I just walked around town and got tired and hungry. I'll be going back to my folks' tent now. They'll be worried about me."

"That so? Where is your tent?"

"Over a couple of streets, higher on the mountain."

"Up on Bennet Avenue, or is it over on Meyers Avenue?"

"Uh. . . . Meyers Avenue."

"The other side of the barbershop, or this side?"

"Uh . . . never seen the barbershop."

"Good, there isn't one on Meyers Avenue." Alexander watched the boy a minute. He squirmed. Alexander waited.

"You want to tell me about it?"

"Tell you about what?"

"Why you ran away from home? We get lot of kids come here thinking this is some big wild adventure. Ain't nothing like that. Just some holes in the ground, lots of hard work, and once in a while somebody finds a gold mine. That's when the real work begins, digging those shafts and tunnels and drifts. Damn hard work."

He was right. Harry knew he was right. This wasn't at all what she figured it would be. Harry felt the tears coming. No, a boy didn't cry. Couldn't. She looked up and heard the man still talking.

"I figure you don't really have no folks here, do you?"

Slowly, Harry shook her head.

"And you don't have a job or know anybody here, no friends, nobody to look out for you. That right?"

She nodded.

"So, seein' you don't have no place to stay and you still have your bag there, I can put you up in the back room for a couple of days."

"Don't need no charity. I got money."

"Don't let anybody around here know that. Men get their heads bashed in for ten dollars up here. We don't have much law around yet."

"How'd you know, about me not having folks here?"

Alexander leaned on the back of the chair and chuckled. "I've seen a lot of youngsters roaming around. You all have that same kind of lost look, wondering what's coming next. Done it myself once for a week. Got tired of it and went home. You want to go home?"

"No. I can't. I mean, no."

"Then why don't you stay here tonight. Dark out there already. I got a cot we can set up along the back wall. Couple of blankets if you need them. You think on it. Right now I better close up the store."

The bell tinkled on the front door and a customer came in. Alexander hurried out, shook the man's hand and found out what he needed: some chain with hooks on both ends for his new shaft.

When Alexander came back after closing up and blowing out the eight lanterns in the store, he found the boy with his head on his folded arms on the table fast asleep.

"Yeah, know how you feel," he said softly.

Five minutes later he had the cot set up near the back door and two blankets and a pillow from the store at the head. He touched the boy's shoulder and he came awake surprised.

"What? Hey, what . . ." He shook his head. "Oh, yes, Mr. Alexander. Sorry I got sleepy."

"Back here is that cot. Come along. You have a good sleep and we'll talk in the morning. We'll figure out something when we're both not so tired."

Alexander took one more tour of his small kingdom to make sure all was safe and secure, then flopped on a chair by the small table in the back section of the store he had partitioned off as his living quarters. He saw the boy on the cot. One blanket lay under him, the other over him. The top blanket was more for protection, Alexander decided, than for warmth. Although at Cripple Creek's 10,500-foot altitude, it always turned chilly at night, even in the summer.

Alexander took a deep breath. He should count up the day's receipts. He'd been doing well lately. Taking in far more money here than they ever had in the family-run store back East.

The idea of getting some help had been nagging at him for a month now. He put in 12 to 14 hours a day, and sometimes he had to drag himself into bed well after midnight. He made a cup of coffee on the small wood-burning cook stove and waited for the grounds to settle after boiling.

He did need some help.

Twice he looked over at the boy. He was slight, no more than five feet two maybe. Just a kid. But he spoke well. Naw, just wouldn't work out. He'd steal the place blind and be gone some dark night.

Maybe not. Alexander would talk to the boy in the morning. The idea that he'd have a place to live and get fed and a little bit of wages might be enough to keep him honest for a few months. In the morning.

When Harry woke up the next morning, she smelled bacon and coffee and something else. She sat on the edge of the cot. She hadn't taken off anything but her shoes when she tucked into the blankets the night before. Now she rubbed the sleep from her eyes and stood.

Alexander turned from the stove. "Breakfast in about two minutes. The privy is out back case you want to use it. Wash pan and a towel out back on a stand. You want breakfast, you better scoot."

Five minutes later, Alexander watched the kid eating. Three eggs, country-fried potatoes, three strips of bacon, two slices of toast and strawberry jam and two glasses of milk.

"Glad you weren't hungry," Alexander said. "You clean up things here and I'll get the store open. I'm ten minutes late. After that we'll talk again."

There were four men standing at the front door when he opened it. He waited on the men, all miners and claim owners needing gear for their work. They paid in cash and Alexander figured it would be a good day. Then he remembered the kid.

When he stepped into the back part of the store, he found the dishes washed and dried, the table cleared and the floor swept and clean. The boy stood to one side.

"Figured I could pay for my breakfast this way," Harry said.

Alexander plunged right in. "You want to stay here and work in the store with me? I need another hand or two at times. Not a lot to learn. You seem bright enough. What's a dollar and a quarter added to thirty-nine cents?"

Harry looked up and nodded. "That's a dollar and sixty-four. I'm good with figures."

"I like that. Can you read and write too?"

"Yes, sir. I've had some schooling."

"Read a newspaper?"

"Yes."

He tossed the boy a package of flour. "Read the label."

The boy caught the two-pound package. "White all-purpose flour made from the finest wheat under strict supervision of our scientists and packaged by careful people to bring the finest flour to you for your cooking pleasures."

"That's enough. You can read and cipher, you'll be a big help. I'll pay you a dollar a day and all you can eat and a place to sleep. You want to stay and work here?"

"Your name is Abe Alexander?" the boy asked.

The merchant nodded. "What's your name?"

"I'm Harry Carson and I'm sixteen years old, going on seventeen in September."

"I hope you'll stay. I really need help. This place is getting too big too fast for one man."

Harry walked forward and held out his hand. "For a dollar a day, I'll be glad to work for you."

"Good. First thing I want you to do is to wander around the store and learn where everything is. I'll have you putting up stock too when things come in. That way you'll learn it faster. I'll call you Harry and you call me Abe. All right?"

Harry smiled. "Yes, sir, Abe. I'm going to like working in your store."

As she walked around the crowded store trying to remember where different things were, she marveled at her good fortune. By all rights she should be still shivering from the cold of last night after spending the night in the open. She couldn't take a room at a hotel, she had decided. Her father's snoopers would be here soon.

But work? She'd never done a lick of work in her life. Not at home, not at school. People had been hired to do everything for her. Now she was. . . . working!

In a way it was a thrilling idea. Something totally new, different. Wasn't that what she had wanted? Now she could see what she could do on her own. It would be no problem hiding her real identity from Abe Alexander. He seemed like a good man, kind and thoughtful.

Then a wagon came in with supplies. She found out the driver's name was Shorty and he brought freight in for Abe from the railroad. Most of the goods came from wholesale houses in Denver.

They carried the boxes and packages in from the

wagon and stacked them in a pile just inside the back door.

When it was all unloaded, Abe tossed her an apple. "Now the work really starts. We have to mark the price on everything and then put it up on the counters and shelves. You unpack it, I'll mark it and you start getting it put up."

He grinned at her and laughed. "Of course we'll do this when we don't have customers to wait on. Before, it would be after midnight before I could get everything put up. Okay, we better get at it. Let's start with the food. That's our biggest seller right now."

They worked all day between customers, and after supper again until eight o'clock, when everything was put on the shelves.

"Well, good work," Abe said. "That's earlier than I've ever got it done before. I think you're going to be a big help to me."

Harry heard only part of what Alexander said. She had sat on her cot in the back room and slowly toppled over and dropped off to sleep before her head touched the pillow.

Abe grinned, took the blanket that had been folded neatly at the bottom of the cot and spread it over the sleeping figure.

"Yes," he said softly. "I think this is going to work out nicely."

Chapter Five

Buckskin Lee Morgan peered past the corner of the saloon he had just left. The round had come from across the street somewhere by the sound of it. A six-gun shot from that range was stupid. It was 50 feet to the stores across Bennett Avenue. He found the small puff of white smoke wafting skyward from the roof of the one-story lawyer's office across the street.

Buckskin surged away from the saloon's protection, zigzagged across the open space of the street, but took no fire. He sprinted over the boardwalk and through a vacant lot next to the lawyer's office. By the time he got to the back of the 60-foot-long building the gunman had dropped off the ladder to the ground and turned. He saw Buckskin and snapped another shot from 40 feet that had no chance to touch flesh.

Buckskin dug his toes into the hard dirt and sprinted forward, his arms pumping, his lungs burning. He ran the man down in 30 yards, slamming into his back, arms laced round the man's chest as their feet tangled and they rolled over and over in the dirt.

Buckskin kept the man's arms pinned to his sides. When they stopped rolling, Buckskin kicked the ground and rolled over on top of the man. He let go of his own wrist and slammed his fist into the back of the man's neck twice. Buckskin then jumped up and cocked his six-gun, putting the muzzle in the man's ear.

"You want to talk now or let me just go ahead and blow your head off?"

"Easy, damnit. I didn't hurt you. Just supposed to scare you."

"Oh, yeah, sure, and I'm the Queen of England. Who hired you?"

"Don't rightly know." The man looked at Buckskin. He was in his thirties, hadn't shaved for a few days and looked like he was down on his luck.

Buckskin jerked the barrel out of the man's ear. The front sight caught it and tore a long slice through the flesh.

"Gawd damn, that hurt! Why'en hell you do that?"

Buckskin stood and kicked the man in the side. He groaned and rolled over on his back.

"Told you I don't know who hired me," he said. "The back room at the saloon was dark. He told me who you were, where you were and to scare you, not to hurt anybody. Then they pushed me out of the room. Two or three in there, but I couldn't see any faces, not even any shoes or boots. I just don't know who they were. I took the ten dollars and found my six-gun."

Buckskin cocked his Colt and fired a shot between the man's legs, missing his crotch by three inches.

"Oh, damn . . . oh, damn."

"You better get out of town. If I see you in Cripple Creek again, I'll kill you."

The man scrabbled backward pushing with his heels, hoisting his body off the ground with his arms. He stopped, eyes wild as he watched Buckskin.

"I . . . I can go?"

"Get out of here before I change my mind." The man stood and looked at Buckskin once more, then ran hard down the alley in back of the stores toward the cross street half a block away.

Buckskin dusted off his clothes, pounded his hat on his knee and then reshaped the Stetson. Now he really did have to talk with the sheriff's deputy.

No one was in the one room that had a sign outside claiming it was a sheriff's substation. The door was locked. The sign said a deputy sheriff would be in town "from time to time." Anything serious should be reported to Sheriff Blount in Colorado Springs.

Buckskin inquired at three stores before he found a man who could help him.

"Yes, sir, we have a town marshal. He's part-time. Also runs the barbershop down on Bennett

Avenue. Name's Tarento. Somebody said he's from Spain. I don't know."

Buckskin found the barbershop on the first street over from Meyers Avenue, the more populated Bennett Avenue. The streets were named after the men who'd plotted the townsite two years ago.

No one sat in the barber chair. A bell over the screen door jangled as Buckskin walked in and a sprightly man in his mid-fifties, slender as a swamp reed, bounded through a doorway from a back room.

"Yes, yes, what a beautiful head of black hair. I can cut, trim and shape it for you so the ladies will all go mad, yes?"

"No, but thanks. I understand you're the town marshal. Is that right?"

"Mostly ceremonial duties. I have no gun, no deputies, no policemen, no jail, no laws to uphold. It is an honor, not a lawman's job."

"So there's no lawman in town at all?"

"Usually, yes. Once a deputy U.S. marshal came, but he just arrested somebody and took him back to Denver."

Buckskin nodded. What the hell now? He waved at the barber and headed back for the hotel. He needed something to go on, some kind of a lead, a clue.

The idea came to him, and at first he rejected it. Then it settled in as a possibility, and within half a block he knew it was his next step. He ran the last half block to the station where the stagecoach came in. He was told that, yes, there was one more eastbound train that afternoon down at Florisant.

The man at the small stage station went on. "We've got one more stage leaving here in about half an hour that will make connections with that 7:35 at Florisant." Buckskin bought a ticket and waited.

That night he stayed in the best hotel in Colorado Springs and ate a delicious pheasant-under-glass late supper. He felt refreshed and ready when he finished breakfast at seven the next morning and began his rounds.

He worked his own hotel first, but no one could remember a young blond girl of 18 who had registered a week ago. Not even her picture helped. He tried four hotels before he had any luck.

The young desk clerk at the last hotel nodded.

"Yes, that's the girl. She checked in here on the twelfth and then out on the fifteenth. Something strange about that girl. I never knew what. She had long hair but it always was hidden under a rather ugly hat she wore. She was pretty. I guessed she must be moneyed so I wouldn't even be able to meet her. But I wanted to.

"She never really signed out, she just left. Then the maids brought down something that was strange. Under the bed they found two long locks of blond hair. More than a foot long and pretty blond hair. I'd say it's the same shade that I see in these pictures."

Buckskin frowned slightly and closed his eyes a moment. "You're telling me that the girl might have cut off her long hair while she was here?"

"Exactly what I'm saying. There was something else. I made some notes because I thought the police might want to know, but nobody ever turned up. Yes, here it is. The maid reported that there were dark brown stains in the wash bowl and some more on the windowsill."

"Dark brown stains? Bloodstains?"

"Oh, my, no. The maid said she was almost sure it was hair dye of some kind. Brown hair dye."

"Did you ever see her with short brown hair?" Buckskin asked.

"Oh, my, no. I think she must have worn the hat after she did the cutting. That way I wouldn't know."

Buckskin thanked the clerk, gave him two dollars for his trouble and hurried for the train station. Now he had a little more to go on. The girl now might be sporting short brown hair. It gave him a whole new angle of attack.

That same afternoon at Cripple Creek the new dance hall singer arrived in town. Her name was Katherine Flowers, but she had cut it short to Kat. She had been singing now and then at fancy parties and salons in Colorado Springs for the rich folks. Now she wanted to make some money and get rich herself. She had arranged with the owner of the largest saloon in town to sing twice a night six nights a week.

Kat was five-four, with long blond hair, a pleasing face and a slender body with large breasts. Her voice was pleasant, if on the small side, but she looked good on a stage and that hushed her audience so she had no trouble being heard.

She had arranged to make a grand entrance. She'd hired a man to plaster red broadsides over half the walls in town a week before she was due to start singing. The notices trumpeted her arrival.

Kat rolled into town in a fancy carriage rented in Florissant and driven by a Negro man in top hat and tails. The rig stopped just outside town for decorating with pink and blue bunting and streamers. A man sat in back blasting out popular songs of the day on his brass trumpet.

Kat sat up front with the driver. She wore a tight-fitting yellow party dress off the shoulders that showed a glorious amount of cleavage. She waved at the people along the half-mile street. Small boys ran along behind, and the driver slowed so they could catch up.

By the time she got to the Cripple Emporium Saloon, Kat had 100 men and boys tagging along beside the fancy carriage. At the saloon, she stood in the rig and sang "Oh, When Is My Johnny Coming Home," a sad tale of a woman whose man went West to find his fortune.

When she finished the song, the crowd around the wagon had increased to more than 300. The men cheered and clapped and called for another song.

Kat smiled sweetly for them. "Gentlemen, gentlemen, I thank you for your warm and friendly reception. If you want to hear more of my songs, please come to the Cripple Emporium Saloon tonight. I'll be singing there every day but Sunday at seven in the evening and again at ten o'clock. I hope to see all of you there. I'm sure you will all act the true gentlemen that I know you are."

Miles Kelton hurried through the crowd and handed Kat down from the carriage, and a path opened ahead of them as he led her to the front door of the Cripple Emporium Saloon and inside.

The establishment had an upstairs, but not for fancy ladies. The owner's wife lived up there with her three children. It was the family home. They had built several back rooms and it had worked out nicely. Kat would have a room there rent free and would take her meals with the family. The contract stipulated all of that.

Abe Alexander came out of his store two doors down from the saloon to check on the excitement. He saw the carriage, remembered the broadsides and figured this had to be the songbird. He edged closer and listened as she sang. He decided she would please the locals with her ordinary songs that the people in town would appreciate. He headed back inside his store as a customer called out to him.

That night at the Cripple Emporium Saloon, Kat Flowers came on the small stage at precisely seven o'clock. She wore a showy blue dress that pinched in tightly at her waist and flared below, stopping two inches off the floor in a flurry of petticoats. The bodice was tight, showing off her firm breasts and teasing the men with a three-inch slash of cleavage.

She wore blue slippers and blue ribbons in her glorious long golden hair. It cascaded around her shoulders and halfway down her back. She was the picture of the ideal woman that every man had left at home or dreamed of finding some day.

The moment she stepped on stage from the small wings, the talking and chatter slowed, then stopped. Men packed into the saloon and gambling emporium so tightly no one could walk around. For the last hour the whole place had done a roaring business, with the men coming early to get good seats and standing places for the show. They drank and gambled to pass the time.

The piano player's name was Chops. He was a small black man with a frilly white shirt and red suspenders. Kat had practiced with him for an hour that afternoon. He'd said he'd stay with her no matter what song she sang or in what key. She had liked him at once.

Into the sudden silence created when Kat stepped out, Chops drummed a few chords. Then Kat turned to the audience and smiled. That brought loud cheering and clapping and hoots and yells from half the men jammed into the 60-foot-long room with its high ceiling.

Kat held up one hand and the sounds died at once. She smiled again at the audience.

"I'm thrilled to be here tonight, to be singing for you those songs you know and love. From time to time, I'll do requests from the audience, so think of your favorite. Now to start, I have a song for all of you men out there from Ohio."

She looked at Chops and he hit the opening chord. A moment later she launched into a song that would be heard often from her in the future, "The Girl I Left Behind in Ohio." Chops banged away loudly for a moment, then softened, and her clear, sweet voice surged into the cavern of a hall and carried to the men still crowding in the front door.

To the girl I left behind in Ohio,
To the one who's always meant the most to me.
Someday soon I'll go back and marry her,
And we'll be together as we're meant to be."

As she finished the first four lines, a young miner in the front row of chairs broke into sobs. Kat smiled down at him, let the piano take eight measures and then came back with the longer second verse. When she finished all six stanzas of the song, the Emporium exploded with cheering and clapping.

Miles Kelton pushed up beside the saloon owner, Jonathan Richmond, who stood at the bar. "Mr. Richmond, I'm Miles Kelton. I represent your gold mine up there on the stage, Kat Flowers. Just a reminder that Kat is to be paid each night after the last show."

Richmond, 50, rough as a just-shelled corncob, had a knife scar on his cheek that hadn't healed right. His nose had been flattened an even dozen times and now resembled more a smashed carrot than a nose. Richmond snorted, gulped down a shot of whiskey and shook his head. His wild brown hair and full beard swayed with the motion.

"Hell, no. I never do that. She'll draw her pay like the rest of my people. I pay every two weeks. Makes their money go farther that way."

Kelton poked Richmond in the shoulder with his finger.

"Mr. Richmond, I don't think you've read your contract with Miss Flowers carefully enough. She gets five percent of your daily gross receipts and she's to be paid in cash every night after the late show when we tally up your take."

Richmond had grown up in his father's pool room and saloon in Michigan. He'd handled almost all kinds of drunks, panhandlers and confidence men. Kelton looked different, but he was still just another bum trying to take him for money.

Richmond belched, blew cigar smoke in the lawyer's face and snorted. "Damn you, Kelton, get the hell out of here. Kat is working for me. You ain't. I don't take orders from a sad-assed, broken-down, belly-crawling, pint-sized little pettifogger the likes of you. Now get out of here before I have Willy pitch you out by the scruff of your neck."

"Can you read, Mr. Richmond?"

"Damn right I can read."

"Did you read the contract you signed with Kat Flowers?"

"Not all of it, I guess, no."

"You should. It stipulates that, if you don't pay Miss Flowers the five percent of your gross receipts daily, Miss Flowers is entitled to a five-percent penalty of each stipulated day when you do not pay her. I suggest you read that part carefully.

"I'll be back to see you right after the ten o'clock show to assist you in an honest tally of your gross receipts, and to figure my client's wages. I'm sure we can work this out. You signed the contract. If you don't pay Miss Flowers and abide by the conditions of the contract, you void the agreement. Then I take Kat's singing to another saloon in town. Tonight you're doing five times the business you usually do. You owe it to her."

Miles Kelton turned, reset his black derby hat precisely and worked his way around the men packed into the saloon. He figured there were over 200 men in there. He pushed his way to the front row near the stage and jingled a stack of quarters in his pocket, waiting.

Kat sang three more songs, then took a break standing beside the piano, watching the men. They watched her right back, grinning and waving. She had hesitated before taking the job in this little scratchy town. But she'd heard that some singers in halls like this one at other mining camps were thrown pokes of gold dust and nuggets.

She frowned now, remembering those were placer mining strikes where men dug the gold out of the river sand. Here it was hardrock mining. Even so, Mr. Kelton had told her what to do. He'd said it would work.

Kat set her slender jaw. Somehow she must figure out how to get rich. That was all she wanted to do, to sing her heart out and to get rich. She didn't care if she had to marry somebody she could hardly stand to become wealthy. Maybe the first millionaire in Cripple Creek would be a bachelor.

Chops, the piano man, repeated the introduction to her next set of four numbers and she grinned and walked to the center of the stage using her ballet training.

Her second set included "Zizzy Ze Zum" and "Sugar Baby." Then she went back to some old standards, and finished the set with a smile and a big bow. The applause was loud and raucous and delightful to Kat's ears. The men wouldn't stop clapping until she nodded at Chops and he chorded down to a new song in a series they had set up as an encore.

She sang six more songs before she stopped. This time when the applause trailed off, she bowed.

Miles Kelton threw a quarter on the stage. It clanked on the wooden floor. He tossed another quarter on the stage and then a third and a fourth. Some of the men in the front of the hall grinned and pitched coins to the singer.

Just the way Miles told her to do, Kat took the sides of her pretty blue skirt and lifted them slightly so she could catch the coins. A man in the first row stood and tossed a silver dollar and she caught it in her skirt. Somebody whooped in the crowd and a dozen more coins fell on the stage or landed in her skirt.

Kat knew well that her lifted skirt showed off her blue slippers and a foot of her bare leg. A small tease, but the men responded to it. Chops played some fast-paced music as the coins rained down. Then Chops hit a strong chord and came from the piano with a broom and swept the coins into a pile, picked them up and dropped them in Kat's held-up skirt.

The men whooped and yelled as she hurried off the stage to the left. There a small room had been built for a dressing area. Kat's place for between the shows had a small cot, two chairs, a table with water and towels and a mirror.

Just inside the door she paused, still holding up her blue skirt. She grinned and let the coins roll out onto the comforter spread on the cot.

She spied one five-dollar gold piece, three silver dollars and loads of quarters and 50-cent pieces.

Miles Kelton knocked and came in. They counted the coins. There was over 16 dollars worth of coins

"Oh, my, that is fine," Kat whispered. "For two shows that would be over thirty dollars!"

Kelton nodded. "Less my fifteen percent. I'd guess the boss must have taken in a thousand dollars tonight in drinks and gambling profits. You know what five percent of a thousand dollars is?"

Kat shook her head.

"It's another fifty dollars."

Kat's eyes went wide. "So I could make eighty dollars a day?"

"Less my fifteen percent or twenty dollars." He'd figured it quickly, cheating her a lot, but she'd never know. "That still leaves you with sixty dollars for an evening's work. Not bad at all. For six days that's three hundred and sixty dollars. As much as some men make for working all year."

"I'm overwhelmed."

"So overwhelmed you'd be extra nice to me?" He

bent and kissed her lips. She didn't respond or protest. His hand slid down to her bare breast tops showing over her dress. She slapped his hand away and stood.

"I'm not that overwhelmed. I told you I want to get rich. I won't get involved with any man who isn't rich. When you own a few gold mines, we'll talk about it. Until then this is strictly a business arrangement between us."

Kelton held up his hands. "I know, I know. I'm trying as hard as I can to get rich."

Kat Flowers looked at him coolly. "Fine, but try harder." She held the door open for him and he left. She sat down beside her stacks of coins and laughed softly.

Chapter Six

Buckskin Lee Morgan arrived back in Cripple Creek from his Colorado Springs trip just before noon the day after he'd left. He had a quick lunch, then checked the hotel again asking about a young girl with short brown hair.

The hotel clerk couldn't remember anyone of that age, size and hair coloring who had registered alone in the past two weeks. But the young clerk was interested.

"That the same girl you were hunting a few days ago?"

"Yes. I think she may have cut her hair. Make her harder to find. Sometimes I wonder why she would run away from a fortune like that."

Next he turned to the boardinghouses. The first one he stopped at he remembered from before. A handsome woman in her thirties ran the place.

She was widowed, she'd told him, and didn't have any children.

Her name was Emily Johnson. He knocked on the door and she let him in and smiled.

"Well, Mr. Morgan. I'm so pleased to see you. Still hunting that runaway girl?"

He told her he was and gave her the new description.

"Land sakes, I don't have any female boarders 'tall here. It just led to too many complications. The men seem to be steadier, not so much turnover." She waved him inside and shut the door firmly.

"Matter of fact, I have a nice room available. You probably staying at that hotel where they charge you two dollars a day for almost nothing. I can put you up here. Clean sheets every Monday, two square meals a day, three if you're around and about at noontime, and a friendly atmosphere. What more could a man want?"

"Mrs. Johnson, I admit it does sound fine, but I won't be in town long. Soon as I find this girl . . ."

She shushed him with a wave of her hand, "I won't hear of it. We need to make our important visitors feel more at home in Cripple Creek. Let me show you the room. It's on the ground floor, matter of fact. Used to be the parlor before I redid things a little. Right this way, Mr. Morgan. At least let me show you the place."

He grinned and motioned for her to go first. "Right behind you, Mrs. Johnson." He followed her, admiring the womanly sway of her firm tight hips. She still had her girlish figure. She opened a

71

door and showed him into the room.

It was pleasant, with a window looking out on the street, a good bed with a hand-quilted blanket on it and a chair, small table and washstand.

"Nice, quite nice, Mrs. Johnson, but . . ."

She quieted him again with her hand. "Fact is, the rent's been paid through the end of the month. I'd be pleased if you'd be my guest here for that time. Like you said, you probably will be gone before then anyway. Test out that bed."

She sat down on it and patted a spot beside her. He sat down, and as he did she leaned in so that he brushed her shoulder.

"Excuse me," he said.

"Oh, that's all right. Fine, in fact. A woman in my situation does tend to get a bit lonesome from time to time." She leaned toward him slightly and he caught her shoulders and moved his face slowly toward hers. She nodded and reached out. The kiss was short and sharp and he pulled back surprised.

"Oh, my," Mrs. Johnson said.

They moved together again, and this time the kiss was hard and insistent and she put her arms around him and pulled him tightly against her breasts. The kiss lasted and lasted and she murmured softly. When their lips came apart she still held him close.

"Oh, my, Mr. Morgan, but that was fine. I so hope that you'll be my guest here for the next few weeks. I wanted to offer you a room when you stopped by before, but I was all full. Could you see your way to stay here?"

She had her chin on his shoulder and he eased her away from him so he could see her.

"A lady does get lonesome . . . for some male companionship from time to time," she said.

Buckskin reached in, kissed her soft lips twice quickly and stood.

"Mrs. Johnson, save this room for me. I'll move out of the hotel and be over before supper."

She beamed and stood beside him. "I'm so glad. You won't be disappointed by the bed or the food—or the special benefits, Mr. Morgan." She picked up one of his hands and put it over her right breast and held it there. "The special benefits will be a true blessing for me and I hope exciting for you."

He massaged her breast gently, then withdrew his hand.

"So, business first," he said. "I need to check on the other boardinghouse to be sure I'm not over-looking anything. I'll be back before supper."

She reached up and pecked a kiss on his cheek. "I'll make something special for tonight," she said.

Once outside, he hurried to the other boarding-house he knew about. No one there had seen a girl with short brown hair. He went back to his hotel room to move out. It was nearly three in the afternoon.

Inside his room, he stopped and drew his six-gun. The place was a mess. Somebody had searched it, evidently looking for something. He saw no one was there, and holstered his gun and began picking up things. He packed as he went and saw that nothing was missing. He had a spare

73

Colt .45 in a false bottom in his carpetbag, but that was still in place. Even the bed had been torn apart and the sheets thrown across the room. He checked it all again to be sure nothing was missing, and went down, reported it to the room clerk and left.

Who would tear up his room and what were they hunting? If they had wanted to scare him away they would have tried something else. This seemed to have some purpose.

On his way to the Johnson boardinghouse, he passed the Alexander Hardware and General Store. A small gift for his new landlady would be a nice touch. He had no idea what it might be. Inside the store he wandered around the aisles. Most of the items there were practical, essential to frontier life and the art of mining. Few if any luxury items had places on the shelves.

On the clothing table, he discovered some silk scarves. A blue one with an interesting pattern caught his eye. Just the thing. He took it back to the counter. The young boy stood there, with his cap off this time.

"So, clerking now, are you?" Buckskin asked.

The youth nodded. He looked at the tag on the scarf. "That will be sixty-five cents, unless you want something else."

"No, that's all."

The boy took the scarf, folded it neatly and handed it to Buckskin. Then the boy made change for a dollar and counted it back to him.

"You been clerking long?" Buckskin asked. "You do it quite well."

"Thank you. I'm learning."

Buckskin saw the hint of a smile edge onto the young face, but thought nothing of it. He took his change and hurried out the front door of the store, hoping he wouldn't be late for supper at the boardinghouse. That was when he realized he didn't know when meals were at the Johnson place.

He walked quickly along the uneven boardwalk. Each merchant was responsible for building a boardwalk in front of his store. Some did, some didn't. Often there was a step up or one down between different parts of the boardwalk. Where there had been no store put up yet, there was no boardwalk at all.

He had just stepped down to a vacant section beyond the hardware store when two men came out of the shadows. Both were as tall as Buckskin thick in the shoulders and they walked directly toward him.

He knew it was trouble. He could stop them with a quick draw, but a little exercise might do him good. The two split up and came at him from both sides. He had picked the taller one as the weakest of the two. He was rangy more than muscled, heavy but with too much fat to be tagged as a fighter.

Buckskin stopped, pushed the scarf deeper into his pants pocket and waved at the tall one.

"Hey, stranger, can you tell me how to find the sheriff's office?"

The question caught the man by surprise and he faltered. He shot a quick look at his partner, and that was when Buckskin lunged forward. The side of his right hand chopped hard into the exposed neck. The blow caught the man by surprise and he gurgled, stared at Buckskin for a second, then slid to the ground unconscious before he rolled in the dirt.

Buckskin turned to face the tougher opponent.

"Think you're pretty smart, huh?" the man growled.

Buckskin waited for him. He came in a rush, and Buckskin sidestepped the charge and slammed a kidney blow into the attacker's side as he slanted past.

"Bastard, stand still and fight," the man barked as he turned and stalked Buckskin again. This time he drove in, stopped and feinted with a left fist, then swung his right. Buckskin stepped ahead inside the blow before it got there, jolted a hard fist into the point of the man's chin and smashed him backwards.

The thickset attacker fell back on his heels, then took two quick steps to the rear and scowled. Buckskin saw that the man on the ground hadn't moved.

Buckskin took the lead now, working in close with short, sure steps, his guard up, watching the other one. Half-a-dozen men had gathered around. Buckskin heard two arranging a bet.

He bored in hard, taking a light blow to the shoulder, exchanging it for a solid smash into the man's soft gut, then a cross to the side of his face. The man was a brawler, not a boxer. He backed up again, and Buckskin powered in with a light jab to his nose. Then his right fist came up from his beltline and thundered into his opponent's jaw in an uppercut that lifted him off his heels to his toes, then dumped him backward.

He hit the dirt of the alley, tried to get up, fell back to his knees and then rolled over on his back.

Buckskin was on him like a wolf, one knee on his chest pinning him down. He picked up the man's head with a handful of hair and back-handed him across the face.

"Who hired you?" Buckskin spat.

The man's eyes flickered, then came open to stay. "Can't say. Can't tell."

Buckskin drew his Colt, cocked it and waved it in front of the man. "Then you die right here. You lost the fight. Just like in Roman times, the loser dies. Caesar has said so." He pushed the muzzle of the Colt under the man's chin and forced it upward in the soft flesh until he heard a yowel of pain.

"Who?"

"Goddamn. Amos. It was Amos," the downed man said.

"Amos who?"

"Don't know. Never saw him before. Gave us five bucks each to pick a fight with you."

"If you're lying to me, you're a dead man. Remember that." Buckskin backhanded him on the other cheek and dropped him back in the dirt. A dozen men stood around watching. Buckskin stood, holstering the Colt.

"Anyone know a man named Amos in town?" Buckskin asked.

Most of the men shook their heads. One

frowned, then nodded. Buckskin walked up to him.

"Amos who?" Buckskin said.

"Two of them I know of. One is Amos Evers. Runs the saddle and leather goods store down the street. Then there's an Amos Ronson who works in the All American mine as a mucker."

Buckskin thanked the man. "Don't worry about them two. They ain't hurt, just a little pounded. Should be able to work by morning."

He turned and walked away toward the Johnson house. Nothing like a little exercise to whet a man's appetite. A few steps later he changed his mind and walked in the other direction toward the saddle shop. He'd always had a weakness for good leather-work. The smell of fresh-cut cowhide and the tanning chemicals set his blood to surging. He'd never taken the time to see if he could learn the trade of saddle-making.

He found the place a half block down from the Cripple Creek National Bank. The moment he stepped inside he caught the fever again. Directly in front of him sat a new saddle on display on a wooden rail. It was magnificent, with silver tooled into it in several locations but not too much to make it too expensive for an ordinary rider to own.

A man came out of a back room through a door hung with strips of leather lacing. He looked part-Indian, had a pleasant smile and watched Buckskin looking at the saddle.

"That's a fifty-five-dollar saddle, but you can have it on special for only forty-five."

"I'd pay you the fifty-five if I could use it, but

lately I've been doing too much riding the rails to own a good saddle." Buckskin looked up, the ease, the smile gone. "You Amos Evers?"

"Yep, that's what my pa tells me."

"You know me?"

"Can't say as I do. Lots of new folks in Cripple Creek, and not enough horses to my way of thinking. Leastwise saddle horses. Sure, I make harnesses too. But I'd rather do more saddles."

"You just send two men to beat me to a bloody stump?"

Amos Evers grinned and shook his head. "Now, why would I want to do that since I have no idea who you are?"

"You positive of that?"

"Damn sure. I make saddles and sell leather. I don't get people beat up."

"Know any other men named Amos in town?"

"Heard of one miner, then somebody said he heard of another one. I never met neither of them." He paused. "For just being in a fight, you don't look too bad off. I walked by just after it started."

"Sometimes I get lucky." Buckskin grinned. He liked this leathersmith. "You do good work. That's a beautiful saddle."

"Rides well too."

"Look, I'm new in town. Who would be trying to scare me away? Is anything big brewing around here?"

The leather worker frowned and rubbed his jaw, then shook his head. "Not that I can figure. Everyone is concentrating on finding an upthrust and then getting enough money together to make it a paying mine. Takes up most of the energy."

"What I figured. But somebody sure as hell doesn't want me in town, and I can't figure out why."

"Figure the why and shouldn't be too hard to come up with the man behind it."

Buckskin grinned. "Yeah, I been working on that. Thanks for your help. Sure like to buy that saddle." He waved and walked out. He was going to be late for supper. If he was lucky, the Widow Johnson would hold dinner for him. He smiled and he remembered his hand on her breast that afternoon. She was truly in need and he'd take care of that need tonight, if he was any judge of women. Yes, it would be tonight.

Chapter Seven

Miles Kelton slammed his palm down on the table so hard it made the cups of coffee jump. His face showed calmness but his voice seethed with anger.

"By God no, Douglas. We can't have this. You gave away another eighth of the Lucky Lady. Lost it in a poker game, you asshole. I've warned you twice before, remember?"

"Hell, I had a damn good hand and I was only a dollar short, and they said no light bets. Oh, hell."

Kelton had been hovering over the miner, who sat in a chair in the back room of the Deep Shaft Saloon. Kelton owned half of the place, but no one knew it. He grabbed Douglas by the face, his thumb under his chin pressing upward painfully.

"You stupid son of a bitch! You gave away an

eighth of our claim for a one-dollar bet? You are shit dumb. I bought half of your claim two weeks ago. This is the fifth time that you've sold or kicked away a one-eighth share. That means you don't own any of the claim anymore if those people ever come around to collect. Besides that, you sold more than you own. That could land you in prison, you stupid bastard."

"I . . . I lost track. Sure as hell I did, Mr. Kelton. I just lost track. Didn't mean to do no harm."

Kelton let go of his face and pushed him sideways. Douglas had to grab the table to keep from falling to the floor with the chair.

Kelton paced to the near wall and back. He was of average height, 32 years old, a lawyer by trade, and had been one of the first on site in the Cripple Creek gold rush. He'd staked out six claims and had hired men working them enough to keep the claims in force. So far he hadn't found an upthrust.

He had black hair that he let grow a little longer than the fashion and a heavy mustache. His left hand showed the effects of a bullet slamming through it. He had only partial use of his thumb and first two fingers. The other two were locked together and couldn't bend. It had been the last of his youthful tries at forming an outlaw gang. Their first and last robbery had netted the three youths 25 dollars and a shot-up hand. He had been furious at all of mankind ever since.

Kelton came back and stared at Larry Douglas until the younger man in the chair squirmed and looked away. "I didn't mean to do anything wrong," Douglas said.

Someone came in the far door, walked to Kelton and spoke to him so the others in the room couldn't hear.

Kelton nodded. "All right. Keep Douglas here. Bring him a beer and keep him quiet. I've got an appointment I'd forgotten about. I'll be back in half an hour."

Five minutes later, in his office on the second floor over the barbershop, Miles Kelton smiled at the sturdy woman sitting in his leather guest's chair.

"Blanche, sorry I'm late. Had some small problems to clear up. As I remember, you said you had something of a credit problem. I didn't know you worked on anything but a cash basis."

Blanche smiled. She had bright red hair and wore a tight blue dress cut low enough to show a four-inch slice of cleavage between her massive breasts.

"Sometimes with gentlemen I know and respect, I extend some credit. But this one gent, I'm worried about."

Kelton was no stranger to Blanche. For the first six wild months in Cripple Creek she was the only whore in town, and her rates went from five dollars to 15 and she could have worked 24 hours a day if she'd wanted to. Kelton had found her a worthy opponent for his type of hard-driving, fast-paced sex. Right now she had the one hole in town that was producing lots of gold.

"I got me this one sweet guy who don't have

much cash," she said. "Now and then I let him give me a paper—an I.O.U. he called them. Brought them along for you to look at. See, I don't know if they any good. Maybe he's just shuckin' me."

"You have one of them with you, Blanche?"

"Oh, yes." she reached in her reticule and brought out a piece of paper. It had been torn off a larger sheet and had writing on it. She handed it to the lawyer, who turned up the wick of the lamp on his desk.

He read it: "I owe Blanche Barton one-eighth share in my gold claim, the Lucky Lady in the Cripple Creek Mining District. Dated June 10, 1892." It was signed by Larry Douglas.

"Damn!" the lawyer exploded. He slammed his hand down on the desk. "You mean this guy gave you this paper for a free poking?"

"Yeah. I like the guy. He's sweet. Everybody else pays cash or the poking hole is closed."

"The man's an idiot. If his claim hit an upthrust you could be a wealthy lady . . . if this paper was any good."

"Yeah, about what I figured. I don't read none too good, but he told me what it said. Still, I couldn't be sure, and I didn't trust nobody else in town to look at them."

"Them? You have more than this one?"

"Land sakes, yes." She reached in her reticule and took out a sheaf of papers held together with a safety pin. "Don't know how many, I never counted them. Go back most of a year, I'd say."

Kelton had to hold his hand back from ripping the papers out of her hand. What had that idiot

Douglas done this time? He took the papers gently, undid the pin and went through the odd-sized papers. Some were torn from a newspaper, some from a book. He read each one. When he finished he had trouble controlling himself.

There were 18 slips of paper. Each one gave to Blanche Barton a one-eighth share in the Lucky Lady claim. She owned the claim more than twice over. The miserable, double-crossing bastard.

When he could speak, Kelton looked up. "Sorry, Blanche. Like I said before, these aren't worth a thing. He cheated you, and I'd say he owes you at least two hundred dollars. Depending what your rates were over the past year."

Blanche shrugged. "Yeah, about what I figured. I don't need the money. You know I been doing right well. Got me a bank account in the Springs and all. I might just retire over there in a year or so. Poor Larry. I didn't mean to get him in no trouble. Just wanted to know if them papers was any good."

Kelton stood, his time-honored way to get rid of someone from his office. Blanche Barton didn't take the hint.

"Blanche, that's about all I can do for you today. Oh, that will be two dollars for the office visit."

Blanche grinned. "I charge a lot more than you do, lawyer man. You should raise your rates."

She gave him two dollars and he let her out to the hallway that led to the steps down to the street.

He sat behind his desk for a moment, the fury building in him. He roared in anger, pushed the chair back so hard it slammed into the wall, then stalked toward the door.

It took him only three minutes to walk to the back room at the Deep Shaft Saloon.

Larry Douglas had just finished the mug of beer. He looked up. "I should get back to the shaft. Down near fifteen feet now and starting my laterals."

"You won't ever . . ." Kelton stopped. "The shaft. Yeah, good idea. I'll come with you. Haven't seen the work you're doing on our claim."

Douglas started to stand. "It's all right then for me to go? Got a lot of work to do over there. Putting on a windlass to wind up my dirt and rocks. Still easy digging."

Kelton nodded. "Yeah, let's go. Lars, you come with us. Might be some cleanup work to do over there."

It was just a little past eight o'clock in the evening when the three men walked up to the sign that said this was the Lucky Lady claim. A small shack on one side served as living quarters for Douglas. The open shaft dropped into the ground a short distance away. The new windlass and half-inch rope was in place but not quite ready to use.

The claim had been laid out below the all American, the first mine in the district to start producing ore. With any luck there would be an upthrust or two near the mine above. No other claim was nearby.

Kelton went to his knees beside the open shaft and looked down. Douglas had fired up a kerosene lantern, and lowered it down the shaft on the windlass rope. Soon they could see the bottom.

"Pull the light back up, I thought I saw something," Kelton said. Douglas hoisted the lantern a little at a time until Kelton stopped him.

"There, right there on the side. Douglas, look at that. I swear that's a vein of gold right there. A small vein, but damn, that's gold ore, I'd swear."

Douglas knelt beside him and looked. "Down there about six feet on the far side?" Kelton asked.

"That's a blotch of quartz." Douglas said.

"No, just under that. Look closer." Kelton stared around at the treeless slope of mountain. He couldn't see anyone in the darkness. Nobody close enough to see them clearly. He looked back at Douglas.

"Just a little lower, see it?"

As Douglas bent lower over the mine shaft, Kelton drew the heavy .45 from his gunbelt and slammed the butt down hard on Douglas's head. The man cried out sharply, grabbing the side of the shaft. Kelton hit him twice more with the butt of the revolver, slamming him off the edge and dumping him downward into the hole.

Lars had been standing behind them, shielding the action from any possible viewer.

"Let's move," Kelton said. He and Lars walked away without checking on the man below. Kelton's skull had split open with the second blow from the steel gun butt and he'd died before he hit the bottom of his own mine shaft.

Buckskin missed supper. He came in the front door after the four other boarders had left for the evening or gone back to their rooms. He eased into the kitchen and found Emily Johnson cleaning up.

She turned and smiled when she saw him. She wore a dress that showed off her breasts and her flat tummy. She crooked a finger at him.

"Buck, you want some supper you come over here and ask me nice for it."

From her grin, he knew she didn't want any words. He moved close to her, then bent and kissed her breasts, blowing his hot breath on them and searching for her nipple with his hand.

"Now, you're getting the idea" she said. "Oh, lordy, yes, you've got the idea down to a fare-thee-well." She took several deep breaths and lifted his face away.

"Best you stop that this instant before I lay down right here on the kitchen floor and pull off my bloomers." She patted her hair and smiled again. "Just a little bit later for more of that. First, you have some supper. I saved it warm for you in the oven. Nice thing about a wood stove, the oven stays hot for just ever so long."

Supper was fried chicken, biscuits, chicken giblet gravy, fresh peas, mashed potatoes, golden-brown fried carrots and parsnips and cherry pie for desert.

She watched him eat, one hand on his leg. "Don't you dare eat so much you can't get it up or I'll kill you. I been dreaming about this all day. Damn, but I like the way you look. Can't wait to check you out naked as a hootencatcher."

He frowned. "What's a hootencatcher?"

"Beats me. My mother always used to use that word."

By the time he finished eating, she had the rest of the kitchen cleaned up and put his dishes on a small counter. "I'll get those in the morning. You want your room or mine?"

A half hour later, they lay on her bed trying to catch their breath. She traced the thick hair on his chest and sighed.

"Just 'bout perfect. I knew you'd be a lot better than anybody I knew around here." She looked up. "Not that I do this a lot. Did with my husband, of course. Must have been at least twice a day that first six months. He poked me regular. Course he wasn't all that good in bed. Different since he got killed at the mine. Actually now and then a girl gets to . . . you know, wanting a little poking."

He traced a line with his finger around one breast, then the other one, and tweaked her nipples. They roused up and stood tall again.

"You don't have to go to your room," she said. "I want you to stay all night. It's been, what, two years since I had somebody for the whole fucking night."

She giggled and covered her mouth. "Usual I don't talk dirty, but when I've just been poked it seems more natural. From talking with the other women around, I guess I like to fuck more than some of them. I love it. You figured out how we're going to do it the second time?"

Buckskin grinned. "I have." He rolled out of her bed, caught her hand and led her to the inside wall beside the door. He pushed her against the wall. She frowned at him.

"I tried it standing up once, can't be done."

"Can," he said. "If you're ever really hurting to be fucked and don't have a bed, try it this way."

He put her hands around his neck. "Lock your fingers together and hang on," he said. "Now jump up and put your legs around my back and lock them together."

"Strange," she said, then nodded. "Yeah, now I see it changes the angle."

As she spoke Buckskin caught her hips, eased her back a little, then rammed hard forward into her slot and sank into the hilt.

"Good Lord!" Emily whispered. "That's fantastic. How did you learn to do it this way?" She shook her head. "No, don't tell me, just get on with the poking. I've never been done this way."

Buckskin went to the task at hand, and soon had her panting and moaning and squealing as he drilled her hard and fast. She cried out in a small voice, then exploded as she spasmed again and again, shattering every nerve ending in her body and pushing in hard against him to make it last as long as possible.

Before she finished he felt his own world collapsing. The jetting stream shot through his tubes and he panted and moaned in rapture. Then the climax came and he brayed and thrust hard with his hips a dozen times as the world shattered around him and it sent him spinning through the stars to far-off planets and new worlds and people before he came down to Earth against her and eased away from her so she could unlatch her legs.

They fell on her bed panting again for five minutes before they came back to life and looked at one another.

"Now that was . . . what?" Emily looked up at him. "How can I describe it? Weird, I guess. I've never been fucked that way before, but I'll be game to try it again. You have any more strange ideas for fucking picked up in your travels?"

"A few," he said. "You want to get any sleep tonight at all?"

Emily laughed. "Not a wink. I can have a nap tomorrow. I'm going to make the best of you while you're here. You could find that little girl tomorrow and be on the train tomorrow night for Denver."

"True," he said. "But right now I don't have the faintest idea where she is or even if she's still in Cripple Creek."

"She has gold fever?"

"What her father told me. Talked about nothing else for a year."

"Then she's here. She might be keeping house for one of the mine owners who hit it big. Or maybe cooking in one of the brothels. All she needs is to be in town, to be near the gold rush, to hear the talk, to look at the mines, to see the claims. It's a kind of a fever that don't burn out easily."

"Let's hope so. I'll get paid well if I find her."

"If you don't?"

"Then I just get my daily wages and expenses."

"I should have charged you more rent."

"More than nothing wouldn't be hard."

She rolled over on top of him, her naked flesh nesting with his. She kissed his lips quickly, then sighed. "Damn, but I wish you were staying around. I just love being with you. You're fun even when we're not fucking."

"Well, thank you. You're fun all the time, especially when your legs are locked around my back."

"I'd blush but I forgot how. Wanting it so bad sometimes kills off all those girlish blushes."

Buckskin nodded. "Know the feeling." He paused. "Hey, didn't you bring some of that cherry pie in here?"

"I wondered how many times it would take to make you hungry. Cherry pie and lemonade right behind us on the dresser. You mind standing up to eat?"

They finished the last two pieces of the pie she had made for supper and then stretched out on the big bed again. She kissed him and eased away, her breasts pressed against his chest.

"My turn to pick the position," she said. "My ideas might not be as wild as yours. We'll have to see."

"You trying to set a record?" he asked.

"A record for how many times in one night? Hadn't thought of it. Now that you bring it up, I'm stuck on five. I hope you have lots of staying power."

He did.

The next morning she was gone when he woke up at 6:30. He slipped from her bedroom and into his room, changed clothes and came out just as the last of the breakfasting boarders headed out the front door for work.

She had hotcakes, eggs and bacon for breakfast, and he ate in a hurry, kissed her good-bye and hiked three blocks to the small newspaper office he had seen. It was just eight o'clock as he tried the door, found it open and ran into a young man wearing a stiff collar, a tie and a black suit and hat and on his way out.

"You the editor?" Buckskin asked.

"Indeed I am, and I'm on the way to cover a story. If you want to talk, you'll have to come along."

"A story?" Buckskin asked. "What story?"

"Oh, I thought you knew. Somehow a miner managed to fall down his own shaft last night and get himself killed. The body hasn't been moved yet, so if we hurry maybe we'll find some clues."

The editor had picked up the pace of his walk as they slanted uphill and to the west.

"Who was the dead man?" Buckskin asked.

"Oh, right, you don't know. He was Larry Douglas, the owner of the Lucky Lady claim. It didn't prove lucky for him. Now the question is did he commit suicide, have a fatal accident or was he murdered?"

"Larry Douglas," Buckskin said. He took the I.O.U. out of his pocket. That was the name. The dead man was the same one Buckskin had won a one-eighth share of the Lucky Lady claim from in the poker game two nights ago. Now he was dead. Why?

Chapter Eight

At least 30 men were crowded around the shaft when Buckskin and the newsman arrived. Buckskin had found out the editor's name was Ray Ewing. He'd started the newspaper three months ago and was still losing money on it. As usual he bewailed the lack of any kind of advertising.

Buckskin pushed through the crowd until he came to the edge of the shaft. No one looked official.

"Who's in charge here?" Buckskin bellowed. The crowd quieted and Buckskin called out the question again. A lot of men shrugged and two men looked away from his glance.

"I forgot, no law in this town. Where's the town marshal, is he here?"

"Tony Tarento?" somebody asked. "What good would he do?"

"He's the only thing like a lawman we have. Who found the body?"

A boy no more than 16 held up his hand like he was in school. "I did, sir."

"Why?"

"I worked for Mr. Douglas. I dug on a tunnel we're running looking for an upthrust. I dug mostly and he mucked out and hauled the dirt and rocks up."

"When did you find him?"

"This morning when I come to work, about an hour ago."

"You go down the hole?"

"Oh, no, sir. Dead bodies scare me. Can I go now?"

"Go where?"

"Back to Denver. I done seen enough of a gold rush to last me all my life."

"You have train fare?"

"No, sir."

"Give me your hat, boy."

The youth brought over his hat and Buckskin put a dollar bill in it. "His hat's coming around, you men. Give the kid some train fare back home. A quarter a man should do it."

Buckskin looked at the hole and the windless. The rope had been anchored on one side but not set up yet on the barrel. He gave the rope a tug. It was solid. He stepped out over the hole and holding tight to the rope, walked down the side of the shaft to the bottom.

He spent five minutes examining the body. Now and again a clod of dirt fell down, kicked over the edge above by some of the curious. He discovered two things at once. There were two deep wounds on the man's head that could have been inflicted by the butt of a revolver. He put the butt of his .45 up to the wounds. It matched perfectly. Probably not more than three or four hundred revolvers that fit the wounds in town.

The second thing he spotted was that there was no blood on the bottom of the shaft. Douglas had died before he came down or maybe on impact. Either way the blows to the head would have been more than enough to kill him.

Buck tied the end of the rope around Douglas, making a loop of the end of the rope under his arms, and looked up.

"Hoist him away. Wrap the rope around the windlass and save your backs some strain."

A few moments later the remains of Larry Douglas were lifted slowly out of the premature grave. When the rope came back down, Buckskin grabbed it, tugged and then walked up the side of the wall by working up the rope hand-over-hand.

On top he found Tarento, still with his apron on, staring at the body. He looked at Buckskin.

"What am I supposed to do now?"

"Send somebody to Florissant to wire the sheriff to come. Tell him there's been a murder here of an owner of a claim, and that there's a U.S. marshal here who wants to see him."

Tarento looked up sharply. "You a U.S. marshal?"

"Didn't say I was. That should get him blasted

out of the Springs and over here. You have an undertaker in town?"

"Yeah, sure."

"Have him come get the body and lay it out on two slabs of ice from the icehouse. Keep Douglas there chilled until the sheriff can get a good look at him."

A man in a bright red shirt and a red top hat stepped forward. "I'm the undertaker here. Proctor R. Oakes. I can take care of refrigerating the body for up to four days. No more."

"Should be time enough even for a sheriff." Buckskin looked around the group. He saw no one he knew. "Was this claim owned jointly by any partners with Mr. Douglas?"

There was silence for a moment and then somebody called out from the back of the group.

"Hell, yes, I won a one-eighth share from Douglas one night in a poker game. He signed it so I guess it's legal."

Would you come up here, please?" Buckskin asked.

Another man came up and waved a paper. "I got me a one-eighth share too, but what good is part of nothing? Told him this wasn't a good spot for a claim."

"If that's true, why did someone kill him?" Buckskin asked.

Another man from the crowd came forward. He was tall with blond hair. He nodded to Buckskin.

"Douglas was short of money last month. He sold me half interest in his claim. I got the paper at home."

Buckskin put him beside the other two. "So it looks like Douglas sold three-quarters of his claim. Didn't leave him much. Do you suppose the killers did in the wrong man? Just a thought."

He looked around the crowd. "Seems the excitement is over, folks. Time to get back to your own work and let these gents work out what to do with this claim." The crowd began to thin as the men wandered back to their own digs.

Buckskin turned to the three men left by the hole. "Now it seems that this claim has new owners. Fact is, I own one-eighth of this claim myself. Looks like the Lucky Lady didn't really belong to Larry Douglas at all." He turned to the blond man. "I didn't catch your name."

The big man blinked. "I'm Lars Zacherias and I own half, so what I say goes. I'm bringing in two men to keep digging the drifts and tunnels. I still think there's an upthrust on this claim. Oh, I'll be dividing up your share of the expenses for the work to each of you gents, unless you want to sell your one-eighth rights. I'm offering to pay a hundred dollars each."

"A hundred for a one-eighth of an unproved claim," one of the men said. "Hey, show me your money, I'm selling."

"You got the paper with you?" Lars asked.

"Hell, no."

"Get it and meet me at the Deep Shaft Saloon. I'll be there the rest of the morning."

The man hurried away. Lars looked at Buckskin and the other man. "How about the two of you?"

"You control it with your five-eighths," Buckskin said. "Why do you need our shares?"

"Just in case. Price I'm paying right now just went up to a hundred and fifty dollars."

"Not a chance," the other miner said. "I'll hold on to it and watch to see that you work this dig right."

"I'm not selling either," Buckskin said. "You can be sure I'll be watching you careful. Lars, did you kill Douglas?"

The tall, blond man surged three steps toward Buckskin before he stopped. His face went red and he scowled, barely able to control his anger.

"Hell, no, did you?" Lars said. Then he turned and walked down the slope toward the business section of Cripple Creek. Buckskin and the other man looked at each other and Buckskin grinned.

"You're the poker player the other night in that game with Douglas when I won that share."

The man lifted one hand and nodded. "Wondered when you would figure that out. Looks like we're partners. Name's Don Casemore." He held out his hand. Buckskin took it and shook.

"I'm Buckskin Morgan. You can probably show me a lot about this town and the claim. Want to take a look at our hole in the ground?"

A half hour later they had explored the two tunnels that had been dug off the main shaft. At the bottom of the shaft were three lanterns, some picks and shovels and an assortment of five-and ten-gallon buckets for lifting out the dirt and rocks.

"So, what do you think of our hole?" Buckskin asked.

"It's a possible. Hell, everytime you go down fifteen feet and start pushing tunnels out, it's a possible strike. This used to be an old volcano in here. Blew its top a million years ago or so and left all of these cracks where the molten rock boiled up for a while. They cooled and formed these upthrusts of solid rock. Lots of them have gold in them."

"Volcano, huh?"

"That's what the experts say. It was more than six miles across when it blew, so we have a six-mile-wide gold-dig area. Gold might be anywhere."

"How did the upthrusts get covered up?"

"Years and years of erosion, maybe dust storms, floods, hurricanes. Lots of things can happen to a chunk of ground in thirty or forty thousand years."

Casemore motioned with one hand. "You real busy or you got time to meet a friend of mine?"

"Not what you'd call busy at all. Who is this friend?"

They crawled out of the hole using the rope and went downtown to the Cripple Emporium Saloon. They picked up mugs of beer from the barkeep. Casemore took two. They went to a side table where a man sat talking to a newcomer with clean clothes and no sunburn.

"Bob, looks like your beer is about gone," Casemore said to the older man. "You have time for another one?"

"Casemore, you old grave robber, always time for a beer. Sit down and take a load off your boots."

The newcomer stood, shook the older man's hand and hurried away.

"They all want to know how to find an upthrust quick and easy," the man at the table said.

Casemore and Buckskin sat down. The man on the other side of the table was big and heavily muscled. Buckskin figured he was a little over six feet tall. He had black hair and a receding hairline and looked to be about 50 years old. He had larger than normal ears, and a prominent nose with flaring nostrils. Dark, deep-set eyes surveyed Buckskin from under hooded brows.

"Who's this greenhorn?" the man asked.

"Bob Womack, I'd like you to meet Buckskin Morgan," Casemore said. "He's new in town. Wanted him to meet the man who found the first upthrust in the whole area and started the Cripple Creek gold rush."

Womack didn't offer to shake hands. He stared at Buckskin for a moment and then nodded.

"It's an honor to meet you, Mr. Womack," Buckskin said. "You sure did stir up a lot of people with your gold find. You must be proud."

"Hell, proud ain't the word. Disgruntled, disgusted. A little mad that nobody believed me at first. Not even after that first piece of float tested out at two hundred and fifty dollars a ton. Then when I hit the upthrust, we still couldn't get any financing."

He took a long pull on the beer, then hunched his heavy shoulders forward. "See the thing is, in hardrock mining, it don't do no good just to find a vein of gold. You got to get somebody to put up

101

fifty to a hundred thousand dollars so you can start to dig that gold ore out and ship it to the smelter. Costs money all along the line. Hell, I didn't have no money. Hell, I couldn't raise no hundred thousand dollars."

They talked for a half hour, with Bob Womack telling how hard it was in the beginning and how his dentist friend from Colorado Springs, Dr. John P. Grannis, had financed him so he could even afford to find the first upthrust.

Buckskin had the itch to move. He looked around and saw three men waiting to talk to Bob Womack. He had become a legend in Cripple Creek and would offer free advice to anyone who asked.

Casemore brought another beer for Bob, and then he and Buckskin went out and sat in the chairs outside of the hardware store.

Buckskin told Casemore his real job in town, and the miner said he was a part-time miner. He had two claims but no upthrust yet. He also drove a wagon part-time for Nat Purvis, a mine owner who'd hit it big and was hauling out gold ore to the rail line in Florissant.

"He usually loads up two wagons and sends them together. He lost one wagon a week ago. Gold ore and all. Each one of them big heavy wagons packs two tons of gold ore. That ore is worth about two hundred dollars a ton. So that's a possible eight hundred dollars on each trip."

"He lost a wagon load of gold ore?"

"Yep. Don't know how it happened. Found the wagon but it was empty. Never did find the driver.

We're guessing the driver sold the gold ore to somebody for cash and went up the steel rails to Denver."

"He should have somebody riding shotgun," Buckskin said. "Now, you have any idea where I can find my runaway little rich girl in this wild mining town?"

"Did she have any money with her?"

"My guess is that she did. She must have planned this for a time."

"Why come here? Oh, you said she had gold fever. It burns out fast in a lot of people, especially the young ones. It's work here, drudgery in those tunnels. Although she wouldn't be down there."

"You know this town, Casemore. Where could she be?"

"From what you said, you've covered all the probable places. It would be hard for a young girl to hide in a town this small."

"I won't give up," Buckskin said.

Casemore chuckled. "Figured you wouldn't. And now you're the owner of part of a claim. I'll put my wife to working on your problem. We've got a wee bit of a house here."

"A house and a wife. That makes you a rich man in Cripple Creek no matter how much cash you have."

"Not much of that, I'm afraid. The sheriff should be here before dark tonight, if he comes. We're the poor country cousins to him even though we've struck gold."

Buckskin pushed his long legs out on the boardwalk and crossed them at his ankles. He laced his fingers behind his head and tipped his Stetson down so it barely let him see under the front brim. "What I can't figure out is why somebody killed Larry Douglas for an unproved claim. Must be three or four hundred such claims around here."

"At least that many. Good point. I've been thinking along the same lines, but we checked out that claim. It don't show no signs of an upthrust that is showing any place."

Buckskin came down from where he rested on the back two legs of the chair and hit all four legs on the boardwalk. He tipped his hat back. "Casemore, wasn't there a lot of loose dirt and rocks at the end of that short tunnel?"

"Yep. Way some guys work. Dig out a bunch and then haul it up a bucketful at a time."

"Yes. Now, have you played poker with Douglas before when he offered I.O.U.'s on his claim when he ran out of cash?"

Casemore rubbed his chin a moment, then nodded. "Yep, I'd say I have six or eight times. I liked playing with him because he usually lost."

"We know he gave out at least three of those I.O.U.'s on the claim. What if he gave out a dozen, maybe more?"

"He'd be in big trouble," Casemore said. "Be in big trouble with the law if we had any here and with his partner who had bought half the claim."

"Maybe he spread around a dozen or more of those I.O.U.'s and the tunnel hit something worthwhile. Right then the partners could decide that Douglas was too much of a problem to deal with. I don't know if a dead man's I.O.U. is any good or not. But ours seem to be worth a hundred and fifty dollars."

"But we looked at that claim, both tunnels and the shaft. I saw nothing that indicated anything valuable."

"Does the mining apex law hold here in Colorado?" Buckskin asked.

"Sure, basic mining law. You mean that to own a vein it must come to the surface and the man who owns that land or has claim to it owns the vein no matter where it goes underground? Even if it runs right through another man's mine?"

"That's the one. What if Douglas dug into a vein of ore that didn't surface on his claim? He could have covered it up with some more digging down in the end of that tunnel until he and his partner decided what to do about it."

Casemore nodded. "So the partner decides to cut his losses with the unpredictable partner and dump him dead down his own claim shaft."

Buckskin tapped his boot on the boardwalk. "This is starting to get interesting. How would you like to crawl back into that short tunnel with three bright kerosene lanterns and have a better look around?"

Casemore stood and grinned. "Being part owner of that claim, I'd be delighted to go with you for another look. Let's hope that the majority shareholder of the claim isn't back yet."

They walked up to the claim and found two men working on the windlass. Lars Zacherias came out of the shack holding a shotgun.

Chapter Nine

Harriet Braithwaite chided herself for ever agreeing to meet the boy after the store closed. She hardly knew him. Of course he thought she was Harry Carson. She had been friendly to him the first day he came into the store and tried to steal a loaf of bread. She'd taken it away from him and pushed him out the door. He'd turned around and come back in and told her he was hungry and hadn't eaten all day.

Harriet had given him a quarter and told him to buy the bread from the store owner, Mr. Alexander. He did, and stood around and talked as he ate the bread.

"I'm just in from Denver. Actually I've been here about a month. I worked for some guy in his mine until he gave up and left. I worked a couple of days more thinking I could sign on the claim, but they say you have to be eighteen. I'm just seventeen."

He looked at her and saw a boy younger than himself. "What about you? Why did you run away from home?"

"Who said I ran away? I might be an orphan."

"Are you?"

Harriet laughed, and she knew it sounded too much like a girl. She lowered her voice and shook her head. "No, I'm not an orphan."

"So you're working here. You get paid?"

"Sure, a dollar a day. I'm worth it."

He grinned. "I don't even know your name. What is it?"

"I'm Harry, Harry Carson."

"Good, I'll call you Kit. I'm Stan."

He left then, and she didn't know where he went. After that he came in every day. Usually he bought a loaf of bread. Sometimes he had a dollar and bought more food. He usually ate some of it and talked with Harry.

Then that afternoon he said he had an adventure planned and wanted Harry to come along with him.

"What kind of adventure?" Harry asked.

"It's a surprise. You'll love it." Stan lowered his voice and looked around. Nobody was near them in the clothes section of the Alexander Hardware and General Store. "Hey, you ever seen a girl naked, you know, without any clothes on?"

"Maybe. Why?"

"Oh, I just get to feeling sort of hot and bothered sometimes, you know, wondering what it'd be like. At home I never had a chance. Small little town.

Everybody knew everybody and if I even touched a girl's tits, she'd run and tell her mother and I'd get fried for a year."

"Oh, what small town?"

"I ain't saying where it is. So, you seen a naked girl or not?"

"Well, yes. She didn't look so much different than us."

"But she was old enough to have boobs, you know, tits?"

Harriet wanted to giggle, but she didn't. "Sure, that and long hair, that's about the only difference."

"Yeah, what I've heard. Tonight, right after you get off work, I'll have two surprises for you."

Harriet shivered, but it didn't show. "Yeah, sure. At the back door at just after eight o'clock."

Now Harriet Braithwaite wondered if it had been a good idea to say she would go with him. He might be wild or rob a saloon or something. No, she'd never seen him have a gun. She leaned against the side of the wooden back door to the store and wondered if she should go back inside.

Then she saw a shadow move up the alley and he was there.

"Hi, Harry. Glad you didn't disappoint me. Are we gonna have ourselves some fun!"

Harry shrugged. "Yeah, I guess. What are we going to do?"

"Hey, you'll see. We don't even need any money. Come on."

They walked down the alley, and Harry had to hurry to keep up.

"Where we going? You got to tell me."

Stan grinned in the half light coming from a pale moon. "We're going over two blocks and up the alley."

"So, what's so much fun about that?" Harry asked. She was getting more worried now. Maybe he knew she was a girl. Maybe he had figured it out and was going to get her alone in the dark alley and do all sorts of wild things to her. Maybe . . .

"You really want to know?"

"Yeah, right now."

"Okay, one word. Tits."

Harry scowled and shook her head. "Don't make no sense. How we gonna see naked girls in the alley?"

"You'll find out."

Stan started to trot then and Harry did likewise. They rounded the corner of Bennett and went down to Meyers Avenue on Second Street. Half a block down past Meyers they turned into the alley and Stan wailed. "Holy damn, I'm getting a hard-on already just thinking about it! Right down here. We got to be quiet now. Not a sound. You'll see what's what."

The building they were behind was two stories and had ten windows on the ground floor. Stan took off his hat, sidled up near the building and lifted up so he could look over the windowsill. A lamp burned in the room. He dropped down and shook his head and moved to the next window.

"What are we . . ." Harry began, but Stan turned and grabbed her mouth shutting off the words. He put his finger over his lips, then let go of Harry

109

and went to the next window. Now Harry saw that every one of the windows had light in it. Stan edged up to the next window and lifted up as before and looked inside.

"Oh, shit!" He dropped down and grinned. Take a look."

Harry lifted slowly beside the window and stared inside. What she saw was fascinating. A naked woman stood there as if showing off to someone. She turned slowly. She wasn't slender by any means. She had a fat little tummy, full breasts that swung as she turned and heavy legs and hips.

A naked man lay on the bed. Harry had heard about men and their privates, she'd seen pictures of a penis in a book once, but this one the man had was stiff and looked hard and must be eight inches long. He waved to the woman and said something, and she moved over to the bed and knelt over on top of him, then lay down full-length right on him.

Harry eased down. She could feel sweat beading on her forehead and under her arms. Naked people. What in the world? Then she knew. It was a brothel where the women sold their bodies to the men for money. Five dollars for half an hour. She'd heard the men talking about it more than once.

She looked at Stan. He still watched over the windowsill. There was no curtain on the window. Stan took a quick look at Harry and grinned.

"Told you it was about tits. Did you see those jugs on that whore? Man, they were big ones, huge, with red rings and everything. Even nipples."

Harry took another look. The man had rolled over on top of the woman and seemed to be pushing at her crotch. They were doing it! Like the girls at school talked about. Making love, they had called it. Having sex. She heard Stan panting and looked at him. He turned away from her and had his hands down by his waist. His hips pushed in and out.

"What are you doing?" Harry asked.

"What do you think? I'm jerking off. Go ahead. Watch them in there. Get your dick out of your pants and whang it off. You'll never get another chance like this. He's fucking her in there right now!" Stan groaned and thrust his hips ahead hard four, then five times. He panted like a steam locomotive, and then he shivered and sagged against the window. "Oh, damn. Oh, damn. Oh, damn, but that was fine."

Harry lifted up for one more look. The woman had locked her legs around the man's back and she humped up to meet the hard thrusts of the man's hips.

Stan caught Harry's arm.

"Come on, we better get out of here. They have a big ugly half-wit who prowls around back here watching for peepers. First time I ever tried it. Damn, did you see them big swingers of tits?"

They trotted to the end of the alley where they had come in and went down half a block on Second Street, then turned into the next alley behind

Bennett Avenue. Most of the main stores and saloons fronted Bennett.

"Why we going back here?" Harry asked. She was still seeing the naked man on the bed with the huge erection and then the two of them pounding away on the bed.

"Hard to tell what you can find back here. Drunks come out to go to the pisser. Sometimes they pass out."

"So you help them?" Harry asked.

Stan snorted. "Boy, kid, you've got a lot to learn. Why'n hell should I help them?"

They paused near the back door to a saloon. An outhouse had been strategically placed between two saloons. A man staggered out the door of one the drinking establishments, looked around in the pale moonlight and spotted the outhouse. He stumbled once getting there, but made it without falling down. The two crouched in shadows behind some packing boxes and waited.

"Maybe we should go," Harry whispered.

"Hell, no, the good part's coming up."

A short time later the man came out of the outhouse. He staggered more now, fell once and giggled. He rolled over and stood, then fell down again. This time he couldn't get up.

"Oh, hell," he said, then put his hand under his face to keep it out of the dirt and went to sleep.

"Yeah, just the way I like them," Stan said. "Come on." They walked up to the man. Stan nudged him with his toe, but he didn't wake up. Stan knelt beside the drunk and rifled his pockets. He laughed softly when he found two folded dollar bills and some change. A door down the other way leading to the other saloon slammed and Stan looked up. A man walked toward the outhouse.

"Let's get out of here," Stan whispered.

"Hey, you two. What the hell you doing?"

They stood when the man shouted.

"Hold it right there you robbers!" the man called.

"Run," Stan yelped, and both took off down the alley away from the second man. Behind them they heard another shout, then the boom of a six-gun. Harry thought she heard hot lead cut through the air over her head. Another shot blasted into the alley, but by that time they were far enough down the alley so the gunman couldn't see them and they were out of range.

Harry's teeth chattered. Sweat poured from her forehead and ran into her eyes. That man had actually *shot a revolver at them.* She could have been killed. For a second she didn't believe any of this had happened, but it had.

They ran to the end of the block, then across Bennett Avenue, and rested against a building half a block beyond Bennett. When Harry got her breath back she scowled at Stan.

"You stole that man's money? Stan, that makes you a sneak thief. You got us shot at. He could have killed us. How could you do that?"

Stan took a deep breath and shook his head. "What do you mean how? You just saw me. He had passed out. Hell, only three dollars or so. He'll never miss it. Figure he drank it up before he passed out."

"But you stole money from him."

"Sure. How do you suppose I've been getting money to buy enough to eat so I don't starve?"

"I'm going home." Harry turned and hurried away toward Bennett. Stan caught up with her and grabbed her shoulder and turned her around.

"You don't say nothing to nobody about this, you hear? I don't do no worse than thirty or forty others in town. Why are you such a goody-goody boy all of a sudden? Oh, sure, you don't need to steal to live. I do until I get a job where I can earn some money."

Harry put hands on her hips and shook her head at him. "You just don't come into the store anymore. If you do, I won't wait on you and I'll tell Mr. Alexander what you did to that poor man in the alley. He'll get the committee to run you out of town. He can do it. He has a lot of influence in Cripple Creek."

"You do that and I'll beat you up so bad your own mother wouldn't recognize your ugly face. It's quits with us. I figured you were a little more of a man, not some snot-nosed kid. Damn, was I wrong. Hell, good riddance."

Harry hurried down Bennett Avenue, stayed well on the street side of the boardwalk as she went past the saloons and soon got to the back door of the store. She used a key Mr. Alexander had given her and slipped inside. He was working in the office doing the books.

"Oh, you're back. Good. I'll put the bar on the back door. Have an interesting walk? You should be careful out at night. Some of the men get a little wild out there. I heard some shooting a few minutes ago."

Harriet mumbled, saying she was tired and going to bed. She sat on her bunk and took off her heavy shoes, massaging her toes and feet. The few days she had been there she had learned a lot, becoming physically stronger from lifting all the boxes, and she felt great. Yes, she missed home, but this was all so exciting.

Until tonight. She slipped out of her heavy outer shirt and pants and slid under the covers wearing her undershirt and some of the men's short cotton underwear she had adopted. She no longer bound her breasts. The heavy cotton shirts were baggy enough to conceal her upper figure, and it felt better.

She lay there in the semi-darkness. She still hadn't decided what to think about the whore she had seen. They were *doing it* right there in that room with the window unshuttered. Amazing. She'd heard about it before, but never seen anything like that. It wasn't a scene she'd soon forget.

Rifling the drunk's pockets for his money was outrageous. She wished she had been big enough to fight with Stan and make him give the man his money back. Not a chance of that. That had been the most shocking and surprising part of her wild night in Cripple Creek. But she frowned. Stan was right in a way. She had never been in a position where she had to steal to get enough money for food. She wondered what she would do in the same situation.

Slowly she shook her head. No. She had been in

virtually the same kind of a fix here when she first came. She had found a job to take care of her needs. Yes, Stan could do the same thing if he wanted to. He had taken the easy way out. She hoped that she never saw him again.

For just a moment she thought of home. It was grand and so easy and soft. Not at all like working ten hours a day here in the store. She frowned. Still, she felt secure and happy here. She felt as if she were earning her way, that she was doing something to help others, even if just assisting them to find the tool or bit of hardware they needed. Useful. Yes, she felt useful. For the first time in her life Harriet Braithwaite felt as if she was doing something useful.

Harriet smiled, turned on her side and went to sleep.

Chapter Ten

Buckskin Morgan and Don Casemore watched Lars Zacherias just outside the shack at the Lucky Lady claim. The muzzle aimed downward but the weapon could be brought up quickly.

"Lars, I see you've got our men working already," Buckskin said, covering up his surprise at the weapon.

"What the hell you want?" Lars asked.

"Want? We own a piece of this claim. Just came out to take another look at our property."

"I own the controlling shares, remember?" Lars asked. "What I say goes, and I say I don't want you two anywhere near the Lucky Lady."

"We've got rights," Buckskin said. "I suggest you think through what you just said. I can go to the Springs and get a court order giving the minority shareholders access to this claim any time they want."

"Don't know about that. This twelve-gauge is all the authority I need. This scattergun says you don't get to look over the Lucky Lady. Understand plain talk?"

"Wanted to tell you, Lars, that I have a witness to the killing here last night. As soon as the sheriff gets here, I'll have a talk with him and then you'll be arrested. My witness saw you and another man drinking with Douglas in the Deep Shaft Saloon last night. Then on his way home he saw the same three men walk out and go up to the Lucky Lady. He said only two men left the claim."

Buckskin watched Lars critically. He was bluffing. He'd used the saloon since that was where Lars had told the man with the share of the claim for sale to meet him. The rest had been pure bluff. He hoped it worked.

"Not a word of truth in it," Lars said. "I was in my room last night with a lady who will vouch for me. I don't know your game, but it won't work with me. Now get off my property. You'll be getting a bill from me about charges for your share of the development work. I expect you to pay it promptly. If we hit an upthrust I'll let you know. That's all a judge would make me do. Now beat it." He lifted the shotgun so it covered both of them from 20 feet away. That was a deadly range for a shotgun.

Buckskin held up his hands. "Go ahead and shoot. I told three people we were coming up here to see you. You'll hang before the sheriff gets here.

We're asking to inspect our claim. Are you refusing?"

Lars lifted the twin barrels of the shotgun and fired into the air well over their heads. He quickly lowered the muzzles to cover them with the other barrel.

"Git!"

"Let's go," Buckskin said to Casemore. As they walked away he added in a low voice, "I think we've got the big man worried. Let's find the closest building to this end of the mountain and we'll watch and see where Lars goes. If he's working with somebody on this, I bet he'll hightail it straight to his partner."

"Lars don't look smart enough to pull any kind of a swindle," Casemore said. "He could do the killing, but he's not known around town as being too bright."

"Who does he run with? He have any friends, work for anyone?"

Casemore shrugged as they walked toward the end of Meyers Street where they could hide behind the blacksmith shop. "Lars is sort of a stray cat. He wanders around, works for first one and then another man. Never done any mining. Don't guess he's ever filed on a claim."

Five minutes later they stepped around the side of the big barn at the blacksmith shop. They were out of sight of the Lucky Lady claim. Buckskin peered around the corner of the wooden building and saw Lars walking away from the claim.

"Here he comes. Now all we have to do is follow him and see where he goes."

They split up. Buckskin sent Casemore two blocks up on Bennett Avenue to watch for Lars. Buckskin would be close behind Lars as he came into the little town and would follow him. Lars probably wouldn't even look behind him. He'd have no reason to think anyone might be trailing him.

Buckskin hurried down Meyers and picked up the tall blond man as he turned off Third Street and up Bennett Avenue. He closed to within 20 yards of Lars and settled in to track him. The hunt lasted only a block. Then Lars vanished up the stairs beside the barbershop.

Buckskin let him get to the top, waited a little more and then went up the wooden steps slowly and without a sound. When he could look over the top of the steps, he saw there was a short hallway on the second floor that led to one office.

A neat sign on the door proclaimed the tenant. "Law Offices of Miles Kelton" it said. "Please Come In."

Buckskin eased down the steps and went to find Casemore. He was half a block up Bennett reading a newspaper in front of the tinware store.

Buckskin took a chair beside him. "What do you know about Miles Kelton, a lawyer?" Buckskin asked.

"Kelton, slick and slippery. One of three or four lawyers in town. Kelton is the worst one. He'll represent anyone for any problem. He'll sue you for the smallest cause. He's obtained at least two claims by representing men on lawsuits, and then taking the claims when they couldn't pay him. Not our number-one upstanding citizen."

"Lars went up the steps over the barbershop and the only office up there is Kelton's."

"Figures. I didn't think Lars was smart enough to do anything cleverly illegal. Think Lars and Kelton killed Douglas?"

"Bet my poke on it, but we've got no proof. That witness thing I told Lars was just to get him moving. I made up the whole thing."

A man walked by and slowed, then stopped and turned back. He looked at the men in the chairs, then walked over to them.

"Buckskin Morgan. What the hell you doing in Cripple Creek?"

Buckskin looked up and smiled. "Nate Purvis. Last time I knew you was in Denver two years ago when you hired me to watch your business partner." Buckskin stood and they shook hands.

"Watch him you did, and we nailed the cheating rat. I'm in a new business now. You know Casemore here?"

"Met him this morning."

"He tell you about the trouble I'm having?"

"Trouble? You're the mine owner who lost the load of ore?"

Purvis scowled. He rubbed his face with his hand and nodded. "The damn same. I've got three wagons heading out in a few hours. Wanted to find Casemore here to drive one of them."

Casemore stood. "Mr. Purvis, Buckskin here suggested that you put some shotgun guards on the wagons. You've got considerable value going down that road. Since you lost that one load . . ."

"I agree with you. First, Casemore, I need you to take a load down the road. Want to do it at night, might throw off anybody trying to grab this shipment. Also, I'm going to have two guards riding each wagon. Like you to go along as one of the guards, Buckskin."

"Thanks for the offer Purvis, but I'm on another case right now."

"So take a day off, can't hurt. I really need you on this one. If I've got a loose mouth somewhere at my mine, I need to find out and close it up."

"Who knows the rigs are rolling tonight?" Buckskin asked.

"Only me, our wrangler, and the three drivers. The shotgun guards I'm picking up an hour before we roll. The start-out time I ain't figured yet."

Buckskin growled. "Look, I've got two problems in town right now. I don't need a third one. I'm trying to find this girl who ran away from home, and now somebody got murdered and I own a share of the claim and things are getting to feel like a cut hand with alcohol poured over it."

"So take off a day and let it stew. You told me in Denver that when you were on a real hard case, you'd go fishing for a day and when you came back, the pieces began to fall in place. You have a rifle?"

"No."

"Don't matter. I'll bring one for you. I'm having a shotgun on the front and a rifle on the back of each load of ore. Yes, I'll have a couple of blankets so your butt won't get sore."

Buckskin rubbed his jaw and nodded. "Okay.

Where you picking up us killer guards?"

"Far edge of town on the Florissant road."

"Good. You trailing a riding horse behind each wagon? Then if we get hit, we got something to chase them on."

"Yeah, good idea." He turned to the other man. "Casemore, have a big supper and report to the mine at ten tonight. We'll go sometime after that. Buckskin, instead of the edge of town, I'll see you at the Cripple Emporium Saloon around midnight. Just don't gamble too much. I'm only paying you seven dollars a day for the two-day job. You'll go out tonight, unload in the morning and drive the rigs back tomorrow. Should be here by noon."

The men nodded and Purvis hurried away down the boardwalk, then swung into a saloon.

"Well, looks like I got you a job, Buckskin."

"Yeah, one I really don't want and don't need. I guess I stuck with it. Purvis treated me right in Denver."

The two men sat back in the chairs. "So, what about Kelton?" Buckskin asked.

"Slick, smart, unprincipled. Do anything to make or steal a dollar."

"Think he's the one who bought those four shares from Douglas?" Buckskin asked.

"Could be, but you'll have a hell of a time proving it. Still, it makes him the prime suspect in the killing."

Buckskin nodded and motioned to Casemore. "You know a good place to eat? Investigating a killing always makes me hungry."

After they had big sandwiches at a small diner,

Buckskin took the piece of paper from his pocket that showed he owned a one-eighth share of the Lucky Lady mine.

"Think I'll pay a call on Miles Kelton. Ask him if this IOU is any good and what I might do with it. See what kind of a reaction I get from him."

"Isn't that a little risky, knowing what happened to Douglas?" Casemore asked.

"Not the way I'm going to play it. I'll be a complete dolt with this piece of paper I don't know nothing about nohow and ask the learned man for his advice."

Casemore raised his brows and scratched his chin. "Hell, worth a try. I got some things to do. See you tonight probably around midnight sometime. Even with a team of four up it's gonna take us six hours to drive down there. So we miss the 8:42 out of Florissant. Have to unload. They've got a slant board they use. Works fine. Back the wagon onto this platform. We lock it in place, unhitch the horses, and they crank up the platform to a forty-five-degree angle and open the tailgate.

"Damn ore slides down the slope of the wagon bottom and into the railroad car below. Hey, you'll see it tomorrow." Casemore waved and walked down the street.

Buckskin thought about his plan to confront Kelton in his own office. It could be productive. He grinned. Especially if he found Lars there. Yeah. He turned the wrong way, then headed back down Bennett Avenue until he spotted the barbershop. He crossed over the wide dirt street, missing a series of cow pies from a team of oxen, and made it to the far boardwalk safely. He took the steps two at a time and knocked on the lawyer's door, then turned the knob and walked inside.

The office was plain, with a wooden floor and conservative wallpaper. The desk was expensive, solid cherry from the first look and with a clean top. Only two manila folders lay there. The man sitting behind the desk looked up with a curious expression and nodded.

"Be with you in just a minute. Why don't you sit down."

He looked just over 30 years old to Buckskin, with black hair and a mustache and spectacles. He wrote on a pad with his right hand, and Buckskin saw that his left had been injured and the last two fingers were stiff and frozen together.

Kelton put down the pencil and looked up. "And who might you be?"

"Oh, I'm Buckskin Morgan and I've got a small problem, hoped to hell you could straighten me out on."

"Do the best I can. Two dollars an hour is my fee. Can you pay it?"

"Oh, yes, sir. Money ain't the problem. See I was in this poker game a week or so ago, and in one pot I won me a piece of paper. Warn't no bank note. Not real money. It just said I owe you so much. And was signed. Is that any good? I mean, can I get money for it?"

Kelton took a short breath and nodded. "If it's signed by an adult, and there's a sum of money designated, and the document is dated, it's legal enough for most any court. How much was the I.O.U. written for?"

"Oh, it wasn't money. Another question I had was what happens if the man who wrote me the I.O.U. paper thing up and died before I could collect? Would the paper still be good? Could I claim what he said he owed?"

"Of course, if it was a legal document. That would be considered as a liability against the estate of the deceased and any court in the land would back you up on it."

Buckskin reached in his pocket and took out two of the one-dollar gold coins he won in the poker game. He dropped them on the cherry-wood desk and stood.

"Well, I guess that's about it. Got me this I.O.U. but I don't know what to do about it. Long as you say it's good, I reckon I'll just hang on to it."

"You didn't tell me what the promise was for. What the I.O.U. promised to give to you."

"Oh, that, just some old mine claim. You know how they are, must be four or five hundred of them."

"Could I see your I.O.U.?" Kelton asked.

"Why?"

"Just curious. Wondered what claim."

"You know them all?"

"Of course not, just wondered."

"Oh, then I kin tell you. It's the Lucky Lady. The mine that was owned by that Douglas fella who got himself killed last night. Just glad to know that the promise is still true. Who knows, that claim might hit it rich and I could retire somewhere and kick my feet up and play all night long with two pretty girls."

Buckskin had watched Kelton as he gave the name of the claim. Kelton had held himself in check fairly well. But he had given himself away when his eyes had squinted just a little and a new wrinkle showed in his forehead.

Kelton nodded. "You're right, I've heard of that one because of all the talk about Douglas. You don't have to worry, your claim is good. Any judge would say so. What's it for, a one eighth of the claim?"

"Don't rightly recall, but that sounds reasonable. Got it tucked away in my bible back in my tent."

Buckskin moved toward the door. "I thank you for your aid. These legal things leave me confused. I'll protect my retirement and watch for developments. I hear somebody owned half of the claim. I guess he'll be taking over." Buckskin paused and watched the expression of irritation that the lawyer let slip over his face.

Buckskin went to the door, turned and waved, then stepped into the hall. There were no other doors in the short hallway. He walked down the stairs with an even step. He didn't want to make it hard for whoever Kelton sent to follow him. There would be someone, and Buckskin would double back and try to surprise the man. If only it could be Lars Zacherias, it would make it all so much more simple.

He knew it wouldn't be Lars. Buckskin spent some time looking in windows up and down the street, then crossed over, watched in the reflection of a store window and spotted a man crossing 50 feet down to the right. It was the same man with a black hat, tan shirt and tan vest he had seen behind him along the street before. Buckskin went into a mining supply store and turned to watch out the front window. The man paused at the edge of the building and waited.

Buckskin looked around the store at the various implements and tools of the mining trade, then checked out the window again. The man was still there, only he had moved to the other side of the store front. Buckskin left the store and walked quickly to a 40-foot wide slot between buildings where nothing had been built yet. He stepped just around the corner, drew his six-gun and pressed against the wall.

The man came around the corner of the store walking fast and had no chance to stop when he saw Buckskin.

"That's it, friend, just keep coming. You and me gonna have ourselves a nice chat back here in the alley. No! Keep your hand away from that iron unless you want to get planted out on the hill. No man can beat an already drawn hog-leg. Easy now, fold your arms on your chest and walk up here."

They were in the space between the buildings but only 20 feet from the street when a second man in a black hat jumped into the void and lifted a shotgun aimed directly at Buckskin. The detective knew the shotgunner was going to pull the trigger. He shifted his sights to the right and fired.

Chapter Eleven

Buckskin Morgan dove to the left as he fired, toward the man who had been following him. He had fired automatically, without much of an aim. He hit the ground and smelled the dust in his nose as he rolled. He was aware of a dozen pinpricks on his skin and some pressure against his clothes, but nothing disastrous. Buckshot—but he didn't think any had broken the skin.

It had all happened in the blink of an eye and when he rolled and stopped on his belly, he had the .45 cocked and held out toward the shotgunner. The man was down. He still held the weapon and slowly turned it toward Buckskin.

"Hold it or you're a dead man!" Buckskin roared. The man paid no attention. Buckskin saw the blood on the man's right arm and his chest. The lead slug must have gone through his arm into his chest. The shotgun's aim came closer to him. Buckskin didn't have time to run out of range. He fired again, and saw the slug hit the shotgunner in the chest and pin him against the side of the building.

He hung there for a moment, then slowly slid down the wall leaving a bloody streak. His finger spasmed on the trigger and the shotgun went off into the ground three feet in front of him.

The man who had followed Buckskin sat in the dirt closer to the street. He had evidently dropped to the ground when the shotgun fired. He sat there staring at the dead body across the way.

Buckskin came to his feet and stood over the man who had followed him.

"Who paid you to follow me?"

The man looked up and shook his head. Buckskin kicked him hard in the belly. He screamed, then turned away and vomited. When the retching stopped he looked back and wiped his mouth. His eyes were angry.

"For God's sakes, I didn't try to kill you. I don't know who that man is. I've never seen him in my life. Miles Kelton told me to follow you, find out where you lived. No law against that."

"You weren't working with the dead man?"

"No. I told you. I've never seen him before."

A dozen men and women gathered where the boardwalk should be and stared at the scene.

"Somebody go get the barber, the town marshal, Tarento," Buckskin said. "Tell him he's got another dead body." Buckskin walked over to the dead man and looked in his pockets. They were empty except for a card the size of a business card. On it were two words, "Five Star," and a crude drawing of a five-pointed star.

Buckskin put it in his vest pocket and searched the man again. Nothing else. Not even a dollar in his pocket. Somebody had stripped all of his identification from him before they sent him out on his murder assignment.

Tarento came through the growing crowd, scowled at Buckskin and then looked at the dead man. He had remembered to take off his apron this time and pin the town marshal's badge to his white shirt. He still hadn't rolled down his sleeves, and cuttings of black hair showed on his shirt.

"He's dead, all right. You shoot him?"

"Yes, after he fired one round at me from the shotgun and threatened to finish me with the second one."

"Who's this guy?" Tarento asked, looking at the man sitting in the dirt.

"He says he's not involved. He was following me. I braced him and the killer came around the corner with his shotgun and blasted at me."

"You're damn lucky."

"I'm still alive. Make out a report for the sheriff. He should be here around dark, they said, on the Florisant stage. It was self-defense, ask the yahoo sitting in the dirt. He came close to getting killed too. When he can talk, he'll tell you."

"Where will you be?"

"I'm at Mrs. Johnson's boardinghouse. Part of the afternoon I'll be at the Deep Shaft Saloon. You know the dead man?"

"Not me. Not one of my customers."

Buckskin looked at the crowd of 40 people who crowded around. "Anybody know this dead man? Come up and take a look. I need a name. I want to know who's trying to kill me."

Most of the crowd filed past the man. Everyone shook his or her head. Two women didn't come off the boardwalk on the far side. The line stopped and Buckskin looked at the man staring at the dead man.

"Gawd damnit, it's that son-of-a-bitch Felix Van Dyke. What's he doing back in town. We run him out of here near a year ago."

Buckskin pulled the man to one side. He was in his fifties, and wore mining clothes, boots, and a filthy hat. He had an enlarged nose that showed a pinkish red and his eyes were not too clear.

"Yeah, that's him, Felix Van Dyke. Everybody called him Van. Mean little bastard. Back a year ago we knew damned well he killed a man in cold blood, but we didn't have the evidence to prove it. Rode the bastard out of town on a rail, took his boots, chased him for ten miles down the road toward Florisant."

"You have your own claim?"

"Hell, no, I got a mine. Been taking out gold ore now on the all American for more than a year."

"You have a name? I'm Buckskin Morgan from Denver."

The man held out a knarled and twisted hand that was covered with calluses and blisters. "Proud to meet the man who shot down Van. Lots of folks here will thank you, especially the widow of the last man he killed. I'm Cluny Norman. Call me Cluny."

They shook and Buckskin waved toward the street. "You have time for me to buy you a beer?"

"Always got time for that."

A few minutes later, they sat at a back table at the Deep Shaft Saloon. Buckskin had checked when they came in, but Lars wasn't in the place.

"You've been around Cripple Creek for a while?" Buckskin asked.

"Knew Crazy Bob Womack when he herded cows for his sister's ranch out at Florissant."

"Womack must be rich by now, right?"

Cluny laughed and shook his head. "Not Bob Womack. He owned the first really good gold strike in the whole area. He started the gold rush, but when it came to digging down and finding financing and doing all the business it takes to make an upthrust into a paying gold mine, he simply couldn't be bothered.

"The El Paso was his claim, him and that dentist, Grannis, who owns it now. Bob simply didn't want to go to the trouble of turning it into a paying mine. One day he sold his half of the El Paso for three hundred dollars to the dentist. So far the El Paso has turned out over a hundred thousand dollars in profits and it's just getting started. I'd say that Bob Womack threw away a million and a half in gold on a whim."

"So Bob Womack just sits around saloons talking to the greenhorns?" Buckskin asked.

"Yep. He's a local celebrity. Only now so many

new people are here who never have heard of Bob Womack. It's a shame."

Buckskin reached in his pocket and took out the folded card. "The body of Van Dyke had no identification on it. Glad to know his name. The only thing he carried was this little card in the coin pocket on his jeans. Looks like maybe he forgot to take it out when he removed everything else."

Buckskin opened the card and turned it so Cluny could see the crudely drawn five-pointed star and the two words "Five Star."

Cluny looked at it and closed his eyes. "Oh, damn. I thought we killed off all that trouble a year ago."

"What? Killed off what?"

"Damn, I don't know who they are this time. How could it get going again? Things are a lot more settled down now, more organized, I don't see how it could work again."

"What's this Five Star?"

Cluny emptied his bottle of beer, called for another one from one of the barkeeps and shook his head. He rubbed one hand over his face and took a long, deep breath.

"It started about a year and a half ago, when the first finds were being made and the first mines getting started. Somehow five men got together and decided that they would take over every upthrust that was found. Four men were murdered. Two came up missing, and wills and sales contracts magically showed up so that one of the five took over the upthrusts of the murdered men.

"After three months of that, all that had to be

said on the street was 'Five Star' and men turned pale, sold out their digs at a fraction of the cost and took a fast horse for Florissant and the railroad heading east.

"Most everyone knew who the men were in the Five Star syndicate. It was hard not to know. Then one night after a poker game at my place, six of us got together and pledged to blow apart the syndicate and get rid of the violence. Of course we knew that we'd have to use a little intimidation ourselves to get things rolling.

"During one night three of the Five Star mine operations were either blown up or the aboveground buildings burned to the ground. The most hated of the five was hung after midnight and left hanging from a pole on the roof of the general store for three days. The head killer for the Five Star syndicate was Felix Van Dyke. We gave him his choice. A trial for the murder of the last of the Five Star victims, or a ticket to Denver. He took the ticket and we figured we'd broken the backs of the Five Star."

"You think this card means they're starting to make a comeback?" Buckskin asked.

"Could be. Only two of the original five are still in business here. One has a small operation. The second one has the biggest mine on the mountain, but he's been watched to be sure that all of his luck was legitimate and that he paid a going price for every new claim or upthrust that he took over."

"So what's this new Five Star?"

"I don't have the slightest idea. No guess who's behind it. Maybe it was just an old card he had from a year ago. They used them as a threat. Left one on your front door, nailed one to a post on your claim, cute little tricks like that."

"What about the six men who broke it up before. Are you all still in town?"

"Four of us. One died in an accident, innocent enough. The other one sold out to one of the big mines and went back East."

"I'll leave this card with you. Maybe it's time to get together that old gang of yours so you can bring them up to date." Buckskin hesitated, then plunged ahead. "Oh, did this Five Star bunch have a lawyer in town?"

"They did. The best lawyer they could buy, who turned out to be Miles Kelton. He's still here. We couldn't prove anything against him, so we had a long talk with him one night as he sat on the back of a horse with a noose around his neck and over the second-floor railing of the hotel. He promised he wouldn't work for the remaining members of the Five Star, and we let him go. So far as I know he hasn't given anyone any trouble."

"You heard about Larry Douglas getting killed?" Buckskin asked.

"Yes. Somebody said he was murdered. I don't see how this could tie in with anything the old Five Star would do. They wanted claims that had proved out and with a good-sized vein."

"Maybe they're working up to bigger things," Buckskin said.

Cluny shrugged. "Maybe. Tell you what. I'm going to talk to the others I worked with a year ago to bust up the Five Star. They're gonna be damn interested to see this card and to know that Felix Van Dyke finally got what he so well deserved. I won't tell you who the men are. It was a kind of vigilante situation where we didn't advertise ourselves. The men will be interested."

"I hear the sheriff is coming to town. He know anything about this Five Star outfit?"

"He didn't want to know back then, and he won't want to know now. His main job is getting elected. He doesn't want to make anybody mad by arresting them. By the way, I was up at the Lucky Lady claim this morning when you demanded that Tarento wire for the sheriff to come. Just what's your stake in this whole thing?"

Buckskin explained to him that he was a private detective from Denver trying to find a runaway girl.

"That's a tough one, especially if she's changed her looks. You might have talked to her a dozen times and not even known it."

Cluny finished his beer and stood. "Got some work that needs done." He held out his hand. "Thanks for taking care of Van Dyke. Somebody should have done that years ago. Be sure to stay in touch. Oh, I run the All American mine. Stop by tomorrow and I'll give you a tour."

"Going to go to Florissant, might not be back by tomorrow. I'll look you up when I get in."

They shook hands and Cluny walked out the front door. This Five Star business was really going to mess up finding the girl. But Buckskin was involved now. Whoever had hired Van Dyke wouldn't let their man be gunned down without reacting. Buckskin would be extra careful from now on around dark doorways and shadows and on late-night walks. Why would Five Star mark him for death? He had no idea, which made it all the more interesting.

Back at the Johnson boardinghouse, he went in and straight to his room. He had just taken off his town clothes and changed into range wear when a knock came on the door.

Mrs. Johnson came in quickly and closed the door behind her.

"Well, you finally came back. I have a tremendous dinner for you. A roast that is so tender you can cut it with the back of your hand." She lifted her brows and twisted a white handkerchief in front of her.

"I hope . . . I hope I didn't seem too forward last night. I mean, we did get a little wild there at the last."

"Whatever keeps you happy," Buckskin said.

"How about tonight?"

"Sounds like a fine idea. Not all night, though. I have a job starting at midnight. I'll be back tomorrow sometime."

"That leaves us from now until midnight," she said. She walked toward him unbuttoning her blouse. "My titties would so much like to be chewed on a little to kind of warm up for tonight. Supper's almost ready, but I can spare a few minutes to get you excited and just rock-hard."

Her big breasts tumbled out of her blouse as it came open, and Buckskin chuckled and bent to take care of them. First he gently touched her nipples with his tongue, licking only the dark red pillars until they stood taller and turned a darker red with new blood. Then he worked his tongue around her breasts in a circle and ended it with a kiss on each nipple.

Emily Johnson kept breathing hard as his ministrations continued. "Suck on me, darlin'," she said. "Suck my big tits."

He did and she surged against him, her hips tattooing against his as she trembled and vibrated through a quick climax.

"Oh, lordy, but you are fine. No man ever made me come like that without even touching my cunnie. Damn, but I like you, Buckskin Morgan." She wiped the flush on her cheeks and forehead and tried to quiet her panting.

"Course, I love you when you get buck naked. No time now. I got me a pie to get out of the oven and cooled down some." She looked at a man's watch she took from the pocket of her apron. "Oh, lordy, only a half hour to supper-time. I better get cracking."

She buttoned her blouse on the way to the door, opened the door and hurried out.

Buckskin grinned. It was going to be an interesting evening.

Chapter Twelve

Buckskin walked into the Cripple Creek Saloon that night just after 11:30. The place was still packed. The show by the songbird was nearly over. The girl could sing, Buckskin had to admit. He didn't recognize her name on the placard on the side of the small stage. Kat Flowers. It seemed to fit. He wormed his way toward the stage and saw a man come out at the last line of the last song and begin to pitch coins on the stage. The one who tossed the first coins was Miles Kelton. The idea caught on at once and coins rained on the stage.

Kat Flowers held up her skirt and caught some coins, exposing a delicious slice of bare leg. As Buckskin watched, the woman took another bow, then hurried off the stage. The Negro piano player used a small broom and a dust pan to sweep up the coins and, to the cheers of the crowd, walked off the stage into the back area.

Buckskin saw Miles Kelton watch the process and then go through the small door into the back of the saloon.

Kelton? What did he have to do with the girl, or this saloon? Buckskin had no idea.

About 20 minutes later the saloon had mostly emptied. No more than 20 men remained, most drinking. Two poker games had started, and the other gambling tables were busy. Nate Purvis came in the door and looked around. He saw Buckskin, gave a small nod and left the place. A few moments later, Buckskin went out the front door of the saloon and walked down the street to where Purvis stood.

"Ready when you are," Buckskin said. They went down to the next street, and turned up it for two blocks. Two saddle horses stood tied to a hitching rail. The two men mounted and rode toward the Florissant road.

When they passed the last house, Purvis let out a long breath and spoke for the first time.

"Damn, I'm not sure of this one. I kept it a secret. But I got me a bad feeling. The wagons are a quarter of a mile ahead. I want you on the first wagon with a rifle. It's a Remington repeater with eight rounds. Here's another thirty in case you need them."

They rode a ways without talking.

"Just watch out," Purvis finally said. "There could be some trouble. If it gets bad it would be the men they're after, not the horses. The outlaws would need the horses to haul the gold ore the rest of the way. Just be careful."

"You know something's going to happen?" Buckskin asked.

"Just a hunch. One of my best men was acting a bit strange today. He knew about the shipment. He loaded the wagons out this afternoon."

"Did you confront him?"

"I couldn't. He's married to my sister."

"He's probably just worried about the shipment like you are. Relax. This is going to go off without a shot being fired."

A few minutes later they caught up with the slow-moving wagon train. Two men with weapons on the rear rig had them in their sights until Purvis called out.

Buckskin rode to the front wagon, tied his mount on the tailgate and swung up beside the driver. It was Casemore.

"Finally decided to show up, huh?"

"Right. Where's my rifle?"

The man on the other side of Casemore held out his hand. "Jed Warshaw. Pleased to meet you."

"Yeah, Jed, I'm Buckskin. You're up here with Casemore with the scattergun and I'm on the hind side with the rifle."

The moon had grown to almost full. Buckskin looked at Casemore. "You know the route," he said. "If you wanted to capture these three wagons, where would you hit?"

"Easy. About two miles from Florissant is a little wooded area the road goes through. It's gonna be dark as hell in there. Soon as we come out into the moonlight is where I'd attack."

Buckskin nodded. "Yeah, we'll be tired of watching by then and the horses will be tired. Some of us might even be asleep. Good. This rifle loaded?"

It wasn't. He filled the eight-round magazine and slid one more round into the chamber.

Buckskin found a spot near the back of the load of gold ore where he put down the folded blankets and tried to sit in a comfortable position. There wasn't one. He remembered nothing about the route to Florissant except that it would be a gentle downgrade most of the way.

Buckskin listened to the jangle of the harness, the blowing and snorting of the 12 horses, the sound of the steel-banded wheels on the rocks and gravel of the rough road. He wanted to get familiar with them so if a new sound came, like galloping horses storming up behind them, he would pick it out quickly. He tried for ten minutes, but each time he thought he had the sounds down, a different horse would make a sound or whinny or cough, or a wheel would clatter over a sheet of rock, or a rock would get pushed to the side and bounce off the road into the brush.

After an hour he gave up and sat there maintaining his balance with one hand on each side. The Remington repeater lay across his legs ready for quick use.

After two hours he crawled up to the front with the rifle and blankets so he could talk to Casemore.

"If somebody tries to jump us, it'll be within the next hour," Buckskin said. The shotgun guard snored on the seat beside Casemore.

"I'll wake him if anything happens," Casemore said. "Hit us three hours out? Why?"

"Because then they'll have three hours of darkness to get away if anything goes wrong. They also would have three hours to drive the rigs on to Florissant and the railroad siding so they'll be used to the animals."

Casemore shook his head. "Nope, don't figure. We got it free and easy until at least five hours from town, be about five in the A.M."

"Quiet," Buckskin whispered.

"What?"

"Quiet, horses coming up behind us, riding horses." Buckskin drew his six-gun and fired into the air.

"Horses coming up in the rear!" he bellowed. He heard men behind him react. Then he heard horses coming from the front.

He leveled the rifle past Casemore's shoulder and fired three quick shots straight down the road. He heard a horse scream and someone swearing. The rifleman on the back wagon fired four rounds and Buckskin hoped they were to the rear.

The pounding hooves quiet for a moment.

"They'll come at us from the side," Buckskin said. "Get low to the load and keep down. They'll try to pick us off and not touch the horses."

All was quiet for five minutes as the wagons kept moving down the road. Then pistol fire broke out on both sides of the wagons as dark shapes came galloping at them. Buckskin used the rifle. He knocked one rider out of the saddle, missed a second rider and hit his horse in the head. It went down in a crashing, screaming patch of dust and dirt.

The guards on the other wagons fired as well. Buckskin had no way of knowing how many attackers there were. He was sure he'd disabled three of them.

Suddenly the attackers quit shooting. After a minute, the men on the wagons stopped firing as well.

"Reload," Buckskin shouted. "They'll be back. Stay low on the loads. We take any casualties?"

"Yeah, lost the driver on wagon two," a voice called. "I got the reins. Horses know where to go, I reckon."

"Anybody else hit?"

Nobody answered.

"We surprised them," Buckskin told Casemore. "They figured to box us in front and back, shoot the drivers and take over the wagons with no problems."

Casemore didn't answer.

"Hey, you all right?"

Casemore turned and Buckskin could see the blood on his shoulder. "Caught a round," Casemore said. "Somebody else better drive."

The shotgun guard grabbed the reins and handed his scattergun to Buckskin. Just then Buckskin heard the hoofbeats coming from the sides.

"Here they come again!" he bellowed.

He waited until the riders were closer this time, then used the shotgun, pounding the first load of double-ought buck into a horse and rider, swung the weapon and fired the second barrel and saw both horses and men go down.

Shots from both sides blasted down the line of wagons.

Buckskin heard the snarl of the rifles, the heavier roar of the shotguns and the crack of the six-guns. He used the rifle until it emptied, then drew his six-gun and fired four times before the attackers faded away.

In two minutes it was over and the robbers who were alive rode away up the road toward Cripple Creek.

Buckskin called the rigs to a halt and checked the men. One was dead. Two were wounded. Three out of nine, not bad. He made a torch and went to the side and looked for the outlaws. He found two dead near the road. Further on he heard a groan and found a man shot in the chest. He screamed and then died without saying a word.

"I want one alive," Buckskin said. He told Jed Warshaw, the shotgun on Casemore's wagon, to take the rigs on to the rail siding. "I'm going to ride after them, see what I can find out."

He untied the saddle horse from the back of the first wagon and mounted. It was too dark to make any time. Even on the roadway, a wagon wheel rut hit at the wrong angle by the mount's hoof could break a leg.

He worked forward at a fast walk. The outlaws couldn't be more than 15 minutes ahead of him. Maybe they would stop and lick their wounds.

A half hour later, he could hear talk ahead. He

walked his mount slower and soon saw the start of a small fire to the side of the road. He tied his horse and moved up with caution on foot. He didn't scuff his boots, didn't break a twig. After five minutes, he edged around some brush and saw three men sitting around a fire. Another form lay huddled to one side. Buckskin listened.

"What the hell went wrong?"

"They had guards all over the place. Must have been two dozen guns on those wagons."

"Why didn't somebody tell us?"

"We knew there would be one shotgun guard."

"That don't mean fifteen or twenty guns."

"What the hell we gonna tell Walt?"

"Not worried about Walt. We left three dead men back there, and Hugh don't look too good."

"Don't know about you gents, but I'm heading for Florissant soon as it's light. Them I'm selling my horse and saddle and taking the train to the Springs and then south. Going back to Oklahoma."

One of the men stood.

"Where you going, Jenkins?"

"Going to take a piss. Or do you want me to put out your fire?" The others laughed. Jenkins went into the darkness almost straight toward Buckskin. Buckskin waited until the man was urinating, then he moved up silently, caught his hand around the man's mouth from behind and his arm around his waist and dragged him back in the brush farther.

When he figured they were far enough away,

Buckskin put the muzzle of his six-gun against the man's cheek.

"Jenkins, you listen best you ever have in your life. You make one little sound and you're a dead man. You understand?"

He nodded.

"Who hired you to steal the gold ore?"

"Don't know."

Buckskin moved the six-gun's muzzle to the soft flesh under Jenkin's chin and pushed up hard.

"You ever have the top of your head blown off by a .45 slug, Jenkins? Ain't pretty. Now who hired you?"

"Walt."

"Walt who?"

"Don't know. I come riding into town yesterday and he yelled at me and asked me if I wanted to make ten dollars. Mister, I ain't seen ten dollars in one chunk for six months."

"You hire cheap as a killer."

"Ain't no killer."

"Three of your men are dead, one driver on the wagons died. That makes you a killer. You'll hang. What does Walt look like?"

"Tall, thin as a pencil, wears two guns tied low. Came out of the Deep Shaft Saloon. Black hair, funny little mustache thin like a knife blade and a goatee. He sounded mean as nails."

"Okay, put your hands behind your back."

Buckskin tied them with rawhide laces, then tied his ankles together.

"You make a sound until I call for you and you're dead as those three men you lost. You ken?"

He nodded in the faint moonlight.

Buckskin worked his way back to the fire. The men were talking in low tones.

"Jenkins, everything coming out all right?" one of them called.

"Ke-rist, he must be jerking off again." They all laughed.

Buckskin got within 20 feet of the fire and shot a revolver round over their heads.

"Don't move. I've got both barrels of a shotgun on you and two rounds of double-ought buck loaded. Enough to blast all three of you into Hell. Put your hands up high and stand."

The men did as he told them.

A half hour later he had them all tied up and on their horses. The wounded man at the fire had died. They left him there. Buckskin put a four-rock stack beside the trail to mark the spot, then led the four outlaws up the road toward Cripple Creek. He figured they should get there at daybreak.

A mile outside of town, Buckskin remembered that last night was when the county sheriff was supposed to get into Cripple Creek. If he had, Buckskin would have some more business for him. Four more killers. The youngest one, Jenkins, had agreed to testify against the other three for a lighter sentence, five years in prison.

It was just after 6:30 A.M. when Buckskin stopped his string of horses in front of the Cripple Creek barbershop. It was closed. The town had no jail. He tied the horses to the rail, pulled each of the four tied men off their mounts and tied them to the barber pole, then sat with the Remington rifle across his lap as he waited for the town marshal to get to work. He should know where the sheriff was, if the man had made it to town.

Buckskin nearly dozed off twice, but each time came up with the rifle in both hands and ready to fire. Half-a-dozen locals stopped and asked him what was going on.

"Some killers for the sheriff. Is he still in town?" Nobody knew.

At eight o'clock, Tony Tarento came to open his barbershop.

"Good Lord, what do you have here?" Tarento asked.

"Where's the sheriff?"

"At the hotel."

"Go get him now," Buckskin snapped with enough steel and fire in the words to send Tarento rushing toward the hotel without asking another question.

Ten minutes later, Tarento came back. Buckskin figured the man walking with him was the sheriff. He was short and fat, waddled and wore town clothes and no gun. A proper brown fedora hid most of his brown hair. He was clean-shaven.

Tarento stopped in front of Buckskin, who didn't stand but remained slumped against the front wall of the barbershop.

"Morgan, this is Sheriff Houston. He wants to talk to you about the killing."

"Good. Sit down, Sheriff, and make yourself comfortable. I'm too tired to stand up. You've got more trouble. Over there by the rail are four killers. They attacked three wagons of gold ore on the

Florissant trail about three o'clock this morning. Killed one man on the wagons and lost four dead out of their outfit. The younger one will testify against the other three in exchange for a five-year term in prison instead of hanging. The others should hang. Any questions?"

The sheriff looked startled. Then a bit of a frown stained his round, fleshy face. "Any other witnesses?"

"Eight of us still alive. See mine owner Nate Purvis, he'll tell you who he hired on the wagons. I don't know who the dead guard is. Don Casemore was on the lead wagon and took a round in the shoulder. The prisoners are yours. If you don't have any questions, I'm going to find a bed somewhere and collapse."

"You a deputy United States marshal?" Sheriff Houston asked.

"No. Never claimed to be. Like I said, the prisoners are yours. You should have a full-time deputy sheriff stationed here. Any more questions?"

"We'll want you at the trial. Do it here in two days. Don't leave town."

"I could sleep for two days." Buckskin stood with an effort and walked with pain until his legs uncramped. Then he stepped into the saddle and rode the four blocks to Mrs. Johnson's boarding-house.

She met him at the door and realized his state. "You want a bath before bed or breakfast?"

"Thanks, just the bed. See you this afternoon."

* * *

Back in front of the barbershop, Sheriff Houston watched Buckskin walk away. He scowled at Tarento. "You know anything about that man?"

"Not much. He's a detective from Denver here on a case. I'd say he knows his business."

The sheriff snorted. "So do I. I've dealt with upstarts like him before. You heard me about the trial. It'll be here in two days. I'll get a wire off to Judge Blankenship on the next stage. Who's the lawyer we use here . . . yes, Kelton, Miles Kelton. He'll prosecute for the county. Where is there a place we can lock up these men for the next two days before we hang them?"

Chapter Thirteen

Harriet "Harry" Braithwaite put another nut on the half-inch-by-six-inch machine bolt in the bin at the Alexander Hardware and General Store. It was boring. Work in the store could also be hard and some nights she went to sleep totally exhausted. But her secret was safe. Not even Mr. Alexander knew who she was or, more important, that she was female. Her made-up name of Harry Carson was still working.

She finished the box of bolts and stared out the front window at Cripple Creek. She'd wanted to come here for the thrill of a gold rush, to say that she'd been here when the mines were getting started. It was exciting. The whole little town seemed to vibrate with expectations and hope.

Now she'd done it, experienced a real gold rush. Oh, she was tired. Her back hurt again from lifting those kegs of nails. Maybe it was time she went home. She wouldn't have to work if she were home. Of course her father would try to pack her off to that school again. Now a university, that might be interesting, but she would never go back to that finishing school. She started on another box of bolts, three-eighths of an inch by four inches.

Yes, maybe she had spent enough time masquerading as a boy. But if she became Harriet Braithwaite again, that nice Mr. Buckskin Morgan would come calling and take her directly back to Denver. She wasn't ready for that. Not yet. But what else could she do here in Cripple Creek and still remain hidden?

The little bell jingled over the front door when the screen door opened, and Harriet looked up. A woman came into the store. Harriet wiped off her hands on a small towel she kept nearby for that purpose. She looked at Mr. Alexander and he nodded.

He'd told Harry that he had a good touch with the women who came in. Harriet went up to where the woman looked over the gallon-sized canned goods. Harriet had waited on the woman once before. Her name was Mrs. Johnson and she ran a boardinghouse.

"Good morning, Harry. My, but you have a lot more stock today than you did last time I was here."

"The supply wagon came from the train just last night, Mrs. Johnson, and we loaded the shelves."

"I like the idea of these pre-cooked canned goods, but they are expensive. I could bake up three pots of beans for what this one big can cost." She smiled. "Of course I'd have to sort the rocks out of the beans, then soak them for five hours and then keep them cooking for another four hours. Work. Land sakes, sometimes I think that's my first name."

"You have five boarders again, Mrs. Johnson?"

The woman looked up quickly. "My, but you're a sharp and bright young boy. I must have mentioned that last time. Honestly, I'm getting so tired these days I don't know which way is up or down some times."

"You should hire someone to help you," Harriet said, the idea blossoming in her mind.

"Sure, if I could afford it. But even so, who would work for me twelve hours a day for fifty cents?"

"There might just be somebody out there who might like to work for you. You'd furnish meals and a bed, I'd guess."

Mrs. Johnson smiled and patted Harriet's shoulder. "Boy, you're putting ideas into my mind. Don't see how I could afford it."

"Raise your board-and-room price by fifty cents a week. That would make up most of the three-fifty you'd be spending on help. So it would only cost you a dollar a week."

Emily Johnson laughed and eyed the boy. "Harry, if I had a suspicious mind, I'd think that you were trying to find a job for your sister." She shook her head but grinned. "I think I'll try two of those big cans of beans, and one of green beans, and then two smaller cans of peaches. Now, back in Ohio I could have a garden growing all these things, but the growing season here is so short can't grow much of anything."

That evening as soon as the Alexander store closed, Harriet washed her face, put on a new bill cap and changed into a clean shirt. Then she took a walk. She asked questions until she found where the Johnson boardinghouse was and knocked on the door, waited a moment, then opened the door and went inside.

"Yes?" a voice said from a room to the left.

"Mrs. Johnson?"

"In here, please, come this way."

Harriet was surprised how neat and clean and well furnished the house was. It gave her a pang of memory about her home in Denver. She walked across an entryway and stepped into the living room. Emily Johnson sat in a rocker with a small white cat on her lap. She looked up with surprise.

"Harry? What brings you out this time of night?"

"Mrs. Johnson I need to talk to you." She looked around. "Is there anybody . . ."

"All my boarders are out for the night or in their rooms, boy. What did you want to say?"

"I'd like to come to work for you for fifty cents a day."

Mrs. Johnson frowned and motioned for Harriet to sit down in an upholstered chair nearby.

"But Harry, this is woman's work you're talking about. Making beds and emptying slop jars and baking and cooking and doing dishes."

"I know." Harriet took a deep breath. "Can I tell you a secret? If I tell you will you promise not to

156

tell anyone ever, ever, ever?"

"Of course, Harry. Yes, certainly. A secret between two people is something sacred, tremendously special. No matter what you tell me, I'll never repeat it to another living soul."

"Yes, I believe you. All right." Harriet stood and walked around the room and came back to the chair.

"Dear boy, are you in trouble with the law or something like that?"

"Oh, my, no. Nothing like that. Not the law. Just . . . just my father. I . . . I ran away from home. My father was not kind to me. He made me do things I didn't want to do. I don't want him to find me, not right away. Harry Carson isn't my real name."

"Well, I can assure you, whoever you are, that I will never tell anyone. But if I did have a job here it would be for a woman or a girl, not for a boy."

"That's what I'm trying to tell you. I'm not a boy. I'm . . . I'm a girl, female."

Mrs. Johnson cocked her head to one side. She looked at Harriet's face, touched it. "I certainly don't see a sign of any whiskers. Let me see your hands."

Harriet had washed them with soap carefully and pushed back her cuticles and cleaned her nails. Some were broken, but at least they were clean and well trimmed.

"Oh, my, yes, you have a woman's hands. Small and with long fingers. But I don't understand. Why the masquerade?"

"I knew my father would try to find me. If he

came to Cripple Creek he'd find me easy if I still had long brown hair and worked in a cafe or something. So I got a job with Mr. Alexander."

"How did you . . . I mean how could you conceal that you were a girl?"

"It was easy. I wore these loose shirts. For a while I bound my breasts, but it didn't matter that much 'cause I'm not all that big on top. I had my hair cut and wore boy's clothes and never undressed when Mr. Alexander was there. It wasn't that hard."

Mrs. Jones blinked back tears. "You poor dear. I can't think of anything worse than running away and trying to make a living and then disguising yourself as a boy. Oh, my."

"Could we go into your bedroom or someplace less public for a minute, Mrs. Johnson?"

"You want to . . . oh, my. Yes. of course."

They went into Mrs. Johnson's bedroom and Harriet unbuttoned her shirt and took it off and then lifted the cotton camisole to show her breasts. They were hand-sized, with soft pink nipples and lighter-colored areolas.

"Yes, yes, I see. You've proved to me that you're a girl. Now the only problem is what to do. I won't let you stay one more night under that merchant's roof. You'll come here, of course. My one child is grown and gone. I married young. Then my Will was killed in the mines a year go. Yes, I want you to come here. Yes, I'll pay you fifty cents a day for as long as you can stay. First we figure out how to get you away from that nice Mr. Alexander."

"I have to go back tonight. Tomorrow I'll tell

him I have to leave. To go away." She frowned. "Could we change the color of my hair? That would help. It is growing a little, but if it were red, say, that would change my appearance a lot."

"Just the ticket. I can do it. I used to have red hair myself for a while." She smiled. "And we won't tell a soul who you are or where you're from." She frowned. "No, then people would get curious. You'll be my niece from Kansas City. You'll be Mae Johnson, one of my brother-in-law's children who they can't afford to take care of. Yes. It will work."

"Would it be all right . . ." She stopped. Harriet had rebuttoned her shirt and stood there looking lost. "Would it be all right if I hugged you? I haven't had a hug in a long time."

Emily Johnson blinked back tears and held out her arms. After the long hug, they walked to the living room. "You hurry back to the store. Then tomorrow you leave there and come here by the back door. We'll get some girl clothes for you. Some of my own might cut down nicely."

"Oh, I'm good with a needle and thread."

"Good. One more question. How old are you?"

"I'm eighteen, least I will be in another month. I've done all of my high school and have a diploma."

"My goodness, you're a young woman." Mrs. Johnson stopped before her voice failed her. Tears came in a rush and she hugged the girl again. "I so wanted a little girl, but after my son, the doctor said I couldn't risk getting pregnant again. Then he said my machinery just broke down so I'd never be pregnant again. Maybe you can be the little girl I never could have."

"That would be wonderful, and I'll even learn to like those canned beans."

They both laughed. They talked for another half hour. Then Harriet left to go back to the store for one last night. She promised to be at Mrs. Johnson's back door the next day about ten o'clock. That would give them most of the day before she would be presented to the boarders at supper-time as Mae Johnson, Mrs. Johnson's niece.

That same night, Buckskin Morgan had recovered from his long ride and all-night workout. He had one immediate job, to try to find out who the "Walt" was he'd heard named. Even with the description, it wouldn't be an easy task.

His first stop was the Deep Shaft Saloon. The place seemed to be the focal point of everything that had gone wrong in this case. Was it all chance or was there some deeper connection?

In the saloon, he heard that the Lucky Lady claim had hit a good-sized upthrust, had blasted it and was already mining the gold ore and storing it in one of the tunnels. At first he felt delight. Then he thought about it. That would mean they needed a lot of money to develop the mine. He still didn't discount the idea that Kelton and his henchmen hadn't tapped into someone else's vein of gold. They could disguise it, fake an upthrust and mine the vein until it surfaced on someone else's claim.

But what about development? They would need at least a hundred thousand dollars to develop the mine. Wouldn't the partners be responsible for raising the money? Where would Buckskin get 15 thousand dollars to help develop the mine? He shook his head, finished his bottle of beer and went to see the barkeep.

"Don't have no idea who you're talking about," the barkeep at the Deep Shaft Saloon said.

"He was in here two days ago," Buckskin said. "His name is Walt. He's thin as a sapling, tall, and has a narrow black mustache and a goatee. Not a man easy to miss. You sure you haven't seen him around here?"

"Not likely. Now, you want another beer? I'm busy." He moved down the counter and never looked back at Buckskin, who got another beer and sat at a back table watching everyone who came in. He had done that for two hours before he talked to the barman. If Walt really was a part of this group, he'd now be warned not to show his face around here. So Buckskin was on a dead-end run.

He finished the beer, headed for the back door, then snorted and went out the front door. He remembered that twice someone had tried to kill him. Why would now be any different?

He checked the street just outside the door. Nobody waited for him. No shots snarled. He eased away from the saloon's windows into the welcome darkness and paused getting used to the dimness. Not ten o'clock yet. Lots to do, but he didn't have the slightest idea how to start.

He'd sent a second letter to Hercules B. Braithwaite in Denver telling him his progress. He expected an angry letter in return, but hadn't heard anything yet.

Now he had this damned Five Star mess. He could walk away from it, but the killer had come straight for him with a shotgun. Why? They must think he was a threat to them. Buckskin Morgan still couldn't figure out why they thought that way. Whoever "they" were.

The missing Braithwaite girl.

The damned Five Star.

The Lady Luck mine that he figured must be a swindle.

He had more branding irons in the fire than he had livestock. Maybe it was time he took off the rest of the night and tried to think it all through. He grinned. He'd just about get in bed at the boardinghouse, and Emily Johnson would be there with cheese and crackers and a bottle of cheap wine and wearing a silk robe so thin he could see right through it.

The Lucky Lady claim still bothered him. Then he had an idea. If it was the middle of somebody else's vein they'd hit, it would go two directions. They'd probably seal off one end of the vein and work the end that looked the most productive. All he had to do was get into the mine, rip off the timbers or whatever they used to hide the other end of the vein of gold and prove them to be thieves. Great, he had one problem solved. Now what about the other two?

None of the cafes were still open. One saloon also had a good-sized eating area along one side of the room, but that part had closed down at nine o'clock. He saw a woman walking toward him moving quickly. It wasn't the safest place for a woman at night. She came closer while staring behind her. He tried to miss her, but she shifted directions and the two ran into each other and both fell to the boardwalk.

Buckskin arose quickly and helped the young woman up.

"Miss, I'm sorry."

"Thanks, my fault. I wasn't looking where I was going. Somebody was following me. I guess he got scared off."

She frowned in the dim light from the saloon window.

"Hey, I remember you. At the hotel, the first night you got into town. Buckskin Morgan. Oh, but that was a fantastic night of lovemaking. You going anywhere special? I've got a little house up the street." She leaned up and kissed his lips and her hand rubbed his crotch.

"Buck, I'd be more than happy to take you off the street for a while. Even a quick one. I'm trying not to be so bashful these days." She lifted his hand and put it over one of her breasts.

"You remember what these are, don't you, Buck? Bet you do. Hey, I've got some good Scotch whiskey up there. Come on, make a girl feel good."

Buckskin lifted his brows. Her breasts felt warm and inviting. He didn't have anything else to do. The night was shot for him. He squeezed her breast.

"Yeah, Lois, I'd like that. Which way?"

"You remembered my name. How sweet. Oh, up

here a block and then over two."

About 30 yards behind them, two men came out of the shadows and followed Buckskin and Lois making sure they weren't heard or seen. Both men carried shotguns.

Chapter Fourteen

Just after Buckskin Morgan had left the Deep Shaft Saloon, a hurried conference took place in the back room. The barkeep told them what Buckskin had asked and the three men at the table all looked grim.

"Kill the bastard," the tall thin man with the black goatee said. "He knows my name, knows there's some connection with me and that gold ore robbery attempt. We have to blow him into pieces."

"Hold it," Miles Kelton said. "We think this through. What happens if we do kill this detective? We get some anger from some of the locals. The sheriff won't touch it if I ask him not to. Maybe Walt is right."

The third man shifted in his chair. "I don't like it. Too much killing. First that loudmouth Douglas, then Van Dyke and then the men on that gold wagon disaster. Now maybe Morgan. I don't like it. That's what got us in trouble the time before. I say we take it slow."

The man speaking spread his hands on the table and stabbed a penknife between his spread fingers. "It's so easy to make mistakes in something like this."

"No mistakes, Rudolph," Kelton said. "We'll take care of it. Just a big surprise and a shock that Morgan caught Walt's name. We've spent too much time and too much money setting this up to let one wandering detective stop us."

Godfrey Rudolph on the far side of the table lifted the shot glass and drained the whiskey. A ring glittered on his finger. It was a large white diamond set in a gold nugget. Kelton figured it was worth over ten thousand dollars. Rudolph wiped his mouth, his pale blue eyes wary. "All right. I'll trust you. But I want to be kept up to date on everything that happens."

The mine owner stood and went out the back door. As soon as he had left, Kelton nodded to the two men on the far side of the room.

"You put Lois on him?"

"Right, Boss, soon as he left."

"Follow them and take care of Buckskin Morgan. Better if his body is never found. Dig it in deep somewhere. Down an old claim shaft followed by a stick of dynamite would be ideal." Kelton grinned as the two men left the saloon by the back door carrying shotguns.

They hurried to the cross street, then up to Bennett Avenue, and caught sight of two figures as they passed the next saloon's splash of lamplight onto the boardwalk.

The two men moved up and made sure it was Lois and Buckskin, then followed them from a safe distance. Neither of the walkers ahead looked back.

"What about the woman?" one of the shotgunners whispered.

"Didn't say nothing about her. Let's get them both."

"No way. Lois is too good in bed. I'm getting her for free. No way we kill her. We get him outside."

"How?"

"Hell, I don't know. Might be easier to blast him in the house."

"Lois will raise Old Ned."

"Yeah, who cares. She'll be alive to fuck again."

As they watched the couple enter a small white house set back from the street, the two killers worked out their plan. They nodded and separated, one going to the back door and one to the front and moving so they wouldn't be seen by anyone in the house. Inside the small house, Buckskin kissed Lois as she worked on the buttons on her blouse. Something stirred in his brain and he worried it. Then it flowered and came into words.

"What were you doing out this late at night?"

"I'm not supposed to say. Hell, I guess it don't matter. A girl's got to make a living. Can't working at the hotel. I do some night work. I make house calls on gentlemen who would rather not be seen at a whorehouse."

Buckskin chuckled, but somehow it didn't ring true. He still didn't feel right. Something about it just didn't sit right. Why tonight? Why just after he'd shown his hand by asking about Walt in the Deep Shaft Saloon?

He felt her lifting his six-gun from leather.

"You certainly won't be needing this. I give up, crazed outlaw gunman. Do with my body what you will."

He took the Colt from her hand and pushed it back into its dark leather home. "I never let my weapon far from me, no matter what I'm doing. Right now I need to water the lilly. Your outhouse in back?"

"No, it's in the front yard," she said with a wry grin.

He laughed. "You get in your bedroom and get naked. I want you primed and ready to explode when I get back."

She smiled and went into the next room. He headed for the kitchen and the back door. He still had a strange feeling about this. It seemed too easy, too pat. Why was she in the street just when he was?

He stepped into the dark kitchen quietly. They had lit only two lamps. One sat in the living room. The second Lois had carried into the bedroom. A thin shaft of light stabbed into the kitchen and hit the back door. He could afford to wait a few minutes. Might be nothing, but then again . . . Over the years, he had learned to trust his hunches.

Two or three minutes later, he headed for the

back door just as he saw the knob turn and the panel edge inward.

Buckskin drew his iron and stepped behind the opening door. When it had been pushed two feet inward, he slammed into it with his shoulder blasting it backward. He heard a groan, and something hit the floor. He jerked the door open and stepped around it. A man on his hands and knees on the floor looked up. A shotgun lay between his hands. He grabbed for it.

Buckskin kicked him hard in the face. The toe of his boot hit the gunner under the chin and snapped his head upward and back. Bones cracked and the man fell sideways half in and half out of the kitchen. He didn't move. Buckskin touched his fingers to the man's throat and found no pulse. Broken neck. Buckskin grabbed the shotgun and waited. Why send one when they could send two?

If nobody showed up in a half hour he'd decide he was wrong.

The house remained quiet. Then he heard soft singing coming from the bedroom. He moved without a sound to the kitchen door and looked into the living room. In the small house, he could see the front door. It was closed. He waited.

Buckskin remembered his training with his Indian friend, a Sioux warrior who'd taught him how to be patient beyond all reason. The first element, think of some wonderful time when all was glorious and fantastic. Concentrate on that great feeling.

Portland, out on the Pacific coast two years ago.

169

Two weeks of relaxation and lovemaking and honesty and pure joy. She had been . . .

The front door eased open and a man stepped inside. In the lamplight he looked young, with a beard and black hair under his hat. Workingman's clothes. He held the shotgun ready. Buckskin lifted his Colt and stepped around the door.

"Looking for someone?" he asked.

The man bellowed in protest and brought up the shotgun, but before he could fire Buckskin put two rounds into his chest, pinning him against the wall. His eyes went glassy; then his head dropped to his chest and a last gush of breath came from his lungs as he slumped to the side and fell to the floor. His finger jerked the trigger in a death spasm and the side window shattered as most of the heavy double-ought slugs drilled through it and the rest plowed into the wall.

"Oh, my God!" Lois said when she rushed into the room. She stood there naked with one hand to her mouth, the other one behind her back.

"You killed him," she wailed.

"He was trying to kill me. You know anything about that?"

"Me? Why should I? I was just looking for a good time with a handsome, sexy man."

"Who paid you to set me up for killing, Lois?"

"Paid me? Nonsense. I don't know what you mean. I just happened to run into you and . . ."

"Bring your other hand out, Lois, now."

Buckskin held the Colt easy, aimed at the floor halfway between them.

"Why should I?"

"If you don't, I'm going to shoot you in the leg. You may never walk again without a limp. Oh, don't count on the other one. He's dead in the kitchen."

"You bastard!" She whipped her hand from her back and as soon as her aim came near him, she fired the derringer. Buckskin let her have the first shot. Then he came up with the .45 and fired one shot so fast she didn't have time to pull the trigger on the little gun's second barrel.

Buckskin's round caught her in the chest, just missing her heart, tearing up some vital blood pipelines. She slammed backward against the door frame and fell into the living room. Shock and anger, fear and hatred swept over her face.

"Those little guns ain't much good over two or three feet, Lois. You know that. I wouldn't have hurt you if you didn't shoot first. Who paid you to set me up?"

She looked up, the pain clouding her mind. She blinked, then struggled with the words. At last they came out. "Miles Kelton." She shivered, then screamed from the terrible pain. "Get the bastard for me." She wailed in pain. Then suddenly the sound stopped. Her head rolled to one side in the last movement Lois would ever make.

Buckskin left the three bodies as they were. He went out the back door into the darkness, walked down a deserted street and in a roundabout way to get back to Mrs. Johnson's boardinghouse. The sheriff would have some more bodies to worry about in the morning. There was no way anyone but Miles Kelton could blame the deaths on him.

* * *

Back in the rear room of the Deep Shaft Saloon, Miles Kelton sipped at a glass of whiskey and looked at his gold-filled pocket watch. It had been an hour. Where were the two men he had sent? He had hoped to have good news to report at the meeting tonight.

Ten minutes later he could wait no longer. He sent Walt to Lois's house to see what the trouble was.

Walt came through the back door ten minutes later, his face still showing shock.

"All three dead, Boss. Not a mark on Pete in the kitchen. Homer at the front wall took two slugs in his heart. Lois had a derringer in her hand. She was naked and caught one slug in her chest. Blood all over the place."

"No!" Kelton bellowed. He threw his glass across the room, shattering it against the wall. He tipped over the small table and kicked a chair until it spun to the floor.

"Who the hell is this guy? That's four of my men he's killed here and four on that damn gold-wagon disaster. Who the hell is he?"

Walt preened his blade-thin mustache and shrugged. "Just some detective from Denver."

"And then again, maybe he's a deputy U.S. marshal," Kelton said. "The guy is either damn good or unbelievably lucky." He looked at his watch again. "You stay here and keep out of sight. I've got to go see a man about a fortune. Keep out of sight and wait until I come back."

About 15 minutes later, at the stroke of midnight, Miles Kelton opened a door on the third floor of the hotel with a key and slipped inside. As usual the lamp had been turned so low it almost sputtered out. Three men sat around a small table in the middle of the room. There was no bed or dresser. It had been set up for meetings.

Kelton sat down in the last chair at the table.

"Gentlemen, time to start the meeting," he said. "I had hoped to have some good news for you, but unfortunately, the one big threat against us, Buckskin Morgan, is still alive."

There was some murmured talk, but nothing he could make out. He knew only one of the men at the table. He wore the diamond ring set in a gold nugget, Godfrey Rudolph. He knew the two others were owners of mines in Cripple Creek.

One of the owners took the floor. "We'll get to him later. What's more important to me is the fact that the Five Star symbol has surfaced here in Cripple Creek. I thought we agreed never to use that here again. At least not until the final phase of our plan when it could be used to fine advantage to spread fear."

"Gentlemen, that was my mistake," Kelton said. "When Van Dyke took the job, I made him take everything out of his pockets. The folded card must have been in a coin pocket or somewhere so it was simply missed when he dumped out his things on my desk. It was my mistake, and one that won't be repeated again. As I understand it, only two or three people in town know about the card. Some remember Van Dyke as being with the group, but people tend to forget in a hurry. If it doesn't spread, the fact of that card can't hurt us."

The other voice came then, deep, strong. He was the third man at the table, the one that Kelton didn't know all that well.

"You better be sure of that, Kelton. We agreed there would be no mistakes, no risks this time, until we were fairly well set up."

"It's all under control," Kelton said, smoothing the waters with his sincerity and tone of voice. "I told you I'd take care of it all. I will. Those legal papers are ready for all of you to sign. You know exactly what they are. They are preliminary to articles of incorporation of our new corporate entity that will be the major power in the new mining involvements. The usual type of formalities when individuals or companies get into something together. These are not public documents. Each of you should sign two copies, one for your files and one for me."

He looked around as he distributed the copies.

"Now, about the other small riffle in the stream, Mr. Buckskin Lee Morgan. He is a detective from Denver here to find a girl belonging to a rich man up there. So far he hasn't found her, but he's got in our hair a time or two. He'll be taken care of before our meeting next week.

"I'd like to wait a couple of days so he lets down his guard. Also I can watch his movements, his habits. Then the job will be done because I'll do it myself."

The men signed the papers and returned them to him. He put them in his small case and stood. "Well, then, it looks like that's all I have to bring up. Now, it's your turn. Do any of you have any questions?"

"You say this is foolproof," one man said, "that there is no way that we can be held liable or legally responsible and that the benefits will more than exceed our first projections?"

"Absolutely foolproof. We will be capitalizing on man's major vice, greed. The greed will outlast caution, and in the end we will come up with everything. The way we are setting up the new corporation, there will be no way for any of us to be personally responsible, and no possible legal action will be applicable to any of us. That's a solid guarantee." He looked around.

"And we four are the sole stockholders?" one of the men asked.

"Exactly, and officers of the corporation. No additional stock or shares can be sold without a majority vote of the stockholders, we four who will each hold one hundred thousand shares at a face value of the initial offering price of ten dollars and forty-five cents."

"All right. I wanted to clear that up."

Kelton looked around again, then closed his leather case and walked to the door. "Remember to leave separately. All go out different doors and space it out at five-minute intervals. I'll see you gentlemen next week here at midnight."

Kelton checked the hall. No one was in the third floor hallway of the hotel. He left quickly and walked to the street out the side door. Yes, it would be tonight.

He stopped at the Deep Shaft Saloon's back

door and waved to Walt to come out.

"Small job to do," Kelton said. "You have your tools?"

The thin man with the goatee and thin face nodded.

They walked three blocks up the hill and to the right to what they called millionaires' row. The lots were at least an acre in size, the houses castles with outbuildings. The two men walked up the driveway of one of the smaller of the mansions and stood in shadows next to the stables.

Shortly a rig came up the street, turned into the drive and rolled past them and stopped near the back door. Usually there would be the hired stable boy to take care of the horse, but this night he had been given the night off and Kelton knew it. The mine owner crawled out of the buggy, unhitched the horse and left the harness where it fell, then caught the animal's halter and led her toward the stables.

Kelton positioned Walt near the door. He stood deeper in the stable. When Godfrey Rudolph led the horse into the stables, Walt followed him closely.

Kelton stepped out from where he waited in front of the man and called.

"Mr. Rudolph. Kelton here. Something we need to talk about privately."

Rudolph looked up, startled, then relaxed when he heard the familiar name and voice. "What, man? I'm tired."

Walt used that moment to move up close and

slam his six-gun down hard on the mine owner's head.

"It's him?" Walt asked.

"Dead certain," Kelton said. "Get that ring and his wallet. It has to look good."

Walt rolled the medium-sized man on his back and stabbed him three times in the heart, then cut off his finger and let the ring drop into his hand. He pulled out the mine owner's wallet and nodded.

"Done," he said. The two men left through the rear of the small estate and hurried toward town by a back route so no one would see them. They slipped in the back of the Deep Shaft Saloon, which had closed for the night.

They examined the wallet. There were three 50-dollar bills and six 20s. Kelton gave the 20s to Walt along with a firm handshake.

"A bonus for a job well done. Your next target is the detective, Buckskin Morgan. I'm working on a plan. It won't be anything up close. This will be a long-range killing."

Chapter Fifteen

Buckskin slipped in the front door of the boardinghouse without a sound, stepped lightly to the hallway and back to his room. He could hear someone snoring up the stairs. Maybe it was Mrs. Johnson in her bedroom. He edged open his door a crack and saw light coming from inside.

His frown deepened and he drew his six-gun. When he pushed the door open quickly he found Emily Johnson in a filmy nightgown sitting up in his bed reading. She looked up and smiled.

"Land sakes, I was hoping that you wouldn't take all night to get here. I've got plans for you."

Buckskin closed the door gently and locked it. She had dropped her night-wear and knelt on the bed with her legs apart, her hands on her hips, her big breasts thrown forward.

"Woman, don't you ever get enough poking?"

"Never. Anyway, soon you'll be gone and I'll be a dried-up old maid of a widow again."

Buckskin laughed. "Not true, not a word of it. You'll pick out the best of your boarders and offer him a good deal on his rent money and all the sexy benefits of the ground floor room. Now won't you?"

She smiled.

"You've done it before I came, you'll do it after I leave."

"But you're special."

Buckskin grinned. "Yeah, because I'm here, right now, and you're wanting it."

"You be nice to me and I'll tell you something that will really shock you. Maybe I'll tell you. Depends on how nice you are to me."

She came off the bed and began to undress him. First the brown vest, then the tan shirt. She twirled his black chest hair around her finger and kissed his nipples.

"Damn, but I like a good man."

"Good, otherwise I'd be in a hell of a fix."

"You were going to be nice, remember?"

He kicked out of his pants and the short cotton underwear that everyone in New York and Chicago was wearing.

"Oh, yes, now I remember why I came in here tonight," she said.

"What's the book you're reading?"

"*The Adventures of Sherlock Holmes,* by Arthur Conan Doyle. It's a collection of short stories about this English detective. I bet you'd like them. He can tell the criminal by the smell in a murder room. He's tremendously talented."

"It's easy in a fictional story."

"Show me how it is in real life." Emily dropped on the bed and rolled over. He went down beside her.

"On top," she said. "I love it with me on top."

"You mentioned telling me something that would shock me. What is it?"

"Nope, sorry. I gave my word that I would never, never, never tell. And never's one hell of a long time." She rolled over on top of him and eased one big breast down to his lips. "Now open up like a good boy and do your big mama here a little bit of tit chewing. Big Mama likes it."

He liked it too. It was the start of a roller-coaster ride that wouldn't end. He'd been on a roller coaster in Chicago back in '89 and almost lost his supper.

Their first lovemaking was fast and furious and with lots of squeals and yelps of delight. They rested and she watched him.

"Hear you were mixed up in that gold ore attack down toward Florissant. How'd you get involved in that."

"I was one of the guards."

"Oh, Lord. You could have been killed."

"Wasn't."

"See?" she said quickly. "See what I mean? First a man is there in your bed just pleasuring you no end, and then somebody knocks on your door and your man is gone, dead in a cave in, and your bed is empty and cold and lonely. Could have happened to me again last night. Oh, Lord, you got shot at." She frowned and stared at him a minute, propped up on one elbow and watching him closely.

"You kill anybody yesterday?" she asked.

"Probably. It was dark, so we couldn't say for sure who shot who."

"Oh that really gets me worked up. I mean men shooting at each other. The idea that somebody gets killed. That just makes me so hot and furious to get fucked!"

She wailed and panted. "Damnit, Morgan, hold me tight, no, get inside me right now. Oh, God, no, there ain't no time, I'm coming. Lord, fuck, but it's here right now." Her whole body shook and she roared into a climax without him touching her. Her face twisted and she yelped and moaned and then a high keening shrilled through the room and she came down at last, sweating and panting, totally spent.

When she had recovered, he caressed one breast and kissed her cheek. "Johnson, there's nothing halfway about you. When you go for something you go all the way."

She looked at him from heavy, sexy eyes and sighed. "Never done that before. I didn't even touch my clit. Gawddamn, but that was one hell of a ride. You really did kill some of those attackers, didn't you?"

"Might have. Blew two out of their saddles. Them double-ought buck slugs must have stung something fierce."

"You bastard." She said it with a smile and with a tone that made it a compliment and not a word to start a saloon fight or a showdown at noon on a dusty street.

"You fucking bastard! K-erist but I'd love to have you stay in town and bed me about three times a night. You won't, though, will you? After you find that little girl you told me about, you'll be running back to Denver."

"I live there."

"Yeah, how, in a hotel with maid service in and out of bed?"

"Now and again."

"Get over here and poke me, damn you. I'm starting to feel old. I'll be thirty-five come December." She giggled. "I can just see myself in thirty years trying to proposition a boarder. My tits will be sagging, I'll have a potbelly and liver spots and my hair will be white and falling out. Hell, I'll have to pay them to spread my legs." She shook her head. "So, let's not waste it as long as we have it. Use it or you'll lose it, I heard a man say once. Let's use it."

The next morning at breakfast, a young redheaded girl served the plates of eggs, country-shredded potatoes, flapjacks, bacon, coffee and toast.

Emily came in and cleared her throat. The men looked up from their meal. "For anyone who didn't meet her last night, I'd like to introduce my new helper. This young lady is my niece from Kansas City and her name is Mae Johnson. She'll be helping me out here for a while. Be nice to Mae or I'll pitch you out on your hindside. Clear?"

She smiled and went back to the kitchen to cook up seconds.

Most of the five boarders had seen Mae the night before. They said hello and went back to eating. For just a moment Buckskin thought there was something familiar about the girl's face, but when he looked at her she simply nodded and kept passing a platter of buttered toast. He shrugged, putting his mind back on what he had to do today.

He had set up a meeting with Purvis and Cluny Norman to see what they could work out on the Five Star situation.

Since Purvis had been hit on the trail, and Cluny had told him about the conspiracy of a year ago, Buckskin felt that both of them must be free and clear of any involvement with it now. But who else? And did Miles Kelton figure in any way, or was he just stealing somebody else's gold from that vein?

A short time later, the three men sat in Cluny's office at the All American mine. It was in a separate building up the slope from the mine entrance and the other buildings, had carpet on the floor and was furnished more like a living room than an office. They sat in three large upholstered chairs and puffed on thick brown cigars.

"Yes, I'd say there are five or six men with big mines and even larger egos who might participate in a scheme like this," Cluny said.

"What about the others in your vigilante group" Buckskin asked. "Would any of them help us now?"

Cluny nodded. "I was thinking along the same

lines. Strange, one of them is Godfrey Rudolph. But the last time I saw him he didn't even speak to me. Ignored me completely. He usually knows what's going on in town."

"Could he be in on this new scheme?" Purvis asked.

Cluny took a long pull from his cup of coffee and shook his head. "Who in hell knows these days. Life used to be so simple. Work hard, get some breaks and make something of yourself. Now it depends on who you know and who knows you. I don't like it."

"So who are the others who were in the vigilante group last time?" Buckskin asked.

"Ira Langdon at the Second Strike mining company and then Uriah York up at the Gold Hill. Only York was never a committed man. He came in late and went along only because he felt there wasn't anything else we could do. Things had turned real bad before he joined us. No chance he'd come in now."

Someone knocked on the door, came in and went straight to Cluny. The young man whispered something to Cluny, who frowned, evidently asked him to repeat it, and when he was sure of the message waved the messenger away.

"Well, things just turned a little more complicated. Somebody just found Godfrey Rudolph murdered in his stable at his house. The sheriff's been there already. Godfrey's prized diamond-and-gold-nugget ring was cut off his finger and his wallet is missing. Could be robbery."

"Could be?" Purvis said. "Sounds plain enough

to me. Cut his finger off for that ring. Damn. He used to brag that it was worth over ten thousand dollars."

"Why do you think it might not be robbery?" Buckskin asked.

Cluny scowled and puffed on his cigar. "Because that's one of the ways the Five Star killers did their dirty work a year ago. Started out that way before they came out into the open trying to get the small mine owners to sell out."

"How many mine owners were in on the Five Star before who are still around?"

"There were five of them. Three big ones, two smaller. Two of the five met untimely deaths. Their mines were sold by the estates and I don't see how the new owners could have any current connection. Then the other three. They all had serious talks with the vigilante committee. One of them was perched on top of the third floor of the hotel with his hands tied behind his back. He stood on the ledge and listened closely to those talking to him.

"He had an option. He could jump, or he could tell us all he knew about Five Star. He talked. The other two followed Miles Kelton on the back of a horse with a noose around their necks. They had the same option and talked. One of the three was run out of town by his miners, shot and damn near killed, but he got away. He never came back.

"So that leaves two of the men still in town. Both run fairly small operations and seem to be doing it straight and true as an arrow."

"So our only lead is Miles Kelton," Buckskin

said. "I'm not terribly popular with him right now. He's tried to have me killed at least twice in the past week. Maybe I should have a friendly talk with him."

"Careful," Purvis said. "If he's tried twice and failed, he'll try again. You really don't want him to be successful the next time."

"Why would he gun for you?" Cluny asked. "This could be important."

"I'm a one-eighth share holder in the Lucky Lady claim that just hit an upthrust. Only reason I know."

"He wants the share back?"

"Tried to buy it before they hit the upthrust. If it is an upthrust. He could have hit the middle of a vein."

"So he's worried?"

"Could be that, or something else."

"Like the Five Star," Purvis said.

"How many producing mines in the district?" Buckskin asked.

"Big and little, about thirty, I'd say. Some are hand-to-bucket operations, who work six months to get a wagon load of ore. Some are multi-million-dollar deep-shaft hardrock mines. Everything in between."

"How many of the biggest ones?"

Purvis looked at Cluny. "I'd say mines with at least a million dollar investment, no more than six or seven," Purvis said. Cluny nodded.

"With three of you out of the running, including Rudolph, that leaves three or four who could be in on the conspiracy," Buckskin said.

"What are they trying to do?" Purvis asked.

"You weren't here last year when they tried it the first time," Cluny said. "They tried to grab up all of the little mines they could and make them their own. They did it by threat, by destruction, with dynamite blasts, and in the end by killing two of the mine owners. That's when we went into action to stop it. I'd figure that's what somebody's trying to do again. But for the life of me, I can't figure out who could be the ringleaders."

"I'll work on it," Buckskin said. "We have Ira Langdon at the Second Strike, Uriah York at Gold Hill and who else?"

"There's Quinn Forbes on the Poverty mine and Victor Irwin who operates the Princess mine," Purvis said.

"Got it. Let me do some nosing round and see what I can stir up."

"Watch your back, cowboy," Cluny·said. "From what you've said, these guys don't mind back-shooting a man at all."

Later, Buckskin had just left the New Town Cafe after lunch when the sheriff hailed him.

"Been looking for you, Morgan."

"You found me. Any idea who killed the mine owner?"

"Not a clue. Robbery probably from the looks of things. That makes four bodies in one day, a record even for Cripple Creek."

"Four bodies, Sheriff?"

"Yep. A naked woman in her little house and two gunslingers who must have shot it out over her. One had a broken neck and the other one shot twice. Woman was shot once. From what I hear she was a whore working on her own."

"Happens," Buckskin said. "You mentioned you'd been looking for me."

"True. The trial is set for ten o'clock tomorrow morning in the Cripple Emporium Saloon. Only place in town big enough to hold a good trial. I want you to be on hand to testify."

"Be glad to, Sheriff. Been wondering about that man who tried to shotgun me the other day, Van Dyke. You find out anything about him?"

"Nope. But I want you to fill out a report on the killing. Routine. Van Dyke used to live here. Got run out about a year ago after some killings and a reign of terror. Don't know why he came back."

"You ever hear of the Five Star gang, Sheriff?"

For just a second surprise tainted the sheriff's face. Then it went calm again. "Nope, can't say as I have. It have anything to do with Van Dyke?"

"You got me. I was hoping you might be able to help me."

"Afraid not, Morgan." He frowned slightly. "Don't be late tomorrow. I think the prosecutor will want to start with you."

"Who is prosecuting for the county, Sheriff."

"Local lawyer we hire sometimes by the name of Miles Kelton."

Chapter Sixteen

Buckskin covered up his surprise and the sheriff turned and walked away with his slow waddle. Miles Kelton was prosecuting the case? How could that be? Didn't the sheriff know anything about the man's background?

Buckskin stared after the county's head lawman and set his mouth in a hard line. Maybe that was it. Maybe Sheriff Houston knew all about Miles Kelton. Another thing he'd have to ask one of his local contacts before the trial in the morning.

Buckskin went back to see Cluny Norman at the All American mine. He sounded surprised too.

"So Kelton will prosecute" Cluny said. "I guess I should have expected it. There were rumors that Sheriff Houston was getting paid off plenty during the problems up here a year ago. People said that's why he never came up or stationed a full-time deputy or two up here."

"What will happen at the trial?" Buckskin asked.

"Damned if I know. Sounds like the sheriff wants to make quick work of them. Give them a fair trial and we'll hang them in the morning. Not at all unusual in this part of the country. We still don't hold with them fancy lawyers and their talk and all that shit about appealing verdicts."

"So I'll tell exactly what happened."

"If Miles gives you the chance. He may be careful about what questions he asks. He might not open up enough questions so you can tell the jury exactly what happened."

"I'll be ready for any of his tricks. I've testified in a trial or two myself."

Cluny filled Buckskin's coffee cup from a hot pot on the small stove in the corner of his office. "I've been asking around about the four suspected mine owners. So far I can't find out much about them. Two are new, one came in just after the big mess last year. Might take some time."

Buckskin thanked him and headed for the boardinghouse. Emily might know something about the four mine owners. Gossip usually made the rounds quickly in a small town.

She was working at the sink in the kitchen with her niece. The girl with red hair nodded at Buckskin and hurried out on a chore. Emily knew nothing that could help him about any of the mine owners.

"Different society they travel in," Emily said. "Land sakes, they don't even know us common folks are alive. They consider anything not up on the hill to be trash."

"I was hoping there was stories running round." Buckskin sighed. "If'n it ain't one thing, it's another. I've got to send another letter to my client in Denver."

"Writing paper, pen and ink in that little secretary with the glass doors in the living room. Oh, the front lets down into a writing desk. Help yourself." She smiled. "I don't want you reading my magazines in there. That's my private hoard."

"Take you up on the offer." He bent and kissed her lips and then hurried into the living room. He found the writing gear. He smiled as he looked at the magazines. *The National Police Gazette*, with its lurid accounts of crimes and rapes, *Puck*, with political cartoons, wit and humor. *Woman's Home Journal*, with women's news and stories. And the *Illustrated Police News*, featuring sex crimes and sex scandals.

He pushed them aside and wrote that he continued to search for Harriet Braithwaite, but that every lead he had turned out to be someone else. He hadn't given up hope, but felt that Harriet must be well or there would be some police report about an unknown girl who'd been hurt or killed. But no such report had been made, so he was optimistic about finding Harriet alive and well somewhere.

He signed the letter and folded it into an envelope, hoping that Braithwaite believed the optimistic message he had just sent.

That night at supper, the usual five men sat around the table. Emily always sat at the head of the table near the kitchen so she could bring in seconds and deserts and fill coffee cups. Now Mae, her niece from Kansas City, sat beside her. On the other side of her, Gomer took his usual spot. He ate his supper with the best etiquette, a marked improvement over his usual style.

Tonight he had even combed his hair and kept on his white shirt and tie from work. Knowing glances and a few snorts let it be known that the other men noticed his new manners and dress after work as well.

Buckskin had asked about Gomer before. Emily had told him that the young man was an accountant at the All American mine. He had worked there for almost a year and always paid his bill on time, never caused any trouble and was a perfect boarder.

Buckskin watched him as he ate supper, and he realized that Gomer was totally smitten with the shy, softspoken Mae Johnson. He guessed she was about 18, maybe a bit more. He wondered if her family had sent her here to a relative where no one knew her because she was pregnant out of wedlock. Happened more often than people knew.

At first the two young people didn't even speak to each other. They were so shy and bashful it hurt. Then Gomer asked her to pass the bread. Later she asked him to pass the salt. Halfway through the meal they were chatting away like old friends.

After the rhubarb pie, Buckskin excused himself with the rest of the boarders and went to the front porch for a moment. When he came back to go to his room he saw Emily alone in the kitchen. When he went into the kitchen, she turned expectantly.

"I have to be a witness in the gold ore wagon killings tomorrow," he said. "I figure I better get about nine hours of sleep so I'll be ready for any questions they might ask."

Emily pouted, then lifted her brows. "Fine, I was getting a little sore anyway." She said it softly so no one else could hear. She grinned. "Let's hope it's just a one-day trial."

Buckskin checked his vest pocket for cigars, found he was out of the thin black ones he preferred and waved at Emily and made a quick trip to the general store before it closed. When he came back he found Mae and Gomer sitting on the front porch swing talking. The young man was a fast mover. If Mae had traveled from Kansas City here by herself, she must be able to take care of herself. Of course, her aunt was nearby.

Buckskin went upstairs and closed the door, threw the small bolt and dropped on the bed. He'd have a small nap before bedtime.

The next morning, Buckskin had breakfast with the other men and headed for the saloon where the trial would be held just after 7:30. It would give him some time to talk with the prosecutor and maybe the judge. He had no idea if the judge had any legal training or not. Sometimes these country judges were notoriously lacking in any legal skills.

He didn't have a chance to talk to either man before the saloon was cleared and two long tables made by pushing together four small ones. The judge sat behind another table on the small stage.

Promptly at ten o'clock the black piano player did a fanfare on the piano and the judge in black robes walked in from the back. He sat and slammed a gavel down on the table.

"Here ye, hear ye, this Colorado judicial district court is now in session. The Honorable Emmett C. Blankenship presiding. All be seated."

About 50 people had crowded into the front of the saloon gawking at the judge and his robes.

Buckskin had been in a lot of courtrooms, some worse than this one. The judge looked down at last at the lawyers. There was no bailiff, no formality. Judge Blankenship looked at the sheriff.

"Who is on trial here today, Sheriff?"

"Your Honor, four men have been charged with murder."

"Then let's select a jury." He looked at the man sitting at a table to his left at the front of the room. "Mr. Kelton, you're acting for the district attorney, I'd assume. Has the state selected a panel of jurymen?"

"We have fifteen prospective jurors, Your Honor. If there is no objection from the defense, I'd like to seat the first twelve."

A man sitting at a table over from Kelton rose. "Your Honor, Jeff Samuels for the defense. I would like to hear the names and occupations of the prospective jurors."

"You're right, Mr. Samuels. Challenge whoever you wish and I'll rule on it."

A half hour later, a jury of 12 men had been seated. Samuels had challenged two men who were unemployed and had histories of drunkenness and violence in Cripple Creek.

Judge Blankenship watched the last of the jurors sit in the 12 chairs that had been placed to his right and then nodded. "All right, bring in the defendants and let's hear their pleas."

The sheriff waved and a deputy brought the four men in. All four had wrist irons on and were unshaven and angry. The deputy marched the men in and stood them in front of the judge. The deputy stared at them and read off the four names.

Judge Blankenship scowled down at them like an avenging angel. "You four men have been charged with the murder of one guard on an ore train heading for Florissant and the death of four of your fellow outlaws. You can save the court a lot of time here by pleading guilty. How do you say?"

Jeff Samuels stood and waited until the judge looked up. "Your Honor, I was retained as counsel for these gentlemen only an hour ago. Could I have a moment to confer with my clients before they answer to their pleadings?"

Blankenship sighed and scowled. "Unusual, but I'll allow it. Nobody can say I don't run a fair court. We'll take a ten-minute recess. All be back here ready to proceed at exactly . . ." He checked his watch. "At exactly ten-forty-six."

The young man hurried up to his clients, who grouped around him. Buckskin sat near the middle of six rows of chairs that had been put up across the saloon. He couldn't hear what the lawyer said to the defendants.

Miles Kelton stood at the far table situated in front of the judge. The table on the other side of the room also facing the judge was for the defendants.

The time was up quickly and the judge came back into court holding a bible. He sat behind his table on the stage, arranged his robes and then banged the gavel.

"Court's back in session. You four defendants, how do you plead?"

The first three plead not guilty. The fourth, the youngest and the one Buckskin had talked to, named Dick Jenkins, looked at his lawyer, who nodded.

"Your Honor," Jenkins said, "I'm willing to testify against the other three and plead guilty if the court will give me a prison term. I'm truly sorry for being part of the attack and I aim to be a good citizen from now on. I'll start by testifying against the three defendants."

Judge Blankenship scowled. "You talked to the sheriff about this, Mr. Parsons?"

"Yes, Your Honor. He said this is often done and if you agreed, it could happen."

"Mr. Parsons. You made a mistake, a big one. Five men died. That's not something the court takes lightly."

"Your Honor, may I speak?" Miles Kelton asked as he stood.

"Mr. Kelton."

"Your Honor, the state will have a much stronger case against the defendants if Mr. Jenkins is allowed to testify for us. He was there, he can absolutely testify to the fact that these three men attacked the gold ore wagons. Without him we have the testimony of one other eyewitness. The corroborating testimony of this gentleman would be immensely helpful."

The judge frowned and rubbed his face with his right hand. With his left he drew on the pad of paper in front of him. His deliberations stretched out. No one in the courtroom made a sound.

After a minute, he looked up. "If the state will agree to a ten-year prison term for this defendant, I'll permit his plea and his testimony."

"That seems fair to the state, Your Honor."

The lawyer at the defendants' table talked briefly with the young man, then looked at the judge. "Mr. Jenkins agrees to the ten-year term, Your Honor."

"Very well, the plea is accepted, sentencing will take place after the trial of the other three. Remove Mr. Jenkins to the back of the courtroom but keep him in manacles and guarded."

Judge Blankenship looked at Miles Kelton. "Is the state ready with its case?"

"We are, Your Honor."

"No opening remarks, lets get at it. I don't like to waste time in my courtroom."

"Yes, Your Honor. The state calls Buckskin Lee Morgan to the stand."

Buckskin rose from where he sat and walked to the front of the court to a chair that had been placed just in front, between the two small tables.

"Come up here and put your hand on the bible, Mr. Morgan," the judge said.

Buckskin stepped up on the stage, put his right

hand on the bible and swore he'd tell the truth, the whole truth and nothing but the truth. He returned to the chair and sat down facing the 50 people in the chairs and standing.

"Your name and occupation?" Kelton asked.

"I'm Buckskin Lee Morgan. I'm a professional detective."

"What's your home address?"

"The Lenox Hotel in Denver."

"Are you here working on a case."

"I am."

"What did you do three nights ago?"

"I rode on a three-wagon gold ore train heading for Florissant."

"In what capacity were you there?"

"I was an armed guard to protect the shipment."

"How many guards were there?"

"Six, two on each wagon besides the driver."

"Why so many guards, Mr. Morgan?"

"The owner of the ore, Mr. Purvis, told me he expected trouble. A hunch."

"Was the gold ore valuable?"

"Mr. Purvis told me it was worth about two hundred dollars a ton. We had two tons per wagon. In three wagons we had twelve hundred dollars worth of gold ore."

"You indeed did run into trouble?"

"No, sir. The trouble sought us out and attacked."

"Can you describe the attack itself and the place of the attack?"

Buckskin did, detailing the attack as he remembered it.

"After the outlaws broke off the fight, what did you do?"

"I untied my riding horse from the back of the wagon and followed the killers."

"I object to the word killers, Your Honor," Samuels said. "Nothing has been established to prove that fact."

"Sustained."

"I followed the sound of the horses as the men who shot at us rode directly away from the scene," Buckskin said.

"And did you find these fleeing men where they had stopped?"

"I did, about four miles up the road, more or less."

"How could you be sure they were the same men who shot at the gold wagon train?"

"I slipped up on them. They had made a fire and everyone was yelling at everyone else. They blamed each other for not being able to seize the gold wagons. They described how they attacked the wagons and how they were surprised there were so many guards. Only men who had done that would know about the guards."

Judge Blankenship cleared his throat. "Mr. Morgan. You're not allowed to argue the case. Just present the evidence."

Buckskin went on to tell how he had captured the men and taken them to town and turned them over to the sheriff.

"Now, Mr. Morgan, are you positive that these four men on trial here today are the same men who attacked the gold ore wagons?"

"Yes, sir. They are the same ones. One even told me that he was recruited here in town for the job by someone named Walt. He's thin and tall."

"Move to strike, Your Honor," Samuels said. "This man must be in court if he's one of these four. He can give his own testimony."

"Sustained. Move on, Counselor."

"Now, Mr. Morgan. Are those men you saw around the fire in this courtroom?"

"They are."

"Would you point them out so the jury will know who they are?"

"The three defendants and the one who pleaded guilty."

"Thank you, Mr. Morgan. No more questions."

The defense attorney questioned Buckskin for ten minutes trying to shake his story. He tried to show that the four men could have been coming from Cripple Creek and paused for the rest of the night. What Buckskin heard from the men around the fire could have been talk about hunting deer. Buckskin beat down every suggestion, and in the end the lawyer shook his head and gave up.

The next witness was the kid who pleaded guilty, Dick Jenkins. Kelton took him through the plans for the attack, the attack itself, how three men died and then the retreat and the conversations at the campfire. He wound up his testimony in a half hour and the defense lawyer had no questions.

The defense had no witnesses. The lawyers gave their closing statements and it was up to the jury. The trial had lasted almost two hours.

Buckskin figured about 15 minutes for the 12 good men in the jury to reach a verdict. They came back in ten with a guilty verdict.

The judge sentenced Jenkins to ten years in the state prison and the other three to be hung the following day in Colorado Springs.

"We don't have a gallows here and it would cost too much to build one. We'll transport you back to the Springs this afternoon and come sunup you'll meet your maker. Put shackles on their legs and let's get them to a wagon and down to Florissant before the evening train gets there. Come on, move, gentlemen, we don't have a lot of time to spare."

Later, Buckskin talked to the sheriff. He had the men in a wagon heading for Florissant.

"What about the Larry Douglas killing?"

"Never heard of it. Oh, you mean that accidental death in that claim. A shame, nice young man like him. It was investigated and determined to be an accident."

"He was murdered."

"So you think. The official record shows accidental death."

"What about the three deaths you heard about here in town, the woman and two men?"

"That case is closed too. A simple love triangle. Two men fought over one woman. She chose the wrong one, got herself shot, and then the dying man shot the man who killed the girl. Simple, neat, all wrapped up." He looked at Buckskin and grinned. "Now, Mr. Morgan, can you tell me positively that it happened any other way?"

"Nope, just wondered. Figured you were here in town you'd take care of it." Buckskin turned and walked away. He had been surprised by Kelton. The man was a good trial lawyer. He had done a fine job prosecuting the four men.

Buckskin had wondered if Kelton would do something wrong or forget something so the men would get off. Maybe Kelton wasn't in on the ore stealing at all. Maybe. Buckskin knew Kelton had murdered the Douglas boy to get a paying mine. Was he behind the gold ore stealing and the Five Star scheme? Those were two questions he had to get answers to fast.

Chapter Seventeen

As Mae peeled potatoes in the kitchen at the Johnson boardinghouse she closed her eyes and laughed softly.

"But Aunt Emily, he's just so. . . . so nice!"

"Yes dear, I know he is. Careful to get all the peeling. You never done this much before, have you?"

"No, Aunt Emily. Never peeled many potatoes before. But Gomer is so smart and fun to talk to and just so . . . Nice!"

Emily smiled. "I know what you mean, young lady. This the first boy you've ever felt this way about?"

"Oh, my, yes. I've never been around boys much before. You know an all-girls school, and then when I'm at home my parents are like prison guards. But Gomer. I just can't explain it."

Emily caught Mae's chin in her hand. "I'll explain one thing to you, young lady. You keep your knees together when he's around. Don't let him kiss you more than once and don't you ever let him touch your breasts. We don't want you pregnant, now do we, girl?"

Harriet Baraithwaite remembered the girl who came to finishing school in Denver and three months later was sent home quickly because she'd started to get fat in the belly. To "show," the girls called it. She was pregnant.

"Oh, no, Aunt Emily. I certainly don't want that. But . . . but I like him so much."

"Fine, like him, just make him keep his hands off your body. Slap him if you have to. He'll understand quickly. There are two kinds of girls, Mae. One who is polite and firm and sweet but when she says no to a boy, she means it. The other kind doesn't even bother to say no and gets herself pregnant."

Mae set her mouth firmly and a determined look froze on her face. "Absolutely, Aunt Emily. I can be firm and polite and sweet but also stern. When I say no, he'll stop."

"You be sure he does. You get yourself pregnant and you don't live under my roof no more. I've got my reputation in this little town to think about. You get yourself pregnant and you're out in the street on your own again."

"Yes, Aunt Emily." She smiled remembering. "He hasn't even kissed me yet. But last night he held my hand and I know he wanted to. One kiss, right, I can remember that. Only one kiss and no touching."

As Emily Johnson watched the pretty girl, she knew what a difficult time she was going to have, especially since she seemed so smitten with this young man. Emily frowned for a moment. From now on she was going to be sure that her bedroom door, or Buckskin's, was locked and the bolt thrown when they were together. Wouldn't do for Mae to prance into her aunt's bedroom and find her naked, on her back on the bed with both legs aimed at the ceiling and a naked Buckskin pounding away at her crotch.

That evening, right after supper dishes were washed and dried and the kitchen cleaned up, Harriet Braithwaite, hiding as Mae, went out to the front porch for a breath of air.

Gomer Haskel sat on the swing smoking a just-rolled cigarette. He dumped it on the porch floor and ground it out with his boot, then stood and smiled at Mae.

"Good evening, Miss Mae. Out for some night air?"

"Indeed I am, Mr. Haskel. I see you're still smoking those foul cigarettes."

"I'm quitting right now if'n you want me to, Miss Mae."

"Good. Is the swing being used?"

"Not so you could notice. I had to boot Charlie off it about half an hour ago, but it's available right now."

She smiled and sat down in the porch swing and

pushed it gently with her foot so it swung back and forth in a gentle arc.

"Could I have the pleasure of swinging with you, Miss Mae?"

"I would certainly think so. Plenty of room."

He sat down beside her and took over pushing the swing.

"No moon tonight, Mr. Haskel."

"Not yet, maybe later when it gets full dark, we can see it."

He moved a little closer to her on the swing.

"Mr. Haskel, if I remember correctly, you said you're an accountant, a bookkeeper for the All American mining company."

"That's right. I'm the head bookkeeper and accountant. I check all the books to make sure the others do their work right."

"Does that pay well?"

He smiled. "Now, money matters are no subject for a woman. I get paid well enough."

"But what about your future? Do you always want to be an accountant?"

"I don't see why not. It's an honorable profession. I'm good at it and I enjoy it. What more can a man want?"

"Why, a family, of course. You do want a family, don't you?"

Gomer Haskel frowned, ran his finger around his white collar and blinked. He felt sweat bead his forehead. "Sure, sometime I figure I want a family. Yes."

"Well, Mr. Haskel, that is good news. I'm sure all the girls in Cripple Creek are just lining up hoping that you'll dance with them."

Gomer grinned and moved a little closer. "Miss Johnson, we don't have many dances in Cripple Creek. I can only remember one in the past six months, and then there ain't almost no young girls in town a'tall."

"Oh." The word came out small and soft and she turned and smiled at him. "I'm sorry you don't get to go to dances. They are just loads of fun."

"I . . . I don't know much about dancing."

"I could teach you."

"First we'd have to have music. I don't think so. I'm not much of a mind about dancing."

"Oh. Well, if you don't want me to teach you."

"Now, didn't say that a'tall. Guess it would be fine. Just don't know where." He looked at her and moved a little closer until his leg touched her skirt.

"Miss Mae. Would it be all right if I held your hand?"

She sucked in a quick breath, her heart pounding. She took another breath, then nodded. "Yes, I think that would be permitted, Mr. Haskel."

He caught her hand, held it gently and pulled it toward him so their hands lay on his thigh.

She smiled. "Yes, I . . . I like that, Gomer."

"It does feel good, doesn't it? I could just sit here a long time this way." A quiet came between them. At last he broke it. "You like it here better than Kansas City?"

"Oh, yes. Much better. I lived in Chicago too. I didn't like it there at all."

"Chicago. That's a real big city, isn't it? I've never

even been to Kansas City. Been in Denver. Used to live there."

He moved closer and squeezed her hand. He looked at her and found she was staring at him. "Would it be all right, Mae, if I kissed your cheek?"

"I don't know, Gomer. This is all happening just so fast. I only met you yesterday."

"I kissed your cheek last night."

"I know and it was sweet and nice. . . . " She sighed. "Yes, I think it would be all right."

She leaned toward him and he stretched over toward her. His lips touched her cheek and stayed there. Harriet knew she had closed her eyes. A moment later she eased away from him.

"Nice," she said. "That was sweet and nice, Gomer Haskel."

"Yes, nice." He gave a sigh. "I sure wish . . ." He stopped and shrugged.

"What do you wish, Gomer?"

"Oh, it wouldn't do no good to ask."

"Depends on what you ask. You just never can tell. I might surprise you."

He lifted his brows. It was nearly dark. The moon hadn't come up yet. He sat close to her, his thigh touching hers. He still held her hand on his lap.

"I . . . I just wish I could kiss you on the lips. A real kiss. Would that be all right?"

"Gomer, that is a lot to ask. Most girls don't get kissed until they plan on getting married. You know, a serious kiss."

"Just one?"

"Would that make you happy?"

"Oh, yes. I'd jump over the moon."

"Well, maybe once, just once, but don't tell anyone."

"Oh, never."

She turned toward him and watched his face. Harriet took a deep breath and nodded. "All right, just once."

She leaned in and he pushed toward her. She closed her eyes and their lips met and held for a moment, then eased apart but came back together again. She felt herself falling. Her hands came out and caught his shoulders and she slumped against him, her lips still on his, her breasts pushed against his chest.

They stayed that way for what seemed like hours to Harriet Braithwaite. Then she opened her eyes and pulled back from him with a gasp.

"Oh, my goodness." She frowned and watched him.

"Mae, that was wonderful. That was a real kiss."

"I better go in."

"No, please not yet. I wanted to talk with you. I've got a lot of plans I want to tell you about. We need to talk. I'd like to go back to Denver. I'm saving my money and I want to open up an accounting firm of my own. Hire bookkeepers, become a real businessman. There's so much I want to tell you."

Harriet knew she had to get inside, get away from him. She had melted, completely melted. His kiss had unhinged her. He could have done anything he wanted to right then. Oh, she'd be careful about kissing him again. So powerful. It was more than the girls ever talked about. She felt her breasts still throbbing. She knew that she was damp down below. Goodness sakes, what had she almost let happen?

"I've got to go in, Mr. Haskel. Thank you for a wonderful talk. I really have to go in now."

She stood and he stood and then she hurried inside away from him. In the kitchen she put a cold wet cloth to her face and tired to get calmed down. Would her Aunt Emily notice how she was?

Goodness, she hoped not. She would be extra careful the next time she was with Gomer Haskel. He had a strange effect on her. Strange but nice, nice and cuddly and warm and wanting and . . . and she didn't know what else. Right then she didn't want to find out what else it was.

She hurried into the spare room in back of the kitchen Aunt Emily had fixed up for her to use as a bedroom. She slipped inside, lit the lamp and then pushed the bolt on her door and fell on her bed remembering how that kiss had felt. Goodness.

Earlier that same afternoon, Buckskin Morgan made another attempt to find out what happened to the small blond girl he hunted for Hercules Braithwaite, the powerful and rich man from Denver.

He worked the whorehouses again, those in the saloons and three bawdy houses that had been moved another block back from the main street of Bennett Avenue. Nobody had seen a young girl, especially not one with short brown hair.

"Men like their whores to look like women, not young boys," one madam said. "But if you want one like that I can ask around."

Buckskin shook his head and left the house. He checked the other boardinghouse again without results and went over the hotel register. No one could remember a young girl traveling alone with short brown hair.

"Course most women wear some kind of hat when they travel," the clerk told Buckskin. "Might be that one could slip by I wouldn't notice. Not likely, though."

Buckskin gave up about four that afternoon and went up to the All American mine to talk with Cluny Norman. He found the miner with Nate Purvis. They welcomed him to Cluny's office and filled his coffee cup.

"Not one hell of a lot of progress," Cluny said. "Oh, I dug up a little bit of dirt on one of the mine owners, but I'm not sure it's true. I'm checking it out. Something about charges in two California mining towns for fraud and misrepresentation. I'll let you know."

"At least nothing has happened so far from the bastards if they're trying to get the Five Star operation going again," Buckskin said.

"What about Godfrey Rudolph?" Purvis said. "You really don't think that was a robbery victim, do you?" he asked Cluny.

"I don't know. Course the Five Star killers did use that ruse before," Cluny said.

"Then today a notice went up that a Denver

company has taken over Rudolph's mine," Purvis said.

"What's so unusual about that?" Buckskin asked.

"The president of the company according to the notice is Miles Kelton. Is that a familiar name?"

"Be damned," Buckskin said.

"True enough, and that must make Kelton the mainspring of this Five Star operation," Cluny said.

"Can't be," Purvis said. "Buying out that operation would take at least a million and a half. Where would Kelton get four hundred thousand dollars for his one third of the cost?"

Buckskin waved a hand. "But remember, Kelton is a lawyer. Maybe he did some legal magic with Rudolph, some legal mumbo jumbo that in effect gave Kelton the mine if anything happened to Rudolph."

"The man wasn't stupid," Purvis said. "Why would he sign something like that?"

"He wouldn't if he understood what he was signing. Some of these legal papers start out one way and do a quick turn and you never know where they go unless you read it all."

Cluny nodded. "So it could have happened. At least it puts Kelton right in the middle of our target if the Five Star kicks up again."

"It may not be the first mine he's stolen," Buckskin said. "I'm still sure that he killed Larry Douglas on the Lucky Lady claim. The sheriff said it was officially an accidental death."

"Figures," Purvis said.

"Isn't it about time we take a tour of our new mine?" Buckskin asked Cluny. He looked at Purvis. "Both Cluny and I own a one-eighth share of the Lucky Lady. Cluny bought a one-eighth share from Don Casemore."

"What time is it?" Cluny asked. He looked at his watch. "Too late today. How about first thing tomorrow? Lars is going to want each of the partners to kick in some development money. He must own six of the shares, so that's his part."

"How much is he going to want?" Buckskin asked. "We're talking about Lars Zacharias here, but my money is on Miles Kelton as the real owner of that mine."

"He'll need at least a hundred thousand to set up the mine right, if the size of the vein warrants it. We'll have a look. No way he can keep us out now."

Buckskin did some fast figuring and scowled. "That's twelve thousand five hundred dollars for my share. Not a chance I can raise that even if I sell my rifle and saddle." He shrugged. "Looks like I'm out of the game."

"I'll loan it to you if it comes to that," Cluny said. "Hell, I can afford it. Let's see what happens tomorrow morning when we show up at that mine and demand to be admitted."

"I still think that he spotted a vein and doesn't own it," Buckskin said.

"So he's running the vein, faked an upthrust and now is following one end of the vein to see where it goes."

"What about the other end of that vein?" Buckskin asked. "He must have blocked it off somehow and will come back to it if he gets too close to some other mining operation."

They tried to remember who had mines around the Lucky Lady. Nothing was right on top of it.

"We'll check it out in the morning," Buckskin said. "Meet me at the hotel dining room for breakfast about seven, and we'll take it from there."

They shook hands and Buckskin headed for the boardinghouse, determined tonight not to miss supper.

Chapter Eighteen

At supper that night at the Johnson boarding-house, Emily sailed around in her usual efficient manner. She even forgot to ask her niece, Mae, to bring in the dessert. She looked at Mae, who was talking with Gomer, and grinned. Oh, to be 18 again. What a time Emily would have knowing what she knew now.

She brought in the dessert and served it and Mae didn't even look up. The girl could be irritating at times, like she was the lady of the manor or something. But the way Mae had taken to Gomer was delightful. It had to be her first love. From the way it was going, it looked as if it could be her last.

Buckskin had noticed the pair as well. He recognized the glorious smile on the girl's face, as if she'd just been done good or was about to be. He grinned. That was a cynical adult man talking. When he was 18 that smile meant he was doing something right and the girl really did care for him. Cared maybe enough that he could kiss her and if that went right get a feel of her breasts. Oh, yes, those were the days.

After supper, Buckskin went to his room and wrote down on a big pad of paper everything he knew about the Five Star conspiracy and the death of Larry Douglas. Somehow there had to be a connection there, he just hadn't figured out what it was.

It was past nine o'clock when he heard a faint rap on his door. He'd left it unlocked, and the knob turned and Emily slid inside with a smile a mile and a half wide on her attractive face. She locked the door by throwing the bolt.

"Did you see our two lovebirds at supper?" she asked, walking over and sitting on the bed. "Now there is a pair that's going to be serious. I can tell the signs. I had a long talk with Mae about how a lady acts and not to let him touch her breasts."

Emily laughed as she unbuttoned her blouse and pushed the cloth to the sides showing off her big breasts. "Ain't I the one to be giving a lecture!"

They both laughed, and Buckskin left the small desk in the room and sat on the bed beside her.

"I can't think of anyone better qualified to give sex instruction than you. Look at all of the experience you've had."

She slapped him gently, then kissed his lips. When the hot kiss ended she frowned at him. "Don't just set there, damnit, seduce me or

216

something. I'm in the mood for something damn crazy, wild, really evil, dangerous or downright risky."

"Like I tie you up naked and whip you with my belt until you beg for it?"

"You're getting the idea."

"I don't do that kind of stuff."

"Yeah, me neither, but I think about it sometimes." She screwed up her face thinking. "How about three of us, two men and me, and both of you getting me at the same time."

"Not a chance." He reached down and massaged both of her breasts at once and watched the nipples rise and her breathing quicken.

"How about just you and me on the bed and getting sexy and then you do me doggie-style?" she asked.

"I think that's a great idea."

Emily threw off her blouse and pulled the skirt and two petticoats down, then pushed off her silk bloomers, which came half way to her knees.

"Leave your clothes on," she said, a huskiness creeping into her voice. "Oh, damn, but I like it when you have your clothes on and it's like you jumped me in the park and tore off my clothes and then . . . oh, yes, that sounds delightful."

He pushed her down on the bed and dropped on top of her, his weight forcing her into the thin mattress.

"Oh, yes, love. That's fine. When you push down on my titties that way it just gives me a jolt of wanting you. Your knee up between my legs is fine, yes, so fine. Love the way your clothes give me little scratches and nicks, love it." She reached up and kissed his lips and then smiled.

"Darling Buckskin, would you roll me over and spank my bottom just a little, like I'm a bad girl? Please. Not to hurt me, just so I'll know that you're spanking me. I really love that."

Buckskin sat up. She rolled over and looked over her shoulder. "Hey, big stud, spank me!"

He slapped her round bottom and she yelped. He used his open hand and spanked her a dozen times, bringing a tinge of red over her buttocks.

She looked back at him and there were tears in her eyes. "More, damn you, more and harder!"

He spanked her again, not harder, gentler, and she broke down and sobbed. He rolled her over on her back and helped her sit up.

"Why the tears?"

"Remembering. I was sixteen that summer on the farm and my pa came into my bedroom and sat on the edge of the bed and told me how much he missed my ma. She'd been dead two years by then and he'd never gone to the whores in town. He told me he needed me and it wouldn't hurt and it would be a big help to him. I didn't know what he was talking about at first and then I told him no, and tried to get away.

"He told me he knew I'd been fucked before. He saw the neighbor boy one day in the haymow have his way with me. It was true. I still told him he was my pa and he couldn't, it wasn't right. He said if I didn't say yes, he'd have to spank me. I told him to go ahead, I wouldn't let him do it.

"He spanked me and told me how much pleasure fucking would give me and how nice I looked and how big my tits were already and the more he spanked me the more I wanted it. I forgot he was my pa and I rolled over and pulled up my nightgown and tore open his pants.

"He poked me five times that night and when it was over he told me he never would again. Two nights later I woke up and he had my nightgown up and my legs spread and my little cunny just running wet with juices. He did me twice a week from then on, and I loved it, but I was afraid I might get pregnant. I knew about breeding animals on the farm. So the day I was seventeen, I took all the cash money he'd saved up under his mattress and his gold-filled watch and Ma's diamond ring and ran away from home. I ain't never regretted it.

"So once in a while I guess I need to be spanked for being so evil and liking it when Pa fucked me all those times. Leastwise I never got pregnant. It's hard to make me pregnant. Got to work at it."

She wiped the last of the tears away and leaned against him. "Now, you big stud animal, please fuck me doggie-style so I can get my kicks in and soar over the moon. I want to go now."

She went on her hands and knees and looked over her shoulder at him. "Hey, you ready?"

Buckskin went on his knees and spread her just a moment, then pushed forward and entered her. Emily growled and then wailed softly as he eased in until their bodies met with his bones against her soft buttocks.

"Oh, glory. Yes, yes."

He leaned over her back and reached below, cupping her soft breasts, caressing them, fondling them, making her nipples jump upward and fill with hot blood.

"Yes, Darling Buckskin. Fuck me hard and fast. Make me screech in delight. There's no pain, you can't hurt me, just pound in as hard and fast as you want to."

Buckskin gripped her breasts and began to jolt into her with long hard strokes. She yelped in response. Then he let go of her breasts and caught her bent hips right at her torso. It made a perfect handhold, and he set up a fast pace that left Emily panting and wailing.

He wasn't sure if she climaxed or not. This time he concentrated on his own desires. He felt the beginning and slammed harder and harder into her until he pushed her so far forward she collapsed onto her face in the pillow and her chest against the bed. Her ass still stuck up in the air and he kept pounding.

The stars exploded, creating new planets. The sun dimmed in the sky by the brilliance of the exploding stars. Then they cooled and the sun took over again in this out-of-the-way place in the poor section of the universe, and he felt the end coming.

He powered again and again as he spasmed and he could feel the seed of the race spurt out of him and he growled and then bellowed with the final thrust and fell on top of her pushing her hips to the mattress and they were still lanced together.

Ten minutes later they sat side by side on the bed.

"You ready yet?" she asked.

"No. You never get enough sex, do you, Emily?"

"I'm saving up, storing up memories for the time when I don't get poked for six months or a year."

"Now, why would that be with a houseful of single men?"

"I usually don't waste my time on men who can only afford to live at my place. Hell, I wouldn't live here myself if I could sell this dump. I should move to Denver and get myself a fancy place."

"Then do what?"

"Do? I'd have a boardinghouse and charge three times as much as I do here, that's what." She looked up at him. "Hey, you ready yet?"

"Have you ever had enough fucking, really enough one night so you just didn't want to spread your legs again?"

"Never. No man can keep up with me. Now, if you aren't ready, I am and I want to play with him. Make your little worm there turn into a sword ready to pierce me again and again."

Buckskin chuckled. He fell backward on the bed. "Go ahead, I give up. Do with me whatever you will. I'm your sex slave."

Emily went on her knees beside him. "Now that's more like it. This is going to be a great night."

The next morning at breakfast, Buckskin stayed after the others had hurried off to work. Mae brought him more coffee and smiled.

"Mr. Morgan, I hear you're hunting for some girl here in town. I thought maybe I might see her sometime. What's her name?"

He told her. "But I doubt if she's using that name. She's too smart for that. My guess is she's going by some other name. Have you seen any young girl around town I might talk to?"

"Well, I don't get out much. I go to the store with Aunt Emily. If you tell me what she looks like I'll certainly watch for her. Has she done something bad?"

"No, not at all. Her father is worried about her and wants her to come home, that's all. She hasn't broken any laws or anything like that."

"That's good. She just wanted to run away. Maybe her father beat her, or wasn't good to her."

"No, I don't think that was the case. She was supposed to go to a school for young ladies in Chicago, but she came here instead."

Mae nodded. "Well, I'll be sure to watch for her." Mae took one more look at him and hurried back to the kitchen with the coffeepot. She was almost laughing as she went out the door.

Buckskin checked the clock on the small hutch at the end of the dining room. It was a quarter to seven. He had a meeting in the hotel at seven. He'd have more coffee there.

Buckskin wore his range clothes. Denim pants, a light blue shirt with long sleeves and a brown vest. He tugged at his gunbelt to get it set precisely, then headed for the hotel.

The other two were there when he arrived. Both had coffee in front of them and he ordered the same.

Nate Purvis had on work clothes, so did Cluny

Norman. They looked like a pair of miners, not mine owners.

"Anything special we need to decide before we go up there to the Lucky Lady?" Buckskin asked.

"Just check it out and look for where the other end of that vein goes," Purvis said. "I'd bet they didn't do a good job of punching out a hole in their tunnel where they will pretend that they found the upthrust. I'll check that out too."

"My guess," Cluny said, "is that they have some sort of a timbered wall blocking off the other end of the vein. That way nobody can see it or guess that it's there."

"I'm thinking that if we find some signs that point to an illegal operation, we should keep mum about it," Buckskin said. "There will be a better time when we can use this fact. What do you think?"

"Like when?" Purvis asked.

"Like when we sue them or charge them with a felony of gold ore theft from someone else's vein."

"Mmmmm, yes. I agree." Cluny nodded. "Yes, if we find evidence that it's an illegal dig, we don't talk about it with them."

A half hour later, they stood beside a new shaft that had been cut into the landscape 30 feet from the original shaft. It had a sign in poor printing that identified it as the Lucky Lady Mine, L. Zacherias, owner. A wooden ladder extended down 15 feet to the bottom of the shaft.

"Hello, anyone home?" Buckskin called. Lars Zacherias jolted out of the small building near the first shaft and stared at them. He didn't have the shotgun this time.

"Yeah, what can I do for you?" he called. He didn't move. The three walked over to him.

"We're your partners in this mine, remember? Figured we'd come over and take a look at our new operation and see how much money we're making."

"Yeah, Morgan and Cluny, each one-eighth shareholders of the Lucky Lady. Figured you'd be here before now."

"We've been busy," Buckskin said. "We want some indication of how good the vein is you've uncovered."

"I'm busy right now."

"Then we'll take a look ourselves," Cluny said. "We've been in a mine or two before."

"You can't do that," Lars said.

"Oh, but we can," Buckskin said, his hand dangling beside his six-gun and quivering. "We can do it right now with or without your help. Come or stay here, it's up to you."

Lars shrugged. "I guess I can come. Not much to see yet. Still evaluating and estimating the amount of money we need to put it into real production. Right now we're digging out the vein and storing the gold ore in one of the dry side tunnels."

"Show us," Purvis said.

About 20 minutes later, they had inspected the whole mine. It was just the one tunnel and three dry drifts off it. In the third drift they had piled up gold ore. Cluny took a close look at it with two lanterns.

"I'd say abut a hundred and fifty dollars a ton," he told Lars. "Might get better as you go deeper."

"It turned into a horizontal vein on us this far down," Lars said. "Must be a strata shift that did it."

Cluny tossed a piece of the ore back on the pile. "Strata shifts happen all the time, but not too often in this area."

They checked the face of the tunnel and found two men pounding in holes with five-pound hammers and six-foot-long steel drill bits. They hit the drill once, turned it a quarter of a turn and hit it again.

"You'll need pneumatic drills in here," Cluny said. "That will make it go faster. Any idea where this horizontal vein is going?"

Lars frowned. "Ain't no idea. Expect it to turn again and go deep into the mountain just at any time now."

The men went back to the new shaft. Buckskin wandered past the ladder down the old tunnel. "What's down this way," he asked.

Lars was beside him in an instant. "Just another empty tunnel that turned up nothing."

"That happens in mines. When did you hit the upthrust?"

"About a week ago. We kept it quiet for a while until we could do the blasting and check it out. Then when it took such a slant, it confused us for a while. Expect it to go straight down in another twenty or thirty feet."

"Yeah, then you can get the heavier veins and the offshoots. Some of those are really rich." Buckskin looked down the other way of the tunnel into the darkness, held up his lantern and made sure he saw the widened part of the tunnel and the thick planks walling off part of the side of the tunnel. The original one looked like it had come in at a different angle.

"Well, looks like we've checked out this hole. Now what are you going to do about development money?" Buckskin asked.

Lars shrugged. "Let's talk about it up top. I still ain't all that happy underground. Nothing serious like that claustrophobia stuff I heard about."

Buckskin swung his lantern ahead and they walked back toward the light coming down the open shaft. "I'm not what you'd call a natural-born miner either, Zacherias," he said.

Back on top, the four men talked.

"Had a friend of mine in who knows mines," Lars said. "He said when this strata shift is over and the vein goes straight down again, we'll be ready for the heavy equipment, machinery, pneumatic drills, air fans, steam engines, the whole thing. He says we'll need a hundred thousand to get the thing going, and maybe twice that much before we start turning a profit."

Cluny took over. "So you're saying your first incorporation will be for a hundred thousand. You own the other six shares, I'd say. Can you come up with your seventy-five-thousand-dollar development money?"

"Damn right. I have a backer."

"He gets a percentage of your seventy-five percent of the mine, not any of our share," Cluny said.

"Well, sure, that's the way it works. When I have the cash in hand, I'll call on you two to bring twelve thousand five hundred each, and then we get rolling."

"You have a lawyer handling your end of things?"

"Yeah, sure."

"Who is it?" Buckskin asked. "We might want to use the same man, keep it in the same office."

"Oh, yeah, I see. I'm using the man recommended to me as the best in town, Miles Kelton."

Cluny pointed at the shaft. "You keep digging out that vein, you could have two wagon loads of ore ready to go to the smelter in a week or so. You do any ore hauling out of here, I want to be notified and a strict accounting kept. We're both in on this now. Let's keep it all straight and aboveboard so nobody has to sue anybody else. I don't hesitate to sue if somebody does me wrong."

"Oh, yes. We did plan on taking a two-wagon load. Maybe sometime next week. We'll even let you watch the load-out."

They said their good-byes and the three visitors headed back down the mountain. As soon as they were out of earshot, Cluny spoke first.

"See the other end of that tunnel?"

"The one that led toward the first shaft that had the planks nailed over it?" Buckskin asked.

"You saw it too. Looks like a setup for an outlaw dig."

"You remember the direction that tunnel went?" Buckskin asked.

"Yeah, almost due north, up toward the Princess mine," Purvis said.

"Toward it, but must be a quarter of a mile away. Lots of unclaimed land up that way. Wasn't that tunnel on a gentle upgrade, like it might be aiming toward a real upthrust and its apex?"

"For damn sure," Cluny said. The question is how far before it surfaces, and what will Lars and Miles Kelton do then?"

"Whatever it is, it won't be good," Buckskin said. But even as he said it, the idea hit him and he pondered it. The more he thought of it, the more he decided it would be worth a try.

They parted near the first store. Purvis went toward his mine. Buckskin caught up with Cluny. He needed some advice and Cluny Norman was just the man to give it to him.

Chapter Nineteen

Cluny Norman looked at Buckskin and chuckled. They stood outside a seamstress shop, the place where Buckskin had caught up with the fast-walking mine owner.

"Morgan, you'd make a damn good lawyer. I never thought of the idea. Hell, yes, give it a try. How many? You can stake as many hardrock claims as you want to. I know one man has twenty. None has ever paid off."

"How far would you guess that it might be before that vein will come to its apex?"

"That's the tricky part. That was a good little angle they were working up along the vein. A hundred yards, maybe fifty, maybe two hundred. You know the direction it took away from that shaft, almost due north."

"How about if I go out fifty yards from the end

of that tunnel. My guess they had worked it about thirty yards from the new shaft. Then I stake claims lengthwise from there out to two hundred and fifty yards."

Cluny laughed out loud this time. His face a huge smile. "Damn if that wouldn't be a fit punishment for the crime. They won't notice new stakes out that direction. Put them in tonight after midnight and nobody will notice them. We've got stakes all over the place."

"Don't I have to work each claim?"

"You've got three months to prove up on the first work. They should break out to the surface in a few days."

"All I have to do is stake the claim and file it with the land office?"

"That's it. One filing for each claim and the approximate location."

"Do it tonight. In the meantime, I'm going to watch Miles Kelton, see where he goes, who he talks to, who visits him. Could be interesting."

"Hope it tells us something. I'm going to talk with another mine owner this afternoon and try to find out what he knows about the Five Star. Nothing, I hope. Oh, best place to get stakes is at the general store. They have them and you can write on them. Name, date filed. Do it with one of them heavy carpenter pencils."

Buckskin nodded. "Now if that vein does apex on one of my claims, I own the whole thing, and any digging and ore already dug out, right?"

"Absolutely, and the owner is liable for prosecution for grand theft, or at least robbery."

They waved and went their different ways.

The afternoon watching Kelton's law office proved to be nearly worthless. Buckskin did see one man climb the steps who was distinctive-looking as he sat in a cafe across the street working on one cup of coffee after another. When the man came down the steps Buckskin called the waiter over and asked him if he knew who the man was.

"Sure, that's Mr. Quinn Forbes of the Poverty mine. Doing right well for himself. Why you ask?"

"Been trying to meet him, but didn't know his name. Thanks."

The afternoon was almost over. Buckskin gave up and headed for the Alexander Hardware and General Store. He bought 18 stakes. They were three feet long and two inches square. He also bought two of the carpenter pencils and walked back to the boardinghouse. He left the stakes beside the porch, arriving just in time for supper. He hadn't eaten this well on a trip since that widow lady in Kansas two years ago had provided his meals.

That evening, just after dark, Buckskin took the stakes, a five-pound hammer he borrowed from Mrs. Johnson and his pencil and walked up to the Lucky Lady mine. No one was around. He paced off the 30 yards due north from the shaft, then went another 20 paces and settled down. He paced off 150 feet on each side of the centerline and drove in stakes. Then he paced off 500 feet north on the same center line and to each side until he had his claim of 300 by 500 feet, the normal size for a hardrock claim.

He repeated the process twice more until he had three claims joining each other north of the Lucky Lady shaft. He had come within 500 feet or so of a claim he saw above that was being worked all night. He wrote his mark on the stakes, and the date. He used L. Morgan for his name. First thing in the morning he'd register the claims at the Cripple Creek Land Office.

He finished about eleven o'clock and when he walked down Bennett Avenue on the way back to the boardinghouse, he noticed that lights still burned in Miles Kelton's office. Curious. Buckskin decided to sit and watch the place for a while. He didn't think there was a rear entrance.

After almost an hour, Buckskin came alert across the street when he saw someone leave Kelton's office. The lights went out and a man came to the street. It was Kelton. Buckskin grinned. Might be worthwhile after all.

Miles Kelton left his office and took ten minutes to walk two blocks. He went by a roundabout way and doubled back once, waited in a dark doorway another time and made certain no one followed him. He had seen Buckskin Morgan watching his office that afternoon. The man was definitely suspicious.

He'd had a report from Lars Zacherias about the visit to the Lucky Lady mine that morning. Nosing around. They wouldn't find a thing. All Lars had to do was keep moving and when he hit the upthrust, he would make another claim where it was going to surface. No problem there. He still didn't trust Buckskin Morgan. Why didn't he just find the girl and go home?

Kelton checked up and down the alley again, then walked to the back door of the hotel and slipped inside. His coat collar was up and a hat pulled far down over his face so no one could tell who he was. Kelton climbed the rear stairs to the third floor and saw no one in the hall. He walked quickly to Room 312, opened the door and went inside.

A lamp on a small conference table showed two other men already there. It was turned up bright this time, the two men in plain sight and both working on bottles of beer. A tray on the table held four more bottles and they waved to the beer and nodded.

"About damn time you got here, you're ten minutes late," the larger of the two men said.

"Somebody followed me around this afternoon. I didn't want him following me here, so I had to back track twice to make sure no one tailed me."

"All right, forget it," the other man said. He was smaller, with gray hair, yet only about 45 years of age. He wore a jacket and colored shirt but no tie. A pince-nez perched on his nose and he sniffed as if he had a cold.

"Let's get to the point of this meeting," Forbes said. "We've decided it's time to turn up the heat, to find out who we can bluff and who will fight."

"Fine with me," Kelton said. "I've had a plan all worked out. You both know that."

"One small problem to clear up first," the larger man said. He had black hair, a full beard and eyes almost hidden under thick brows. One massive hand gripped the bottle of beer and he took a quick drink. His name was Uriah York. "What do you know about Godfrey Rudolph's murder?"

"I know what you know. He was stabbed to death in his stable after our last meeting. Evidently it was a robbery since that big ring was taken and his wallet was missing."

"Nothing more?"

"How could I know anything more? I'm not the sheriff. I didn't investigate the death."

"Neither did the sheriff. He put it down as death by the hand of a man or men unknown."

"Then it's official," Kelton said. "Now can we get on with the matter at hand?"

"Not quite yet," the black-bearded man, York, said. "We hear that you're now owner of the Hard Times mine because of some paper that Rudolph signed."

"That's right. A personal matter between him and me. He owed me some money and he gave me the mine."

"I heard it was in his will," Forbes said "You draw up his will, Kelton?" The smaller man stared hard at Kelton.

"Yes, I was his company lawyer. I work for a lot of people."

"Kelton, let me impress upon you that I think you pulled some sneaky legal trick to get that mine," York said. "Don't even think about trying anything like that with me, or you'll be crawling around in the dark without any hands looking for your head that just rolled down the hillside. Do I make myself clear?"

"Gentlemen, we're not angels, agreed? We are not on the Sunday school teacher's list. I don't expect it of you. You shouldn't expect that kind of activity from me. What I do on my own time is my business. We're here to settle some items about our joint business, so let's get on with it." He looked at the men and both nodded. He knew them better now. The big one was Uriah York of the Gold Hill mine, second richest on the mountain. The other man was Quinn Forbes of the Poverty mine, maybe third richest.

"I agree that we should proceed with deliberate speed," Kelton went on. "We can start tomorrow night if you'd like. A new upthrust has just been found south and west of the All American. Looks promising. The owner of the mine will be visited tomorrow night and his good fortune toasted, and eventually he will stumble in front of a pair of horses running through town and suffer a fatal accident.

"There is a grubstake involved of some two thousand dollars that this young miner had that each of you gentlemen contributed to. A clause in the agreement states that if the claim owner can't repay the loan by June 20, 1892, the claim shall revert to the men who advanced the money to search for an upthrust."

"But I didn't advance. . . . " Uriah began.

"Damn right you did, Uriah, and I kicked in the other thousand," Forbes said. "We do that lots. So now we'll have our first joint venture."

Uriah lifted his brows and nodded. "Oh, yeah, I see. We get things done, but the legal end of it is up to Kelton here, who makes it all turn into strawberries and cream for us."

Kelton beamed. "Certainly. For services rendered I'll retain a twenty-five-percent interest in the mine and the new corporation we'll form to develop the strike."

Uriah laughed and drained his bottle of beer. "Damned if you ain't got a tiger by the tail here, Kelton. Damn, but it looks like you know what you're doing." He set the beer bottle down and picked up a full one. "You need any help on any of these arrangements?"

"No. I'll want both of you with firm, airtight alibis. How about a big poker game down at the Deep Shaft Saloon tomorrow night? Play from nine until midnight. It would look better if both of you lost a hundred dollars or so. People would remember you were there."

"Usually I win at poker," Quinn Forbes said.

"That's why people will remember tomorrow night when you lose."

All three men grinned.

"Now that's development money we just spent," Uriah said. "What about a going mine?"

"Harder, but I'm working on it. Victor Irwin down at the Princess looks like our best bet for a going concern. It will take me two days to set it up. Might not pay off the first strike, but if not, we try again. He's not a strong person and I think that he'll break."

Quinn tapped his beer bottle on the table. He looked toward the dark window as he did so. At last he lifted the bottle and emptied it, then put it on the table and stared at Kelton.

"I'm still worried about the law. What if the sheriff comes in here and starts pushing people around. He'd get some charges in short order."

"Sheriff Houston won't do that," Kelton said.

"You can't guarantee that, Kelton," Uriah York growled.

"Damn near it. How many people have been killed in Cripple Creek in the last week or so, not even counting Larry Douglas?"

Quinn looked up. "Five counting Douglas. There was Rudolph and those three in the house last night or a couple of nights ago."

"Right, five dead and how many criminal actions did the sheriff take? None, not a single one. Accident on one, murder by persons unknown on Rudolph and he said the three of them killed each other in that house."

Uriah York grinned.

Quinn Forbes snorted and then gave a belly laugh. "Oh, yeah, sounds good enough to me. Let's get moving on it."

"Gentlemen, I'm pleased," Kelton said. "Too late to do anything tonight, but I assure you tomorrow the plan will move ahead. Now, one matter remains, that of Mr. Buckskin Morgan. He's more than irritating now, he's becoming downright dangerous. Is there some suggestion by the group what to do about him?"

Uriah stood and paced the room. "I don't like to

take any more chances than we need to, but it seems obvious that he must be eliminated as a threat to us. He is a threat, isn't he?"

"Yes, absolutely," Kelton said.

"Then do it, the sooner the better," Quinn Forbes said. "Do it tomorrow."

Kelton shook his head. "No time tomorrow. I have that other matter to arrange. Buckskin Morgan is going to take some doing, something special, not just some wandering shooter who thinks he can do a job."

"Up to you," Uriah said. "Just get it done."

The men stood. "I'll go last this time," Kelton said. He went over and looked out the window at Bennett Avenue. Not much going on down there. He had two jobs to get done. The first one tomorrow would be easier. Then would come Buckskin Morgan. That could be a problem. He didn't want to think about it now. Later.

Two minutes after the second man left the room, Kelton slipped into the hall and went down the stairs and out the back door into the alley. Careful, always be careful was his rule.

Standing in the shadows 20 feet down the alley, Buckskin Morgan nodded with satisfaction. One of the men who came out the back door of the hotel had been the one he'd identified that afternoon outside Kelton's office, Quinn Forbes, the one with the prematurely gray hair. The large man with the black hair and full black beard shouldn't be hard to identify.

The Five Star? Could it be a meeting of the

members of the Five Star? He'd talk to Cluny about it tomorrow.

Ten minutes later he stepped up on the porch at the Johnson boardinghouse and sensed someone in the shadows. He drew his six-gun in a half second and flattened against the wall beside the door. He heard the squeak of the porch swing.

"Who's there? I've got a .45 covering you so don't try anything."

"Oh, God, don't shoot," a voice said.

"It's just Gomer and me, Mae," Mae Johnson said. Her voice high and wavering. "We didn't mean to scare you."

Buckskin grinned and holstered his Colt, letting the hammer down gently on the chamber.

"Sorry, kids. I don't like to be surprised in the dark that way. Somebody out there isn't too fond of me."

"Sorry, Mr. Morgan," Mae said. "Good night."

"Yeah, good night." He opened the door and went inside to his room. He grinned. Mae and that young accountant must be getting serious. At least the boy was.

Out on the front porch, Mae had stopped shaking. Gomer held her tightly in his arms and talked softly to her.

"Hey, it's all over. He's gone. He didn't shoot us or anything. I know I should have been quieter."

"Oh, my, but that was something," Mae whispered. Her heart was still pounding hard. "He had his gun out? I couldn't see it."

"Forget about him. You have to go in soon. One more kiss."

"No, I can't."

"Just one more." He bent and kissed her lips and she didn't protest. As he kissed her his hand came up to one of her breasts and caressed it gently.

Mae broke off the kiss and grabbed his hand but left it where it was. "You can't do that. We agreed. No touching. You promised."

He moved his hand. "Sorry. When you kiss me that way I get so worked up that I just want to . . . you know, to do more. I love touching you."

"You promised."

"Yeah, I know. But every night we make a new agreement. Maybe I won't have to promise tomorrow night."

"I . . . I think that I better go inside. It must be after midnight."

"True. One more kiss and we'll go in."

She lifted away from him and stood. "Not tonight. I think I've given you enough ideas already. Land sakes, but you want things to go so fast. What's the hurry? I want to get to know all about you. Where you're from and who your folks are. Everything. You promise me now that you'll tell me all about yourself tomorrow night."

"Promise."

She kissed his cheek. "Now, you stay out here until I get in my room and lock the door. You understand?"

He nodded in the soft moonlight. "Understand but I hate it."

"Good. I'll see you at breakfast."

Gomer Haskel stood there and watched her move toward the door and vanish inside. He moaned, shook his head and went through the door and to his room.

Chapter Twenty

Buckskin and three other men waited at the land office early the next morning for it to open. They didn't talk. The clerk came five minutes late, opened up and took the men one at a time. Buckskin let the others go first. He wanted to watch the procedure. Nothing to it.

He signed the forms, put down the approximate location as north of the Lady Luck claim and paid his two-dollar filing fee. The clerk didn't even look at the locations, just took his money and stamped the forms as filed and paid, and Buckskin hurried out the door.

Buckskin's curiosity got the better of him and he left the downtown section and walked up the slope until he could see the Lucky Lady mine. Smoke came out of the small shack on the site. He saw two men go down the ladder into the new shaft. So they were working.

Good. He hoped that he'd pounded in the first pair of stakes deep enough so they wouldn't be a beacon that someone else had made a claim to the north. That would really upset Lars and his owner. So far it looked like everything was calm. He walked closer to the place but still couldn't see the stakes. Good. He headed back to town. He should trail Kelton some more today. First he'd find out the name of that other man, the big one he'd seen come out the rear door of the hotel last night.

A short time later in Cluny's mine office, the owner nodded.

"Oh, yes, no doubt about that one. I call him Big Blackie. That's Uriah York, who has the Gold Hill mine, the second-largest-and-richest in the district. At least so far. So he and Quinn Forbes are the big guns behind this revival of the Five Star."

"Looks like it. Would that make Kelton the one who takes care of the killing?"

"Seems to be it. He's been in town long enough to know all the lowlife floating around."

Cluny cleared his throat and stood up from his desk chair and walked to the window. He stared out at the barren hillside. "Now our problem is what to do. I'm not happy about violence again like we had last year. Maybe we can nip this one before it sprouts and take care of it before it grows too much."

"We can't do much until they show their hand," Buckskin said. "I've about decided that the Larry Douglas killing was a private affair by Kelton and

Lars. I don't think it figures into the Five Star at all."

"So what will they do next?"

Buckskin frowned. "If I were them, I'd come after me. I'm the stick in their eyeball right now. I'm the one they know is causing them trouble."

"So you better be doubly on your guard." Cluny hesitated. "You want me to give you a partner who knows how to use a six-gun? I've got the man in mind."

"Not a chance, Cluny. But thanks. I work best alone. Which means I better get to work. One of these days that Denver rich man is going to be on my neck. I don't have a clue where his daughter might be. I'd bet by now she isn't even in Cripple Creek."

"Be a lot easier for her to get by in the Springs," Cluny said.

"Yeah, I'll have to go over there for a couple of days and see what I can dig up. Right now I'm going to work around here again. If she's been hiding here, she might be tired of it by now."

They waved and Buckskin started back down town. He stopped at the hotel, where he had first registered. He'd left it so it looked like he was still signed in there. That way people could leave messages. There was no letter from Braithwaite and Buckskin breathed a little easier.

The clerk told him he still hadn't seen anyone who matched the missing girl's description, either with long blond hair or short brown hair. He reached under the counter and came up with an envelope.

"Oh, this came in this morning and I hadn't put it in your box yet. Evidently someone left it on the desk here."

Buckskin took the envelope, thanked the clerk and walked to a chair where he sat down and looked at it. His name had been printed in block letters on the front. There was no other writing on the envelope. He tore it open and took out a sheet of white paper. He read the words:

Five Star. Interested? I'll help you get the bastards, but I don't want them to know. Meet me a mile down the Florissant trail near the big pine today, Friday, at ten A.M. I'll be on a gray mare. I have facts on a killing that should hang two of the Five Star gang.

It wasn't signed. Buckskin frowned as he folded the letter and put it in his inner vest pocket. The Seth Thomas over the desk showed it was a quarter to nine. Ten o'clock. Possible. Today was Friday. The note must have come early this morning.

He stood and walked out of the hotel. At the Alexander Hardware and General Store, he bought a Spencer repeating rifle from Abe Alexander. He took a box of 20 rounds and an extra tube that held seven rounds of the .52-caliber shells for the Spencer.

"Going hunting?" Abe asked.

"Thought I might try some varmint hunting to keep my shooting eye," Buckskin said. He had 20 rounds for the Colt .45 in his belt. That should do it. He picked up a canteen as well, filled it at the town well and walked to the livery.

Ten minutes later he rode out of town with the canteen over the saddlehorn and the Spencer in a boot. He went past the Florissant road a quarter of a mile to the north, hoping that might give him an even chance. He rode parallel to the road. He had no idea if the note was legitimate or a trap for him. He'd seen both kinds. It just depended. The idea about not wanting to be seen with Buckskin was logical enough. He'd have to wait and see. If he found the gray horse at the big pine tree and no rider, he would be damn suspicious.

Ten minutes out of town, he could see the pine. Not a lot of trees in that area. He saw a horse tied up there but no person. Shortly he came abreast of the horse, but was still nearly a quarter of a mile to the north. He sat on his mount and studied it. Yes, a good spot for an ambush. Anyone waiting for him at the tree and hidden in the rocks above and to either side should be able to see him where he had stopped.

If they wanted to make a try for him it would come soon.

Just then he heard a shot and hot led sped overhead close enough so he could hear it. He ducked and kicked his mount into motion back toward town.

A rider surged around an outcropping 200 yards behind him and between him and town. The rider fired a rifle and rode hard toward Buckskin. Buckskin whirled his mount and rode away from the threat. Another rifle fired to his right and behind him, again between him and town. The only way he could go was toward Florissant and, he hoped, some cover somewhere ahead.

He ducked low on the horse and kicked it in the flanks, urging it to gallop flat out across the uneven ground and toward the road. It would be easier for the horse to gallop there and he'd have a better chance to outrun the two assassins from behind. He heard a third shot then and saw a puff of white smoke near the gray horse at the tree.

Three of them. He had his morning's work all laid out for him. As he rode hard away from the three rifles, he realized this attack had been carefully thought out. They had been behind him so he couldn't turn and ride for town and safety. This was going to be a fight to the death.

He tried to remember the Florissant road. It was bare of trees much of the way. He needed a good two or three more miles before he could find adequate cover. He listened to his mount. She was tiring. The gallop had lasted long enough. He let the mount slow and saw the men behind him do the same thing. They were within rifle range, but shooting from the back of a horse, even a walking one, is a chancy affair.

These men knew that and didn't fire. They moved along steadily, letting their horses rest. The mile ride from town was not a factor in the freshness of his horse. The animals all seemed about equal in speed. It would be endurance that told the tale.

He patted his mount, let her walk for another hundred yards, then lifted her to a canter. Those behind saw his move and matched it. A canter is a more natural speed for a horse and it can go long distances that way and not tire.

Just ahead the road began a steeper downgrade and a deep canyon angled off to the right. He could take the canyon and be out of sight in five minutes, well before the men could ride up.

The problem was, the riders on the road could make much better time on the road than he could in the canyon, and he'd have to come back to the road sometime. Unless he could reduce the odds in the cover of the canyon.

The road made a turn here and for a moment he was out of sight of the other riders. He pulled his mount to the right and went into the canyon. They would see his tracks. Probably send one man after him and the other two would cut him off ahead. Good, the odds were better this way.

His mare stumbled once going down the sharp angle of the ravine, but then it flattened out a hundred feet below the level of the road. He stayed behind the cutbank that cloudbursts had created and listened, stopping his horse. From above he heard some shouts and then evidently they found his trail. He looked for some cover. The gully made a sharp turn to the right again, away from the road. A scattering of cottonwoods sprinkled the canyon ahead. He rode ahead to some willow brush and surged into it. He slid out of the saddle, tied the horse and took the rifle and wormed his way back to the edge of the cover.

Buckskin found a green blush of grass and weeds and parted it enough to see through. From there he could get off a shot without being seen.

Then he waited. He was sure they would send

one man after him into the gully.

Five minutes later, the horse and man came around the bend cautiously. For a moment the horse pulled up. Then the rider dug in his spurs and the horse jolted forward.

Buckskin tracked the man for a dozen feet, led him a hair and fired. The crack of the Spencer boomed through the canyon. The .52-caliber slug hit the bushwhacker in the chest and lifted him far enough out of the saddle so he toppled away and to the ground. He rolled over when he hit and struggled to sit up, then screamed, held his chest and flopped back in the dust of the ravine and didn't move again. Buckskin ran from the cover and caught the horse.

He calmed it and considered his options. He was maybe three miles from town. Not far. If both the riders had gone ahead to cut him off and trap him, he could work his way up the canyon the way he came down, use both horses and gallop one until it tired and switch and ride the fresh one until it tired.

No rider on one horse could keep up with a man with two horses at his command. He untied his own horse and rode her, leading the other animal. He stared at the dead man in the dust as he rode by. He'd never seen him before.

He was halfway up the slant trail that led out of the ravine when he saw movement ahead. Then a rifle barked and hot lead slapped the air beside Buckskin's shoulder. He jerked the horse around and galloped back into the gully.

So they hadn't gambled on their man flushing

him out. Kept one man in reserve protecting against a retreat. The rear guard had been a fool. He should have waited until Buckskin was right on top of him before he fired. Now he'd pay for his mistake.

Buckskin rode hard along the gully floor for five minutes, then found a way up the far side of the gully away from the road. He rode up into some smattering of pines and a little brush. Not enough to hide in.

He rode through them and angled to the rear and upward. He should be able to get back to town this way. The extra horse wouldn't do him any good in this terrain because it was too rough to gallop in. He pushed his mount to a fast walk, and changed horses after half an hour. He figured he had circled around and was still two miles from town. Buckskin checked the sun. Plenty of time yet before dark. He'd get back and turn in the horse and go knock some teeth out of Miles Kelton just on general principles. He knew the killers had been sent out by Kelton. He didn't need any proof.

Buckskin topped a small rise leading the dead man's horse. Two rifle slugs whistled over his head and a moment later he heard the sound of the shots. At once he dove off his mount away from the sound, but by that time more rounds were on the way, and one caught his horse in the head just as he got off her and she went down screaming in mortal pain. He rolled partway down the far slope and out of range.

The other horse!

He worked higher on the slope and found the

bay with its head down chopping on some summer grass. He crawled forward reaching for the reins that dragged on the ground. Almost there. He heard the rounds coming again before the sound of the shots came. The shooters had to be a half mile away. Lucky shots. He lifted up, grabbed the mount's reins and lunged down the reverse slope.

More rounds came and the horse bellowed in pain. Once out of their firing line, Buckskin stopped and checked the mount. The bay had a bullet wound that only creased her big hind quarters leaving a line of blood six inches long.

He tied the horse to some brush and ran for the canteen from his mount and his Spencer. Only seconds later he mounted and rode. The attackers were still between him and town. They had been lucky to spot him. No more skylining himself on a ridgeline. He'd stick to the reverse slopes and gullies as he worked back toward town.

The sun was out hot again today. He stopped and wiped sweat off his forehead and out of the headband inside his hat. He was working in an arc around the town. Sooner or later he would run out of space and come to the mountain. Well before then he had to take a direct shot at town.

He might get past the two watchers and he might run into one of them. He figured by now they had separated and each watched a different section of the hills and gullies to try to spot him.

They knew he'd try to get back to town. He had checked the saddle the dead man had, but it held no overnight provisions. He hadn't brought any either. So these three had intended to kill him quickly, probably at the big pine. Sorry.

He eased up toward the crest of a ridge. Buckskin stopped short of the top, dismounted and crawled to the very crest to look over. Less than a hundred yards down the slope he saw a horse and rider working slowly toward him. He lifted the Spencer and sighted in. Or should he take him alive and question him? A shot would bring the other killer at a gallop. He had to decide if the other man was far enough away to let Buckskin get in the clear again.

He waited. Not yet.

It was five minutes before the man on the horse came close enough for Buckskin to figure he hadn't seen him before. Strangers to do a killing. Figured. He waited until the rider was 20 yards away eyeing the ridgeline.

Then Buckskin put a .52-caliber slug through the saddle horse's head.

As soon as he fired and the horse went down, Buckskin stood up covering the man floundering in the dust.

"Easy or you're as dead as your buddy back there. Hands up away from that hardware."

The man sat in the dust and watched his horse make a few final kicks as it died.

"That was a good horse," the man in the dirt said.

"A man's life is worth a thousand horses any day. You want yours to go one for one?"

"No."

"Who hired you to kill me?"

"Somebody in a saloon. Don't remember who he was. His money was good. A hundred then and a hundred each when we brought back your six-gun, your hat and wallet."

"You're all damn poor killers. Where is your other friend?"

"Out there somewhere with you in his sights."

Buckskin eased back the other side of the ridge so only his head and his rifle showed while he covered the ambusher.

"Get your rifle and throw it over here."

"Why? You're gonna kill me anyway."

"Not if you do what I tell you." The man perked up a little seeing a chance to go on living. He crawled to the dead horse, took the rifle out of the boot and threw it over the ridgeline where Buckskin waited.

"Now your six-gun."

The man shrugged. Buckskin memorized his features. About 30 years old, brown hair, dark eyes, sunbrowned skin, a long nose and a thin mouth. Maybe five-eight and 150 pounds. The man shrugged and pitched his gun and gunbelt over the top of the ridgeline.

"Now your boots," Buckskin said.

"No, by damn, not my boots."

"Keep wearing them and you die where you sit. Toss them over here and you get a shot at walking back to town."

"Shit."

"Some days are like that."

The man scowled, then swore and pulled off his

253

boots. He held them a minute, then threw them over to Buckskin.

"Good, now stand up and start walking. I'd suggest you take the quickest way back to town before your socks wear out."

"Bastard."

"Been called that before. Don't hurt a bit."

"Fucking bastard."

"Yeah, get moving." The man turned and stared at his tormentor a moment, then shrugged and walked along the ridgeback the way he had ridden. Buckskin quickly checked the dead horse. Nothing he could use in the saddle. He took the six-gun, boots and rifle and carried them a quarter mile away as he rode. At last he threw them down a gully and looked at the mountain where Cripple Creek lay.

He could circle another two miles, then cut north. Or he could make his move right then. The sun was moving lower in the sky. Maybe three hours of sunlight left.

Buckskin checked to see that there was a round in his Spencer, then cradled it across the saddle and turned north along the side of a ridge. If the other killer waited somewhere up ahead he'd take him on man-to-man.

Chapter Twenty-one

Buckskin kept to the sides of the hills and small ravines as he worked north toward Cripple Creek. He figured he was still two miles away, but wasn't sure. Distances in the mountains could be so damned tough to figure out.

With searching eyes that never stopped, he kept checking the terrain as he went. If he could spot the other killer, he'd have the advantage. Now the odds on the hunt were down to one to one. He had no idea who the other man was, but it was a good bet that he would try as hard as he could to collect another $100 by killing Buckskin Morgan. That was as much as most miners made in two months.

Ahead, along the rise of the small ridge he quartered, he saw a splash of green that could only mean a spring. There might be enough water to give his horse a drink. He angled that way as he kept searching the landscape, then going back over it to check patiently for any sign of movement or color.

As he thought back, he tried to remember the color of the shirts of the two closest riders he'd seen. The dead man wore a blue shirt, the bootless ambusher had on a gray shirt. Somehow he thought the third one wore a light-colored shirt, maybe a pale yellow. He'd watch for it.

The horse he rode shied to one side. The sudden movement almost unseated Buckskin when it came unexpectedly. He regained the saddle and checked the ground in front of the animal, which had now stopped. He heard the rattle at the same instant and pulled backward on the reins so that the horse backed up three steps.

The remains of a game trail wound along the side of the ridge and at that point came close to an outcropping of flat rocks. The rattlesnake evidently had been crossing from the flat rocks and the horse had seen it at the last moment before he stepped on it.

Now coiled, the rattler commanded the center of the trail, its rattle vibrating, its forked tongue darting out, testing the smell of this new tall creature in front of it.

Buckskin looked ahead ten feet at the flat rock and scowled. The top of the rock was alive, writhing and coiling and crawling and slithering in a convention of rattlesnakes. He'd never seen so many out in the open before. He'd seen a large ball of snakes once in an old mine where they were hibernating, but this gathering on one flat rock evidently must have another purpose besides soaking up as much sun as possible.

He turned the mare off the trail and went 50 feet around the rattlesnake rock, watching ahead so he could see if any more were migrating to or from the assembly point.

A quarter of a mile past the snakes, he found the trail again and continued his searching and scanning of the hills and small valleys for any sign of the third killer. The hills were mostly bare here. Evidently the soil on top of the Rocky Mountains in this area was sparse and not as rich as it could be. He angled more now for the splotch of green, and was still a half mile from it when he pulled his mount to a stop.

A thin wisp of smoke spiraled upward through the tops of the trees in the green area ahead of him. The tree leaves should have dissipated the smoke, but enough came through that he could identify it. Somebody had a fire in that spot. Was it his man? Buckskin remained absolutely still. He was in plain sight, but at half a mile away a horse and man made a small blob on the landscape.

He turned and looked at the small ridge he rode along. The crest was 20 yards above him, and behind that loomed a higher ridge. He could slip over the crest here without skylining himself. Good. He moved the horse directly over the ridgeline, and didn't breathe until he was on the other side.

The ridge led all the way to the green swatch. It climbed a little in the process, working up toward the higher ridges ahead. By staying on this side of the slant, he could keep out of sight of the person in the green. By the time he got to it, he would be a hundred yards or less from the spring.

He had to find out who it was down there. He rode faster at an easy canter until he figured he was across from the green. He dismounted and crawled to the top of the ridgeline. By looking over it from behind a smattering of tall grass, he made sure he wasn't spotted.

He was 50 yards short of the greenery. The brush wasn't as heavy as he had thought from his first sighting. He could see past some of it to the cottonwoods that grew there. He couldn't see any men, but he spotted the smoke of the fire.

Who would camp this close to town? It couldn't be more than two, maybe three miles away. In an hour a man could walk that far. He scanned the area. No obvious way to get to the place without being seen. He could get on his horse and charge down from the ridge, but that would give whoever was in the trees 100 yards to use a rifle and shoot him off his horse.

Buckskin studied the area again. The green was probably from a small spring and it came at the end of a shallow gully that ran north and turned toward the higher ridge to the right, the one he now lay behind.

Maybe.

He rode on up the reverse slope of the ridge for another 300 yards and then up the slope so he could look over the top. Yes. Below he saw where the gully that ended in the green area was at this point out of sight of the trees. He could ride over the ridge into the smaller gully and work up to within 20 yards of the green splotch before he could be seen.

He checked the sun. Two more hours of sunlight. He rode down the slope into the gully and worked ahead as far as possible. Then he stepped off the mare, tired her to a sage and looked ahead. Now he saw cover he could use to get all the way to the first trees on the green. A few large rocks were big enough to shield him. Then the gully had a small cutbank that would keep him safe.

Buckskin moved. It took him 15 minutes to make it to the edge of the trees. He stopped and listened. He could hear no voices. Maybe just one man. He lifted up and stared around the side of a foot-thick cottonwood.

Ahead he spotted the fire and one man with his back to Buckskin roasting a rabbit over the fire. Good. The roasting rabbit would make a little noise cooking. The fire snapping would also help cover his approach.

Using all of his skills learned at the side of an Indian friend, Buckskin faded from one tree to the next, moved across an open spot a short step at a time, his six-gun drawn but not cocked. He was in plain sight of the man now if he turned around. Buckskin nodded. The man wore a light yellow shirt. His hat lay on the ground and a rifle leaned against a tree. He wore a six-gun on his left hip.

Buckskin shifted his weight to his front foot and took another step. Now he didn't move a boot until he was sure that his weight on it would not make a sound. He moved through the leaves and small branches as quiet as any Indian. He held his breath and walked the last few feet directly toward the man, who now had started humming a song. Buckskin pushed the muzzle of his colt against the back of the man's neck.

"Easy, no sudden movements or you're dead."

"What the hell?"

"Stand up easy like and lace your hands together on the top of your head. Do it now, dead man."

They both stood gently. Buckskin lifted the other man's six-gun out of his holster and pushed it in his own belt. Buckskin pushed the man away from him.

"Turn around, keep your hands on your head."

The man turned. Buckskin had never seen him before. "Who the hell are you and why did you try to kill me?"

"You? You the one? How did you slip up on me? Oh, shit, the smoke. It showed over the trees. Damn."

"Answer the questions." Buckskin cocked his .45 and the ominous sound made the man's eyes go wide.

"Easy. You ain't dead. I'm Jody Bascomb. I'm from New Mexico."

"Who hired you to kill me?"

"Damn, don't remember."

Buckskin shot him in the thigh. The round knocked the man into the dirt and he screamed in pain and fury.

His hands tried to stop the flow of blood out the back of his thigh.

"Bastard! You shot me."

"When you go gunning for a man you got to expect that you might get shot yourself. Now, who hired you to kill me?"

"Guy in a saloon. Tall thin gent, with a pencil mustache and a goatee. Black hair. Thin as a whistle."

"His name is Walt."

"Yeah. Heard somebody call him that."

"Tie up your leg so you don't bleed to death. I need you." Buckskin went to the man and frisked him. He found no hideout gun or any knife. He went back to the fire and picked the stick that held the rabbit that had been half roasted out of the edge of the fire.

Jody Bascomb tied up his leg and screeched in pain. When he was done he looked up. "Bleeding has stopped."

"Good." Buckskin had the rabbit back over the fire cooking it the rest of the way. The outside would be burned and the inside a little raw, but enough would be cooked to be satisfying. Enough for one. Jody could go hungry.

It took them two hours to ride into Cripple Creek. Buckskin had wormed from Jody the place the killers were supposed to meet Walt after their job was done.

They left their horses at the end of the alley, and now were just outside the back door of the Deep Shaft Saloon. It had been dark for a half hour. No moon lighted the dank alley.

"This the place?" Buckskin asked.

"Yeah, and when he sees you're alive, he'll kill

me. Give me back my forty-four so I can defend myself."

"I'll do any defending needed. We go just inside the door and you send word to Walt to come out back. I'll be right beside you with my hat down low. Any mistakes and you die right there. Understand?"

"Yeah. Understand."

They pulled open the saloon's back door and stood just inside. One man crowded past them in a hurry to get to the outhouse in back. Jody called over one of the waitress/whores and told her to go tell Walt that he was at the rear door.

"He's probably in the back room," Jody said.

Buckskin pushed the muzzle of his six-gun harder into Jody's back. "Hey, and rush it, can you?" he told the whore. "This is damn important."

"Yeah, sure. Everything's important tonight," the whore said.

They watched the girl flounce to the bar and vanish. A few moments and she was back and nodded in Jody's direction. Buckskin pulled on his shoulder and they went out the back door.

"We'll both stand here, just out of any splash light from the door," Buckskin said. "When he comes, you speak up and call him Walt and tell him you did it and got the stuff off the body he wanted. You remember that?"

"I can remember it. If he shoots I'm going flat in the dirt. You and him got a fight, fine with me. I'm out of it."

"He carry a gun?"

"Just a hideout. From this distance he couldn't hit a horse standing broadside."

They waited.

The man in the outhouse left it and hurried back inside the saloon. The splash of light missed the two men by ten feet.

A moment later, the door swung open and a tall, thin man strode through. Buckskin didn't have a chance to see more than a flash of a face with a black goatee before the door slammed shut.

"Jody, where the hell are you? Dark as the bottom of an outhouse in this alley."

"Over here, Walt. We got the stuff. Lost one man. Nailed the bastard."

"Good, the boss'll be pleased. Where's Morgan's wallet?"

Buckskin pushed Jody down to the ground and drew his Colt. "My wallet is right in my pocket where it belongs, Walt. Good to meet you. You mentioned your boss. Who is that?"

Buckskin cocked his Colt. The clicking sound was enough to stop the thin man from completing his reach into his jacket.

"Go ahead, Walt, draw. Wish to hell you would. Give me an excuse. Course, with you, I don't mind gut-shooting you and watching you suffer for an hour before you die. Who's your boss?"

"I work for myself. No boss."

Buckskin fired a round between the tall man's boots. Walt jumped back a step.

"Tell me now or later. Five men dead on that try at the gold ore wagons. Another one today. Your list of hanging offenses is climbing."

Buckskin thought he heard something down the alley behind him. He listened again. Nothing.

"Work for myself. Don't know what you're talking about. Came out to take a piss."

"Sure you did, asshole."

Buckskin heard the noise behind him again and dove to the side. Just as he hit the ground and rolled the shotgun went off, slamming double-ought buck into the wall of the saloon where Buckskin had been standing. The rounds missed Walt. Buckskin turned on the ground and fired once where he saw smoke from the shotgun blast. He fired once more and heard a scream, then turned back to the saloon's rear door.

His last two shots caught Walt just as the thin man's hand grabbed the back door to the saloon. One round went in under his arm, the other drove through his right ear, turned upward and exploded out the top of his skull showering brains, skull fragments and blood over half the saloon's back wall.

Buckskin came up in a crouch and eyed the black of the alley behind him. He heard someone whimpering. He zigzagged down the alley 20 feet to the sound. A man lay on the ground beside a shotgun. His shoulder gouted with blood and he looked up at Buckskin in the half light.

"Help me," he said. Then he passed out.

Jody knelt down beside the man. "Lordy, it's Hal, I used to drink with him. I'll get him to the doctor. He don't weigh much more than a hundred pounds."

They carried Hal back to the street and hoisted

him on Jody's horse. Buckskin left him and took the horse he'd borrowed from the dead man back to the livery stable. The attendant never knew the difference. A horse was a horse.

Emily had her hands on her hips when Buckskin walked into the kitchen at her boardinghouse.

"So I suppose you want me to fix you a supper? I had a good one and now it's all put away and done." She stopped. "Oh, my God, what happened to you? Come here and sit down and I'll pour you some coffee. I can make you a good sandwich, lots of roast beef left and onions and mustard and lettuce." She frowned and caught his arm and eased him into a kitchen chair.

"What in hell happened to you?"

He sipped the coffee as he told her. "I knew better than to bite on an old trick like that, a meeting out in the country. I'm getting desperate. This damn Five Star business and I don't know where Harriet is. Best go to the Springs and take a look for her there. If she's here, I damn well can't find her. Might as well admit that and wire the father back in Denver."

Emily worked on building the sandwich. "I pick up mail for my boarders. When I was at the post office in the general store I picked it up for today. You got a letter."

"Who from?"

"I didn't read it."

Emily went to the cupboard and took out two letters. She put one back and carried the second one to him.

"Denver postmark. It's typed, so that must mean it's from my client, Mr. Braithwaite."

Emily watched him. He put the letter down beside his plate and picked up the sandwich.

"Ain't you gonna read it?"

"Won't go anywhere. I have an idea what it says. Been almost two weeks now. Time is money, and Mr. Braithwaite is a good businessman."

He ate the sandwich and had another cup of coffee, then tore open the envelope. The letter inside was typed too. A lot of businesses used typewriters now.

He read the message:

Mr. Morgan.

Disappointed that you've made no progress on finding Harriet. You have four more days to find her or you are terminated as my employee. All financial obligations will be met as agreed upon.

Remember, you have just four more days from the day you receive this letter. I thought you could do the job. All information you have concerning Harriet must be turned over to me upon your return to Denver.

Yours Truly,
Hercules Braithwaite/GC

Buckskin read the letter a second time, then handed it to Emily. She read it and gave it back to him.

"The old skinflint seems fair seeing that you don't have any idea where precious little Harriet is," she said. "What are you going to do?"

"I should check out the Springs again. Lots of places for a young girl to work over there and not be obvious."

"Yeah, like a live-in maid for some of the rich folks."

"I'd play Old Ned in Heaven trying to find her in one of those grand houses in the Springs. Must be a hundred of them."

She refilled his coffee cup and sat down at the table beside him. "You too tired to have some company tonight?"

"Tired? Tired? I'm never too tired for a fine woman." His bluster faded and he laughed. "However, tonight just to get undressed and go horizontal on any flat surface and I'd be snoring. Not the best of company."

"I could tell by the way you're talking."

"Anything exciting or wild happen today?"

"Not that I've heard of. No more bodies showing up, no more trials and no hangings."

"Sounds like a dull day." He stood. "I'll see you for breakfast." He hesitated. "How is the young romance going with your niece?"

"Fine, so far. At least she's still a virgin. I've given her all the warnings."

Buckskin snorted. "Yeah, you're gonna take all the fun out of being young. Let the girl have some good times." He waved and headed for his room.

Chapter Twenty-two

That same evening on the front porch of the Johnson boardinghouse, the two young people sat on the platform swing. Harriet Braithwaite, still hiding under the name of Mae, caught Gomer's hand. Her smile was so bright it lit up that end of the darkened porch.

"Gomer, I just like you so much. I don't know what to say or to do or anything. In such a short time you've become so important to me."

"I like you too, Mae. I like you so much it hurts. When I'm not here with you I think about you all the time. I want to be with you, to touch you, to hold you." He put his arm around her and Mae snuggled against him.

"Oh, yes, this is heaven. I'm just so happy." She looked up at him and he bent and kissed her lips. She responded and for a moment the whole world stopped for her and she thought she would either melt or explode.

When their lips parted he held her tighter. His hand crept up on her breasts and before she could protest, he kissed her again. Gently he caressed her breasts, and he could feel the heat in them. When the kiss ended, his hand stayed there.

"Tonight, new rules," he said his voice husky. "I didn't promise not to touch them tonight. I think you like it."

She sighed. "Not supposed to say so." She reached up and kissed his cheek. "Oh, Gomer. No boy has ever done that before. It just feels so wonderful. I know I shouldn't let you, but it makes me feel just delicious."

In her front bedroom, Emily Johnson smiled and rubbed her own breasts. She had opened her window that afternoon hoping that the lovebirds would use the swing again that night. Sure enough. Now she sat there caressing her breasts and listening to the two young people on the platform rocker swing.

Mae murmured and reached around Gomer and hugged him, slowing his hand on her breast. She eased away and he gently unbuttoned one fastener on her blouse.

"Oh, no, don't do that," she said softly. He kissed her again, stopping her mild protest. When the kiss ended he used both hands and undid all the blouse buttons. She wore only a loose camisole under it. Gomer kissed her again, slid his right hand under the camisole and closed it around a breast.

Her lips came off his and she gasped. Then slowly she closed her eyes and continued the kiss. She sighed deeply.

Gomer moved his hips to lessen the pressure on his erection, which had jolted hard and ready the first time he touched her breasts. His hand held still on her breast for another moment. Then he began to caress it, to circle it and tweak the nipple.

Mae sighed again and leaned against the back of the porch swing, watching Gomer's face. She knew that Gomer liked her, but was he saying that just so he could fondle her? No, he wouldn't do that.

His other hand found her breasts and now both hands massaged and caressed her, setting her on fire. She had never felt this way before. It was so exciting. He took her hand and pushed it down to his waist and cupped it over a bulge in his trousers.

"Oh, my," she said. She looked at him. "That's . . ." He nodded.

"Just hold him a minute. I'm touching you, I thought that you'd want to . . ." She nodded.

He fondled her breasts and kissed her hard. Then he pushed his hips against her side and humped forward three times.

"Oh, damn, I want to so bad," he whispered.

"Want to?" she asked.

He put his hand at her waist and then down

to where her skirt bunched at her crotch, and he pushed inward.

"Can I touch you down here?"

"Oh, no. No, sir. You've done more than I should let you now."

He moved his hand and fumbled with his pants a moment. Then in the faintness of the quarter moon, she saw something she'd never seen before. His penis, hard and erect, popped out of his pants.

He caught her hand and moved it toward his erection. She pulled back. He stroked her breasts, kissed her again and then took her hand down to his crotch.

"Hold him, just hold him. He can't hurt you way over here."

She looked at him hard, then sighed and felt his hands warming her breasts again, and she felt the warm glow growing. She nodded and caught hold of his penis. It was so hard and warm, almost hot to her touch. She held him gently.

All at once he began to pant and his hips moved and his penis bounced in her hand.

"Hold him tight," Gomer hissed at her. Now he turned toward her and humped his hips at her as she held his penis. He grunted and moaned and his breath came hot and hard and all the time his penis stroked in and out of her hand.

Then he cried out softly and humped hard at her hand six times before he moaned again and fell against her spent and exhausted.

She held him. Her arms round him. So that's what the girls were talking about. He had . . . what had they called it? He had climaxed. That was it, he had climaxed, the male sex act. Somewhere on her dress or on the swing were his . . . what had they called them? His sperm.

For a moment, Mae wanted to throw up. Then she felt the burning marvelous warmth of her breasts and knew that down below she was all juicy and so hot she almost couldn't stand it. But down there was where a girl got pregnant, and she certainly wasn't going to let that happen. Not even for Gomer.

She held him, stroking his hair, her arms tightly around him where his head lay against her bare breasts. She smiled. Here she was half undressed on the front porch of a house, with a boy resting his head against her bare bosom, and she had just helped him to climax sexually and she was smiling.

Goodness sakes, what a difference a few weeks made. She could have been in Chicago just talking about things like this with the other 18-year-olds.

Gomer gave a sigh and moved. Then she frowned. Gomer was kissing her breast. She pushed him away.

"What in the world?" she whispered.

He looked up. "Just wanted to pay you back for helping me do it. Don't you like to be kissed there?"

She smiled. She did like it. Slowly she nodded. He grinned and went back to her breasts, kissing them both, then nibbling at her nipples. She felt that wonderful roasting heat again, the itch down between her legs. She pulled his head away from her breasts and gave him a hard and demanding kiss. The kiss lasted a long time and she moaned softly and lay sideways on her back in the swing. It was almost long enough for her to lie down completely.

He followed her and lay partly on top of her and kissed her breasts, then sucked on one. She gasped. The itch was more insistent now. She caught his hand and pushed it down to her waist, then slowly spread her legs. His fingers found her crotch through the skirt and rubbed gently. Then his hand snaked under her skit and she made a mild protest. He worked up to her crotch and rubbed her private place through her bloomers. They were so thin it was like nothing was there. She trembled, then trembled again. His fingers hit something and she felt the world explode. She had never known such a surge of joy, such relief, so much emotion and glory all packed into one ecstatic moment.

Mae heard herself shrilling softly, her breath came like a freight train's engine and suddenly her hips pounded upward against his hand. It was a peak of feeling and emotion that she had never felt before. Slowly she came down from it. Now she was aware that Gomer lay almost full length on top of her. She didn't mind.

It felt good, natural. Then she sensed that his penis was hard and full again, that it pressed against her stomach through her clothing.

"Oh, damn!" Gomer said. "God damn, I just got to do it again." His hips began to pump against her. She felt his stick-hard penis prodding against her belly. She moved so he had a little more room. It drove against her time after time. Toward the last she moved her hips upward to meet the thrust of his even though his penis was far from her crotch.

He went faster and faster. Then he growled and thrust harder yet before he panted and sighed and fell on top of her, spent and drained and relaxed. She brought her arms around him and held him tight.

When he could move again, he sat up and she sat beside him. His arm went around her and they held each other.

"Darling Gomer, I love you. There I said it. I love you in a whole new way now, knowing that I can please you."

In her room, Emily Johnson had tears in her eyes. Her hand came up from her crotch and she wiped sweat off her forehead. Damn, but that had been beautiful, listening to a young girl get her first taste of sex. She wasn't sure if they had actually fucked or not, but there had been climaxes, she was sure of that. She sighed and brought her legs together and relaxed there in the chair, her skirt round her waist and her breasts uncovered. There might be more. She listened.

"Darling Gomer, did I tell you that I love you? I do, and I want to be with you every day now for the rest of our lives. Of course that means you'll have to marry me. Would that be all right with you?"

Gomer gulped and looked down at her. She hadn't covered up her breasts. He reached for them, but she pushed his hand away.

"I'm being serious, Gomer Haskel. Time for serious talk."

He cleared his throat. "Mae, I think I love you too, but it's all happening so fast."

"Good things always go fast," Mae said. She smiled. "I have it all thought out. I want you to come back to Denver with me. That's where I'm from. I can get you a good job, because I know a man who owns a lot of businesses. You'll have a good job. We'll introduce you around in Denver and then in two months we'll announce our engagement."

"Now wait a minute. I have a good job. I make twenty dollars a week as head accountant at the All American mine."

"Yes, Darling Gomer, and I'm proud of you, but you can do better. With your training and ability, you should be able to get a job in Denver that will pay you . . . fifty dollars a week."

"Fifty? Not a chance. That's management pay."

"Really. My father is an important man in Denver. He can put you in a wonderful job."

At her bedroom window, Emily perked up as she listened to the talk. Mae's real father an important man in Denver?

Gomer took his arm away from Mae, sat back

275

and listened to her. "So, maybe you should tell me who you really are. First Mrs. Johnson says you're her niece from Kansas city. Now you say that you're from Denver?"

Mae sighed. She wasn't sure what to do. "I can't tell you right yet who I am. It's a secret. But I do know that you and I should leave here and go to Denver, where I'll introduce you to my family. We won't say anything about what happened here on the swing. I'll talk to Daddy and he'll find a good place for you where you can learn one of his businesses and soon move up into management. We'll get engaged and married and then we can really find out about making love. But not until I get that ring on my finger."

Gomer sat there stunned. He bent and kissed her. "You sure you won't change your mind about me in a week or so?"

"No, I'm sure I won't." She took his hand and put it on her bare breast. "I don't let just any Johnny play with my titties this way. As you should know."

He bent and kissed her and started to push her back down on the long swing, but she shook her head.

"Not right yet. First you haven't told me if you want to marry me. This is almost the twentieth century. Women are getting more independent now. Were going to have the vote soon. So don't be old-fashioned and think you have to ask to marry me."

She stopped and looked at him.

Gomer chuckled. "You are something, you know that? You are a glorious combination of beauty and spunk and sexy workings and a brain that's probably sharper than mine. I'd be crazy not to want to marry you. That decided, we'll worry about Denver later on."

"Not too much later. I don't know how long I can fight you off in this lawn swing. You're so insistent. Are all men that way?"

He shrugged. "Probably. You get a man aroused and there's just one thing he wants to do."

She smiled. "I know what it is, and I bet women who do it all the time love it as much as you men do. I'll find out one of these days. Lord knows I've had enough of a sampling tonight to last me for some time."

He frowned. "If I'm going to marry you, young lady, shouldn't I at least be able to know your real name?"

"Oh, dear. That could be a problem." She frowned and shook her head. "If I tell you, you have to promise that you'll never, never, never tell anyone."

"Of course. I just want to know who it is that I'm going to marry. You can understand that."

She nodded.

Behind them near the window of Emily's bedroom, the boardinghouse proprietor sat stiff and tense listening.

"Oh, dear. It's been such a delicious secret." She took his arm and put it around her and snuggled against him.

"All right, but you promised not to tell. My name is Harriet Louise Braithwaite, and I'm from Denver and my father is Hercules Braithwaite, the most important man in Denver, and probably the richest."

In the window, Emily gasped and then covered her mouth. So this little girl was Harriet Braithwaite.

Then Harriet told him the whole thing about arguing with her father, about wanting to come to Cripple Creek, and then about the train trip and her quick change of trains and landing in Cripple Creek.

When she finished the story, Gomer edged back from her and stared hard at her pretty face.

"I just may have to rethink my plans to marry you. You are so sneaky, and willful, and you act so much like a man would. How will I ever be able to tame you?"

"Nice man, you tamed me and broke me and won my heart these last few days. You don't have to worry about that. I'll have a time keeping up with you."

In her bedroom, Emily Johnson moved away from the window. What a secret. It was a delicious secret. Here Buckskin Morgan had been hunting a little girl who was serving him meals twice a day right under his attractive nose and he didn't even realize who she was.

Emily frowned. But could she tell him? Would that destroy all the plans those two fine young people were making? And her father was

Hercules Braithwaite. Everyone in Colorado knew about him, the richest man in the state, a power behind politicians and senators. Wow. What a tough, daring little lady this Harriet Braithwaite really was.

Emily got ready for bed. Now she really did have a secret and one she knew she couldn't keep from Buckskin Morgan for long. She'd have to plan carefully how to let him figure out who Mae really was. Maybe if Emily dropped some hints to Buckskin. She'd work on that.

Chapter Twenty-three

Buckskin came awake early and had shaved and dressed long before breakfast. He waited in the kitchen and couldn't quite figure out the smile Emily gave him.

"How is your search for the girl going?" she asked.

He watched her, but Emily turned back to the stove and broke eggs into a skillet.

"Not going any good, as you know. Sometimes a case just goes sour on me."

"I got to thinking. The girl had short brown hair, you said. Could it be possible that she changed her hair color again, maybe bleached blond or even black. Could be red. A kid can change the color of her hair with one dye job."

"Yeah, possible. I'll check out the idea at the hotels again. After breakfast I have to see my two mine owner friends."

"You're getting pretty highfalutin for me, Morgan."

"Just business. Both are honest and hard-working men."

Mae came in then and Emily handed her a plate of eggs and shredded potatoes, bacon, toast and jelly to give to Buckskin.

She carried it over to the kitchen table and smiled as she gave it to him.

"This will get your day off to a good start, Mr. Morgan," Mae said.

He had to smile back at her youthful enthusiasm. "You seem all pepped up this morning, Mae. I hear you have a gentleman friend."

Mae blushed and hurried out of the kitchen without saying anything.

"Not nice, Morgan. Not nice to tease a sensitive young girl about her first love. It could even be serious."

Buckskin shrugged. "Glad I'm over that stage of development. It can be heaven one day and hell the next. From what you females tell me, it's twice as bad on you."

"Amen to that, Pastor Morgan," Emily said, and sat down across from him. The other breakfast boarders wouldn't be there for half an hour.

"She did seem like she was glowing, didn't she?" Buckskin said. "Yep, I think our little Mae is in love."

"Happens in the best of families."

Buckskin finished the meal a short time later, touched Emily on the shoulder and said he'd see her later that afternoon. He started toward the All American mine. It was still early. Just a little past 6:30. He saw some men gathered around something on Bennett Avenue. He went down that way and saw a body sprawled in the street.

He pushed in past the others for a better look.

"Dead as a tumbleweed in December," a man said who stood up from the body. "Anybody know who he is?"

"Hell, yes," another man said. "That's Earl Jode. Had a claim out on the south slope and hit a good upthrust couple of days ago. Last time I saw him was about one o'clock this morning celebrating with two girls and a jug of whiskey."

The dead man's shirt showed bloody red and his chest had been caved in. Somebody pointed to a track of a heavy wagon.

"Look at that. Wagon track. Could have been old Jode here got drunk and passed out and last night somebody ran over him with a wagon. In the dark along here the driver wouldn't even be able to see him. He'd be one small bump and the rig would be gone."

"Somebody go bring the barber," another man said. "He's gonna be pissed for getting rousted out of bed so early."

Buckskin continued his walk toward the All American mine. He had no idea who Mr. Jode was, but his good luck had evidently run out much too soon. He scowled. Or had it been bad luck? Buckskin did a quick about-face and went back to the dead man. Most of the crowd had left. He opened the buttons on the bloody shirt and looked at the mashed-in chest. That alone would have been fatal. Then he saw what he was looking for. Just above the print of the heavy steel shod wheel he found a small purple hole. It had the black pucker of a bullet wound.

He lifted the man's head and looked at the back of it. There in matted and bloody hair he found another small pucker mark of a bullet wound. Small, probably a .22-caliber. Getting more popular these days for whores and hideouts.

He looked at the barber, who buttoned his shirt as he hurried up to the scene. Tony Tarento scowled as he saw Buckskin.

"Why are you always at the site of a death in this town?" he asked.

Buckskin shook his head. "Lucky, I guess. Look at that bullet hole an inch over the bloody mess. There's another one just like it in the back of the man's head. Earl Jode here did not celebrate himself to death by accident. Somebody murdered him, probably to get his mine."

Buckskin left, and this time walked to the All American mine before he realized that whoever came up as the new owner of the Jode claim would be a prime candidate for the role of Jode's killer.

When he walked into Cluny Norman's office, he found three other visitors already there. He knew Nate Purvis, who owned the First Find

Mine. The other two were strangers to him.

"Buckskin, glad you showed up. You heard about the trouble last night?"

"What trouble? About Earl Jode getting murdered?"

Cluny frowned. "Hadn't heard about that. No about the mine. Last night somebody attacked the Princess mine. Shot dead the guard on duty, then burned down two buildings and blew up another one. Lucky there wasn't any night shift on last night."

Cluny pointed to the man sitting near the window. "Buckskin, I don't think you've met Victor Irwin. He owns the Princess mine. We're here today to help him get back on his feet."

Buckskin nodded at Irwin.

"This other gent is Ira Langdon of the Second Strike mine, my neighbor up the hill a ways. We're all here to help Victor get his mine working again. We each have twenty men over there this morning working on building a new lift house. The machinery is intact, but it's going to take some time to get it working again."

"Whatever you need, Victor, you just ask," Nate Purvis said. "If we don't have it, we'll make it, by damn."

Cluny took back the floor. "Victor, why don't you tell Buckskin what happened yesterday."

Victor stood and came away from the window. He was slender and no more than five feet four inches tall. His heavy shoulders told of his time in the tunnels swinging hammers and picks. He wore an expensive suit and a carefully tied neck-piece. His hair was blond and wavy. Buckskin figured he was no more than 40 years old.

"Two men came into my office yesterday morning and said they had an offer to buy my mine. They had business cards that said they were from Denver. I told them the Princess wasn't for sale, but they kept right on talking. When they got around to the price, they knew what my production had been last year and so far this year in actual gold bullion. They offered me fifty percent of my year's average.

"That's about a fifth of what a good working mine should go for. I always figure ten times net, five times gross. When they wouldn't leave I called in two of my men, who hauled them by the arms to the edge of my property and pushed them on down the hill.

"Neither one said a word after that. They both stared at us for a while, then shook their heads and walked toward town.

"Then last night somebody killed old Ambrose and burned me out and blew up the ore storage shed."

"The Five Star?" Buckskin asked. He looked around. The four men showed grim faces.

"I don't want it to be," Purvis said.

"Not much of a guess to figure that out," Victor Irwin said. "I heard they did this before a year and a half ago."

Ira Langdon shifted in his chair. "I don't go along with the way this Five Star bunch was broken last time. Some folks said that the way we stopped the Five Star was as downright bad as the Five Star themselves."

"Only two died," Cluny said. "The town figured both of them deserved it, and that if we had some law here they would have been charged, tried, convicted and hung." He looked at Buckskin. "Yeah, I figure the gents we talked about before are up to their old tricks."

"Figures," Buckskin said. "Yesterday three of them tried to ventilate my hide with rifles. They missed. One of them won't ever try again." He let that settle in a moment. "What we have here is a sad failure of the legal system. Still no law in Cripple Creek. With your permission, I'll put some pressure on the one man in town we think is the instigator of this problem."

"You mean Miles Kelton?" Victor asked.

"Yes. He's been dealing with two particular mine owners a lot lately. Neither of them are here. A little pressure might do the job."

"I won't hold to no killing," Langdon said. "No assassinations. If it's a shootout and its either him or you, that's different."

Cluny looked around at the mine owners, nodded and shifted his glance to Buckskin. "You're the professional detective here. How much will you charge us?"

Buckskin looked at the others. "Fifty dollars a day if it works. Give it three days. If I can't do the job, no charge." He grinned. "I've got something of a personal stake in this affair myself. I'm an eighth-share owner of the Lucky Lady mine."

He turned to Victor Irwin. "Sorry about your buildings. If I'd started a little sooner we might have prevented this." He moved toward the door. "Now I'll leave the reconstruction up to you men. It's in good hands.

"I have some work to do to get ready for some surprises for our dear friend Miles Kelton." He walked out the door and hurried down to Abe Alexander's Hardware and General store. There were some supplies he needed.

That same morning, he found out where Miles Kelton lived. He had a medium-sized house two blocks from his office up the hill from Bennett Avenue. It stood on a corner lot with no houses near it. Good.

Buckskin then learned where Uriah York lived. Late that afternoon he scouted the big house cautiously so no one would see him. The York mansion had at least 20 rooms. It stood high on the hill with a separate lane leading up to it. At the bottom of the lane stood a heavy gate across the lane with fencing on both sides. Near the upper end of the quarter-mile lane, another gate blocked the way. No one uninvited rode into Uriah York's private domain. Perfect, Buckskin decided.

Quinn Forbes lived not too far away, but lower on the hill and without the protection. His large house, three stories and maybe 15 rooms, was four blocks off Bennett to the north. No fences, no guards. Both men had families, Buckskin knew, and none of them would be put in danger.

He went back to a cafe and had a big supper and worked on his plans again. He had left the supplies at Alexander's store. He told Alexander about the share he owned in the Lucky Lady mine. That was his reason for buying the materials he did. No questions were asked.

Buckskin spent an hour well inside the cafe across the way from Miles Kelton's office. This time the man left just before six o'clock and walked with purpose up the street and to his house. He lived alone. Buckskin had established that. Smoke soon came from the kitchen chimney and as dusk settled, lights came on in the kitchen and then the living room.

Buckskin stashed his goods in the darkness at the side of the house and ran around and knocked on the front door. He at once ran to the kitchen door and pounded on it, then retreated to the side where he picked up two railroad fuses, the kind trainmen used to signal with. He ran to the front porch, lit a fuse and dropped it, then knocked on the front door again.

This time he retreated into the darkness so he could see the front door. Kelton came to the door, edged it open and pushed out a shotgun. The blast of the weapon took Buckskin by surprise, but the shot went far wide of his position. Then the red glow of the burning flare attracted Kelton and he stormed outside and kicked the flare off the porch into the dirt of the yard. He stamped on the floor that had charred and then glared into the night.

"You're a dead man, whoever you are! Dead and

with the snakes!" He backed into the house and slammed the front door.

Buckskin worked silently this time. He climbed up a small woodshed in back of the house to the roof and then to the kitchen chimney on the one-story section of the house. With him he carried two gunny sacks. He stuffed them down the chimney and felt the hot fumes coming up. Good, Kelton hadn't put out the fire. Buckskin stuffed the sacks in until the chimney was fully blocked, then eased off the roof, down the woodshed and back into the darkness.

It took ten minutes before he heard a roar of anger and the kitchen door burst open. Kelton rushed out coughing and rubbing at his eyes. He went back inside and opened the front door and several windows as the smoke billowed out of each of them.

Buckskin grinned. If he'd had more time to prepare, he would have found a skunk and two or three rattlesnakes, but it was too late for that.

He took a can of gasoline and poured it in a circle in the dirt of the front yard, let it sink into the ground and when he had finished the circle he dropped the can in the middle, then struck a match and threw it at the wet ring. The fumes of the vaporized gasoline whooshed into an immediate ring of fire.

Buckskin scurried back out of the new light and fired his six-gun twice into the air.

He saw a curtain on the front window move

and then Kelton stormed out of his house, the shotgun in one hand and a six-gun in the other.

"Damn you to hell!" he shouted. "Whoever you are, you're a dead man. Dead and in hell." He stood there a moment, then fired the shotgun in one direction, turned and fired the second barrel in the other direction.

He seemed to sag a little as he stood in the firelight. The soaked gasoline in the ground kept burning, the ring of fire bringing two neighbors.

"What the hell's going on?" a man from the shadows asked.

"Who are you?" Kelton bellowed.

"Your neighbor who was trying to get some sleep. What's all the shooting and the fire?"

"I don't know," Kelton said. "Some crazy man. He's probably gone. Go back to bed. No more shooting tonight."

The man said something and left. Kelton stood there in the firelight waving his six-gun. "I'm warning you, whoever the hell you are. You're a dead man and half buried. Count on that."

Buckskin dropped to the ground and fired twice quickly in front of Kelton, digging up the fire ring. By the time Kelton swung around to find the gunman, Buckskin's muzzle flashes had long vanished and he had rolled six times to the left.

"Bastard!" Kelton wailed. He waved the six-gun, then fired all five of his rounds in the general direction where he must have thought the rounds had come from. Then he must have realized he was out of loads and rushed for the house.

A good start, Buckskin decided. He went back to his cache of supplies and worked out his next surprise for Kelton. He wouldn't use it yet. He wanted Kelton to settle down thinking the terror was over. It was only beginning.

Buckskin took his gear half a block away and lay down in a patch of grass. He dozed and watched the big dipper work its nightly trip around the north star. When the pointer stars on the lip of the dipper pointing at the star told him it was midnight, he roused and finished his task.

He grinned as he took his surprise toward the Kelton house. He had planned on not burning down the house. At least not this first night. Maybe tomorrow night if it took that long. He moved with no sound and stopped at the back door. There he set up a net of sticky tape that criss-crossed the back door in a sticky web. Once the tape caught on flesh or cloth it was hard to get off.

He went on to the front door and poured a quart of gasoline into a metal bucket and put it near the front door. He wedged the V-shaped wooden block under the door so it couldn't be pushed outward. Then he lit the gasoline in the bucket. He fired a round from the shotgun through the front window so the buckshot peppered the ceiling.

A moment later, he hurried back out of the light of the new gasoline fire and waited.

A piercing scream echoed out of the house. He heard running feet coming toward the front door. The door rattled, then opened a quarter of an inch and stopped as the wedge held. Kelton pounded on the door. Then it was quiet. Buckskin ran toward the back of the house. A moment later the back door blasted open and a figure bare-chested, shoeless and in pants stormed out the door and blundered directly into the net of tape.

Miles Kelton screamed as the tape snared him. It bulged from his weight and some of the anchoring tapes came loose and wrapped around him tighter. He bellowed in fury, anger and fear, and then suddenly the screaming stopped.

Miles Kelton had fainted.

Buckskin grinned, picked up the rest of his supplies and the shotgun and walked back to the boardinghouse. It had been a good night's work.

Chapter Twenty-four

When Miles Kelton regained consciousness, he had no idea where he was. The panic that had seized him inside the house still swirled around in his mind. His eyes jolted open. Dark. Nighttime. He must have passed out. But not for long. Something held him. He looked down at his arms. Something sticky. Tape. He scowled. A trick, the whole thing was a trick. Who would do something like this?

He knew at once. Buckskin Morgan. The bastard. He began to shiver then, a wracking shaking that he couldn't stop. He screamed there in the darkness alone. He screamed again and again until his voice gave out and he started to cry.

He hadn't cried since he was ten years old.

When the tears failed him as well, he pawed at the tape and slowly began to unwind himself from the trap. It took him a half hour to be completely free. Then he walked away from the house. Anywhere but that house.

He found the back door of the Deep Shaft Saloon and pounded on it until someone came and unlocked it. The old drunk they let sleep in the saloon as a kind of night watchman scratched his beard and then his crotch.

He didn't say a word. When Miles stepped inside, still shirtless and with no boots on, the old man shrugged and went back to the blankets he had stretched out in front of the bar.

Miles stood there a moment, then walked to the bar and pushed open the door to the back room. A cot stood in the corner. He dropped on it and tried to relax. The shivers came again, but he stopped them this time before he screamed. What the hell was the matter with him?

He found two blankets and pulled them over him and tried to get some sleep. What in hell? How could Buckskin Morgan know anything about their Five Star plan? He couldn't. Nobody could. Just the four of them. No, three now. He'd have to deal with it in the morning. Yeah, tomorrow. At last he went to sleep.

Breakfast went as usual the next morning. Buckskin was there first, and Mae served him. She brought in a stack of flapjacks, hot syrup, fresh butter and coffee. The first stack of six plate-sized pancakes had two fried eggs on them.

"Morning, Mr. Morgan," Mae said. "Isn't it a bright and wonderful new day?"

Buckskin grinned at the young girl so obviously in love and transferring her joy to the world.

"Yes, Mae, a beautiful morning. Don't rush off. Tell me about your new boyfriend."

She colored just a little, then beat it back and lifted her chin. "He's fine. You know him, Gomer. He's head accountant at the All American mine and doing very well."

"Good. You make the breakfast?"

"Helped some."

She was cute as a button. He nodded and kept eating. Emily came in and sat down across from him. Mae went back to the kitchen.

Then Emily spoke. "I was talking with Mae the other day and she said she used to be a blonde, long honey-blond hair halfway down her back, can you believe that?"

"Mae a blonde? Somehow it doesn't fit."

"A lot of things about Mae might not fit." She stood. "Better get back to my flapjacks. The rush is about to start." She went into the kitchen and found Mae turning over the cakes on the big griddle she'd had the blacksmith make for her. She stood behind Mae and began talking softly.

"Look, I'm not going to tell anybody, but I know who you are. I don't know exactly why you ran away from the fine home you must have in Denver, and it ain't none of my business. But now I think it's time that you thought about it again. You just can't leave your folks wondering what happened to you. That would be cruel, such a hurt they might never get over."

Mae turned and stared at Emily. "You know it

all? How did you find out?"

"Heard you talking with Gomer. Didn't mean to eavesdrop, but I did. Not proud of it, but might be the best for you. You know that Mr. Morgan is hunting for you?"

Harriet Braithwaite laughed. "Oh, yes. I've known since the first day he arrived here and I met him at the general store. It was fun being near him and his not recognizing me."

"The haircut and boy's clothes did it then." Emily paused and reached over Harriet's shoulder, took up six hotcakes and put them on a serving plate. She handed it to Harriet, who vanished into the dining room and returned almost at once.

"Three more are waiting," Emily said.

Six more hotcakes were already cooking on the grill.

"What are you going to do about Gomer?" Emily asked.

"Gomer? I'm going to marry him. We decided last night, or the night before." She held up a hand. "No, I haven't slept with him. I'm still a virgin."

"Good. Now, it's time for you to act as grown-up as your eighteen years demand. You're a grown woman. Don't you think you should start acting like an adult?"

"I am. That's why I left home."

"You were a child then. Now you're a woman. You think about this. You should go back home, take Gomer with you and explain to your parents that you're in love with the young man. That you're still a virgin and you want your parents' blessing to marry him."

Harriet shook her head. "Oh, no, my parents would never hear of it. They want me to marry one of the rich spoiled brats from Denver."

Then they were too busy to talk. Harriet brought more coffee from the kitchen then more warm syrup and butter. The flapjacks piled up on plates and vanished into hungry mouths the moment they hit the table.

About 15 minutes later the rush was over and all the men had hurried off to work. Even Buckskin had left.

Harriet touched Emily's shoulder and stared with a serious expression at the older woman.

"I'd be ever so thankful if you don't tell Mr. Morgan about me. Give me a couple more days to think it through. What I'd like to do is take Gomer home, get him a good job in one of Daddy's firms and then announce our engagement."

"Why can't you?"

"You don't know my father."

"I've heard of him. You might be surprised how considerate he can be when he sees how determined you are. What he wants is what's best for you. You can count on that. You'll have to make up your own mind about what to do."

"I know and it's hard. I've never felt so free or had such a good time as I have since I came to Cripple Creek."

"Maybe it would be different this time when you go home."

"I doubt that. Oh, you have to promise me that

you won't tell anyone who I am, especially Mr. Morgan."

"Oh, dear. Sometimes I talk too much."

Harriet grinned. "Especially when you're in bed with Mr. Morgan. I've heard the wails and moans coming from your bedroom some nights."

"Well, now, you say you don't know anything about that kind of thing."

"Not really. Just on the fringes of it. Experimenting. I'm sure you did some of that."

Emily grinned and gave Harriet a hug. "Oh, yes, do I remember. I promise not to tell Buckskin and I know that you'll do the right thing. Oh, if you do decide to go home, let Buckskin help you get home."

"So he can be successful?"

"Something like that."

By the time Buckskin arrived at the All American mine, the daily meeting of the mine owners was in full swing. There had been no violence the night before. Two more of the miners had been offered the chance the day before to sell out . . . at about half the worth of their operations.

"So I threw the skunk off my property," Ira Langdon said. "Peppered the rocks behind him with some six-gun rounds so he'd know I was serious."

"I'd strongly suggest you put armed guards out tonight as soon as it gets dark," Buckskin said. "Especially you two who were propositioned yesterday. Don't let the guards roam. Put them in defensive positions so they can see most of the operation. Should have at least two guards and be sure they have a good repeating rifles."

"Seems a little drastic," Victor Irwin said.

"Not drastic enough," Cluny said. "If you'd had two guards out that night they might not have been able to destroy your mine buildings."

"Guards," Purvis said. "What else?"

"Let's hit *them* for a change," Buckskin said. "Last night I went visiting at Miles Kelton's house. I don't think he had a wink of sleep all night. Strange things kept happening to his house. No, it didn't burn down, but it could have.

"What I'm suggesting is that if any more salesmen come around trying to buy your mines, you put them under a gun and lock them up in the mine somewhere for the rest of the day and all night before you let them go. No food or water and no lights, of course. Let them see what a little rough treatment is like."

Purvis chuckled. "Damn good idea. Let them sue us, or go get the sheriff. Yeah, I like it." He frowned at Buckskin. "Why in hell did you leave Kelton alive and kicking?"

"Figured he might lead us somewhere beside the two miners we think are involved." He grinned. "Besides, I want to visit his office."

Cluny laughed with the others and then sobered. "All right, now what else can we do to help stop this Five Star?"

Langdon looked around the office and nodded. "All of the biggest mines are represented here but three. We don't have to worry about Godfrey Rudolph who died. That leaves the Gold Hill with

Uriah York and the Poverty with Quinn Forbes. Anything been done about them yet?"

Buckskin nodded and stood. He walked to the window and looked out a minute, then came back. "I'd guess that both York and Forbes have out-buildings of some sort near their mansions. I've heard it's a bad time of the year for fires. Could be that both of them might suffer the same kind of bad luck right after dark tonight."

"For God's sakes, be careful," Cluny said.

"Careful is my middle name. I can't spend all this money I'm making if I'm six feet underground playing with the snakes."

"That's about it, then," Cluny said.

"Don't forget about those guards tonight" Buckskin said. "Give them repeaters, but caution them not to shoot down any of your own men. Oh, is anybody getting ready to haul ore to the rail line? If so, try to put it off three or four days. I hope we can have this all cleared up by then."

The other mine owners hurried out and headed back to their own digs. All of them handled day-to-day operations of their still relatively small operations.

"You going to torch some buildings tonight?" Cluny asked.

"Nothing too big. Just want to get their attention. Let them know that we know which side they're on. Let them remember what happened before to the miners who worked in the Five Star."

"You think Kelton is behind most of this?"

"I'd say he's the instigator. He's ambitious. He wants some established mines quickly, instead of working for them. That reminds me about the Earl Jode mine. When ownership changes hands, doesn't it have to be recorded in the land office."

"Yeah. Might be interesting to see who owns it now."

I'll go down that way. I need to replenish some of my supplies anyway." Buckskin headed for the door. "Thinking about claims and small operations, I wonder how my one eighth of the Lucky Lady is progressing? Heard anything from Lars Zacherias about that development money yet?"

"Not a word. Suppose it's broken through at the apex yet?"

Buckskin grinned. "About what I was thinking. Now wouldn't it be too bad if it broke through with the upthrust right there in the middle of one of my claims?"

A few minutes later at the land office, Buckskin looked up the ownership of the Earl Jode claim. Jode's name had been crossed out and two new names written in. One was Uriah York, the other was Miles Kelton. Buckskin closed his eyes a moment and then went directly to the hardware store. He bought more supplies, including a dozen sticks of 40% dynamite and two one-gallon cans of kerosene. He left them around back of the woodshed at Mrs. Johnson's boardinghouse and slipped inside the house. It wasn't quite noon.

Emily heard him and came out of the kitchen. "Hey, stranger, we're about ready for some lunch. Want some?"

He nodded. In the kitchen, Emily made a third sandwich and put it on a small plate and set it at the kitchen table. Mae sat there munching on a sandwich and watching him.

"Found that girl yet?" she asked.

He shook his head. "Nope. Don't know if I ever will."

"Maybe you're looking in the wrong place," Mae said.

"Probably. I've got some major worries to get out of the way before I can concentrate on that."

"So she isn't important to you anymore?" Mae asked.

"Yes, sure. It's just that she isn't a threat to my life. I got mixed up with something here in town that is dangerous and terrible and I want to put an end to it first. A couple of days." He turned and looked at her with a frown. "Why, you have some idea where she is?"

"I might. It just depends on some other things going on. I should know in a couple of days."

"Somebody you saw here in town?"

"Yeah. But that's all I can say right now. I promised. A person never goes back on a promise." She turned and looked at Emily.

"Oh, right, child. Nobody with any gumption ever goes back on a promise."

They talked about other things then, and Buckskin went to his room for three hours of sleep. He figured he'd be up most of the night and he didn't want to make any mistakes. He had been asleep for a while when he heard someone at the door. From slitted eyes he watched. The door opened quietly and Emily slid inside.

She came to the bed and gently lay down beside

him. She moved against him and sighed. He pretended to move in his sleep and his right arm came across her and his hand found one of her breasts. All this time he breathed deeply, a sleeping sound.

She made a soft little sound in her throat and then laughed.

"I didn't fool you at all, did I, Buckskin? You knew the second I opened the door."

"True."

"I'm not getting sexy here. I just want to have a nap beside you, all close and cuddly and warm."

He squeezed her breast and moved his hand. "Good, just don't oversleep and miss getting supper ready. I'm going to be as hungry as two jackasses on a Colorado mountain trail."

By eight o'clock that night, some clouds had moved in, quickened the coming of darkness and covered the moon.

Buckskin crouched near the main shaft of the claim that Earl Jode had died for and listened. There were no sounds, no lights around the hole. He worked forward slowly and looked in the shaft. A ladder led down. He climbed down the ladder with his gunny sack full of supplies. At the bottom, he made sure there was no one there. He lit a torch he found there still smelling of kerosene, and hurried along one 40-foot tunnel and another 20-footer. Nobody in the mine.

Buckskin placed two five-stick dynamite charges where they would do the most damage. One halfway into the long tunnel, and the other one in the short tunnel six feet in from the shaft.

With any luck both tunnels would collapse and the shaft itself would cave in from all sides blocking the whole mine. It would take weeks to dig it out to where it was tonight. The new owners would have to redo all the work that Earl Jode had done over the past four months.

He set the charges with detonators, pushed three-foot fuses into each charge and lit them both. The fuse was guaranteed to burn a foot a minute. That gave him three minutes to get up the ladder out of the shaft and out of harm's way. He had just made it to the bottom of the shaft and doused the torch when he heard voices overhead. Then a torch showed at the top of the shaft.

"Yeah, Boss. Like I told you, I saw somebody prowling around here fifteen, twenty minutes ago. Suppose he's still down there?"

Buckskin looked back at the burning dynamite fuses. It was too late now to go back and pull out the fuses. He scowled and pulled the six-gun out of leather and looked up the shaft.

Chapter Twenty-five

A torch thrust over the top of the shaft lighted it all the way to the bottom and Buckskin jumped backward into the tunnel. He looked at the closest five-stick dynamite bomb. It would blow him straight into hell if he stayed there. He had to go up.

He'd try to bluff it.

"Hey, what the hell, give me a little light down here. What the fuck you guys trying to do to me. Tell me to come to work and I get here and not a damned person here. No boss, no tools. What the hell kind of outfit is this anyway?"

As Buckskin yelled, he climbed up the ladder. If he could get to the top he could draw and move them back and get out of the way of the explosion. He couldn't even estimate how much time he had to live yet. He had to get over the lip of the shaft or he'd get blown 50 feet into the sky.

"What the hell?" a voice came from above. "I didn't hire anybody. Who hired him? Shit, do you guys fuck up a job. Who the hell told this guy to come out here tonight?"

Buckskin climbed faster and made it to the top. He vaulted the last step and moved out of the shaft. The torch the men had on top had been put out. They stood there in the semi-darkness staring at his shadow.

"Who do I draw my pay from?" he demanded. "I'm not working for a shitty outfit like this anymore. Get your orders right the next time." He began to stalk away. Then over his shoulder he shouted. "I'll be back tomorrow to get my pay and there damn well better be somebody here to pay me."

Buckskin kept walking into the night. Behind him somebody yelled asking his name, but he ignored them and kept going. Buckskin kept waiting for the explosion. He never realized that three minutes could be so long.

Then the blast rocked the ground under him. He looked back at the shaft opening but couldn't see a thing. Some men there screamed, and Buckskin hoped they were far enough away from the shaft so they didn't fall in when the sides crumbled. A moment later he felt rather than heard the second blast that must be the one deep into the long tunnel. Now blocked from the air by the first blast, all of the power came through the ground.

He ran away from the shaft, back toward town. That was when he realized he didn't have the rest of his supplies. The coal oil was what he needed most. He took a chance and went past the hardware and general store. It was closed. He'd have to improvise. First the smaller of the two houses, the Quinn Forbes place.

He found it as he had before, but this time he circled around it and came in through the unfenced back section. The area around the house was about two acres, 200 feet along the front and 400 feet to the rear.

With no moon to help him, Buckskin had to move up close to identify the buildings. The Forbes house was easy. To the left were the stables with horses he could hear stamping. That was out. He checked the next building. It held two buggies and harness. It was far enough away from the horses. Well inside the closed building, he lit a match to see what was there to help him.

In one corner, he saw a bale of hay. Yes, good for a start. In another corner he found a can of oil and a gallon of turpentine. Just right. He poured the turpentine over the corner of the building in back, tore the hay bale apart and scattered it thickly around the back side of the building. Then he lit the turpentine and hurried out the back door. He was a quarter of a mile away when the flames burst through the top of the building and he knew it was too late to save anything inside. One down.

The problem at Uriah York's estate was more formidable. A six-foot wire fence surrounded the back of the land. The house sat on a parcel of about five acres. He scaled the fence and squatted listening. He hadn't seen any dogs before, but there could be one or more. None showed up.

He moved cautiously toward the buildings a hundred yards away. He knew there were guards on both gates. He didn't know if there were any interior guards or not.

The first building he found was an outhouse, evidently for the help who lived in rooms over the stables. Lights showed in windows there. He couldn't burn that. He skirted it and moved toward the next blob of shadow. It stood 40 feet long and half that wide. He found two doors, both unlocked.

Moving an inch at a time, he edged one door open until he could see inside. Blackness. He let his eyes expand even more but still could see nothing. He struck a match and at once almost stumbled over an overstuffed chair. The match flared brighter and he saw that the building was filled with furniture, pictures and household goods. Some were draped, others left to collect dust.

He found some paper, twisted it into a small torch and looked around more. At the side of the building he found a box filled with old newspapers. Some people never threw anything away. He moved the box to the best spot, a back corner where both sides of the wall could burn. He heaped the crumpled-up papers in the corner, put a wooden chair among them, then stacked more wooden chairs with slat-backs on top. The small pieces of wood would burn quickly.

It took him a half hour to set it up. Then he lit the newspapers in two places with matches and saw it catch and burn brightly. When two of the chairs caught on fire, he hurried to the back door slipped through and threw the bolt. He raced to the back fence in two minutes, went across and sat there watching for the fire to break out through the side or roof.

It took more than a half hour, and by then he figured most of the goods inside would be burning as well. An alarm went off at the house, and a dozen men scurried around trying to throw buckets of water on the roaring flames. They had no chance to put it out.

Buckskin took a roundabout route back to the town and Mrs. Johnson's boardinghouse. When he stepped past the front door, he heard the chiming clock strike. It was only eleven o'clock. He locked the door behind him and turned when he saw Emily at her door down the hall. She motioned to him.

He went to her and into her room. She closed the door and pushed on the bolt. A lamp burned low in her bedroom. She turned to him and he saw she wore the see-through silk nightgown. It shimmered where it pressed against her out-thrust breasts.

"Glad you could come. I had a hard day and I'm in need of some relaxation. You kill anybody today?"

"Sorry. I did blow up a mine. You want to hear about that?"

"Oh, God, yes." She laughed softly. "We must control ourselves, though. Mae heard us the last time we played in here."

309

"I'll try to control myself." He undid the two buttons at her throat and the sheath of silk cascaded to the floor. "Oh, yes, now that is what I call the way to relax."

After the first time, they lay in each other's arms. They had recovered and now smiled.

"Getting relaxed?" he asked.

"Starting. I figure three or four more and I'll be putty in your hands. You'll be able to do anything to me you want."

"Sounds interesting. Can I do that even if you're sleeping?"

She frowned. "I've never been done when I slept. I wonder if I would wake up or just cooperate."

"You'd wake up. Every woman I've ever tried to poke when she was sleeping woke up. They all said they wanted to enjoy it, not just lay there."

"Me too," Emily said. "Enjoy it, but this time quietly."

She told him about eavesdropping on the kids when they were petting on the swing. "I swear she was climaxing. Maybe he hit her clit or something. He could have been doing it against her belly."

"Kids do that. No dangers and no problems that way."

"Yeah, for a while. Then they get more curious. I know I sure the hell was."

"You getting sexy again?" he asked.

"Any time Mr. Worm down there can get himself into an upright position, I'll be ready." Her hands went down and she giggled. "I think Mr. Worm became Mr. Lance. He's ready."

They made love gently, reveling in every bit of

it, every caress, every bit of foreplay, then the poking and thrusting and surging of emotions until they were satiated at least for the moment and fell back on the bed, exhausted again.

After the third lovemaking a half hour later, they quietly slipped off to sleep in each other's arms.

The next morning, Buckskin made it to the Lucky Lady mine just before the men went down the ladder. Lars Zacherias saw him coming and started to reach for his hideout gun, but Buckskin drew and put a bullet between his boots, nicking the back of one heel.

"Hold it right there, cowboy, or you'll be singing about the last roundup for St. Peter."

Lars moved his hand back to his side. "What you doing here?"

"Looking over my share of the wealth. How is the digging going? Still on that upslant? Seems damn strange for a vein of ore this close to the surface to be running upward toward the surface. Usually it works the other way around."

He turned to the three workers who had shovels and buckets and looked ready to go to work.

"You men, have you seen anything down there that looks like an upthrust?"

"Mean like when a vein comes up to the surface?"

"Yeah, exactly what I mean."

"Well, sure, we found one. Crazy it being in there so far."

"Shut up, you idiot!" Lars bellowed.

"Interesting. What's your name?"

"I'm Henry."

"Henry, how far would you say this upthrust is from the shaft?"

"Don't rightly know."

"Well, let's all go own and take a look. We can pace it off. It might be interesting."

"No," Lars shouted. "If any of you go into the Lucky Lady you can draw your pay right now. Nobody is going down there. You're all excused for today. Come back to work tomorrow, same time."

"Why? We came to work," one man said.

"Because I'm the boss and I said so. Now leave. Get out of here."

The three men looked at Buckskin, who nodded. They turned and headed back for the main part of town.

"Okay, Lars, It's just you and me. You going to take me down in the tunnel, or would you rather try to get to the doctor with a .45 slug in your right thigh."

"No, you can't do that. You wouldn't shoot me."

Buckskin moved the muzzle of the Colt, aiming at the man's thigh, and cocked the hammer. Lars stared at Buckskin's deadly expression, then down at the revolver. Sweat dripped down his nose.

"All right! All right. Don't shoot, I'll take you down."

"Give me your hideout."

Lars handed over the twin-barreled .22 hideout. "Interesting caliber. Do you know Earl Jode?"

Lars shook his head. Buckskin frisked him quickly and then pushed him toward the mine shaft. "You first. Remember no tricks. I know

312

mines and I've been down here before. One false move and we won't need to dig a hole to bury you. Just throw your worthless body in a drift and cover you up."

Buckskin lit a torch at the bottom of the shaft and pushed Lars ahead. "Now, take me to that upthrust. I want to pace off the distance, so don't be making a lot of conversation. Understand?"

Lars nodded. Buckskin paced down the tunnel noting the slight bend. He counted the paces until they came to the end where an upthrust had been cut off at tunnel level but still showed in the top.

"Yep, about what I expected. I figured all along that you didn't own this vein you worked. You didn't have the apex of it, so you were stealing someone else's gold. Now, let's get topside and do some walking. Eighty-six paces of mine. My pace is almost three feet, so it's about eighty-six yards from the new shaft you dug trying to hide the fact you were on an outlaw vein."

Lars grumbled all the way to the surface. There Buckskin tied his hands behind his back with a boot lace and marched him ahead on a nearly north direction.

Buckskin didn't point out the claim stakes as he walked past them on his way to 86 paces. He was 30 feet inside the first claim he had filed on.

"Well, looks like it's about right here where that upthrust would come to the surface. It will when we dig it out. You know what that means, Lars."

"Don't make no difference to me."

"But your boss, Miles Kelton, is going to be mad as hell, right?"

"Don't know what you're talking about."

Buckskin took him back to the claim stake and pointed it out to him. "Just so you'll understand completely, that upthrust comes to apex on my claim, so I own that vein you've been digging. All the ore you've dug out belongs to me, and to my partners in this mine. It's still the Lucky Lady, but it ain't lucky for you. I'm charging you with grand larceny, claim-jumping, theft of at least eight hundred dollars worth of gold ore, and murder in the death of Larry Douglas and Earl Jode. Now move, you murdering bastard."

Buckskin walked Lars down to the barbershop where Tony Tarento, the Cripple Creek town marshal, was ready for him.

"We built a jail," Tarento said. "Just a one-cell jail attached to the back of my shop. But at least we can keep prisoners locked up until the county comes and gets them."

"Good, stuff this one in there and don't feed him for a couple of days. He doesn't deserve any food."

Buckskin saw Lars safely tucked away. The wooden building had a two-inch-wide hasp on the outside door and no windows. Inside there was a bunk and a slop jar. Buckskin grinned and slammed the steel home and put a heavy padlock through the hasp. He shook hands with the marshal and walked away.

Buckskin made it to the mine owners' meeting late. He told Cluny about the apex and they grinned. "My claim, but you're a fifty-fifty partner in the mine. All you have to do is develop it into a bonanza."

"You didn't hear my good news," Ira Langdon said. "That same pair came back yesterday and offered me twice as much for my Second Strike, but still about half what she's worth. I called in my two best men and they covered them with shotguns and I tied their hands. Both of them are stewing at the eighty-foot level in a dark tunnel. We hear them screaming now and then."

"Let them out and put them on the stage for Florissant," Buckskin said. "Tell them if they show up in Cripple Creek again they get a bullet between their eyes."

They all cheered.

"Hear that Forbes and York both suffered serious fires at their home places last night," Cluny said.

Buckskin lifted his brows. "Really? I hadn't heard anything about it. Too bad. They have such nice places up there."

Cluny grinned. "So, what's our next step? Where do we take the fight from here?"

"What about the Earl Jode killing?" Nate Purvis asked. "I liked that young kid."

"You didn't hear?" Victor asked. "The Jode diggings suffered some kind of an early detonation with some dynamite they had in the tunnel, and the whole thing collapsed. Even the shaft is a mess, about fifteen feet across now. Looks like they'll have to just about start over with a new shaft and then dig out the tunnels before they can get to the gold."

"Unusual, a premature detonation that way and nobody gets killed," Cluny said.

Buckskin shrugged. "It happens." He grinned. "Especially if you place the dynamite in the right spots."

They all laughed.

"Serves the bastards right," Purvis said. "Now, what is next?"

"Next is the joker in this deck, the man who got it all started and those three mine owners worked up about it," Buckskin said. "We take on Miles Kelton head-on in a showdown hand. We've got all the cards."

"When?" two of the men asked at once.

"Just as soon as I get a little more homework done," Buckskin said. "I should be able to get it cleaned up this afternoon and take on Kelton tonight or in the morning."

They broke up. Buckskin went downtown for one last bit of work to get done before the confrontation.

Chapter Twenty-six

Buckskin had just left the general store after looking over some goods he figured he might need, when he heard about a shootout at the Nate Purvis mine. He trotted up the hill and found Nate getting into a buggy. He had a bloody wound on his left shoulder and looked pale.

"What happened?"

"Two of them came into the office with sawed-off shotguns under their jackets. Whipped them out and covered us, then demanded all the cash we had and our mining records. Three of us in the office. I told one gunman I had to get a key to the cash box from my drawer. He watched me.

"I pulled out my six-gun and shot him in the heart before he could pull the trigger. The other one got rammed in the side by my bookkeeper and he dropped the shotgun. It went off and blew out a window. He pulled a handgun and shot me in the shoulder. Then I cut him down with a round in his leg and he lost his gun. We've got him over there. I'm on my way to see Doc Swanson."

The driver nodded at Buckskin and pulled away toward town. Buckskin went to the man on the ground beside the front steps. A young blond man wearing a suit covered him with a six-gun. Buckskin waved the man's gun aside and knelt beside the robber.

"I'm here to see that these men don't kill you," he said. "I'm trying to help you, do you understand that?"

The man frowned, then lifted his brows. "Then get me to a doctor. Damn slug didn't come out of my leg."

Buckskin slapped him hard, bouncing his head one way, then back the other way. The robber shrilled in surprise and pain.

"Who put you up to this anyway?"

The robber looked away and said nothing. Buckskin slammed his fist against the bloody wound on the man's thigh. He bellowed in pain and swung his fist at Buckskin but missed, and tears came to his eyes.

"Bastard," the robber bawled.

"Been called worse. You telling me you'd rather die than let us know who hired you? Nobody in his right mind would try to rob a mine office. They don't have any money on hand except at payday, which this ain't."

Buckskin caught the man's chin in his hand and turned his face so he looked at Buckskin. "Some news for you, hardcase. I'm the designated hangman for the Cripple Creek Vigilantes. I work under some general rules. The first is that if a felony is being committed and someone dies, the perpetrators are all liable for a charge of murder, and the penalty is hanging. That first rule fits you pretty well, don't you think?"

The man's glance shifted from side to side. His face worked. His attitude changed.

"Look, I was just following orders. Pretend to rob the place, shoot it up, then set it on fire. No big deal. Nobody was supposed to get hurt."

"Tough luck, now you hang for it. Way it goes. Just not your lucky day. You want to hang alone, or with the guy who gave you the orders?"

"Yeah, damn him. If I hang, he hangs."

"Who gave you the orders?"

"Miles Kelton, the lawyer guy."

"We've met. Stand up."

Buckskin tied his hands behind his back, recruited the bookkeeper with the gun and had him take the robber down to the one-room jail.

He stood there watching the pair marching down the mountain toward the jail. Without thinking about it, Buckskin eased the Colt up and down an inch in his holster, loosening it. It was a little nervous habit he'd developed lately. He had to stop it. Might give him away one day.

Kelton. It was time.

He walked down the hill with one project in mind, taking Kelton on. He wasn't sure just how. He'd go with the situation as it developed.

When he came to Kelton's upstairs door, he found it locked. He jiggled it a bit, then stepped back and kicked the door where the handle was. It sprung inward a little, then back. The second kick, with the flat of his boot landing flat against the section of the door right by the square black door lock, broke the lock and blasted the door inward.

He went inside with his Colt drawn, but found nobody there. Evidence. He might need some if Kelton lasted long enough for a trial. Buckskin began pulling out drawers, searching through the desk. He found some interesting files including one on the Earl Jode claim. He found nothing that would incriminate Kelton.

Buckskin didn't try to be neat. He dumped files on the floor, emptied the desk, tipped over chairs and pushed over a book rack. He found nothing he could use.

For a moment he stood there surveying the mess. So where was Kelton? If he wasn't here he could be at his house. But with his recent experience there, he might be reluctant to go back there. That left the Deep Shaft Saloon, which seemed to be the focal point for all of his illegal activities.

Some of the saloons didn't open until noon, but the Deep Shaft opened at eight in the morning. Buckskin pushed in through the bat-wing doors and looked around quickly. One drunk

320

had passed out on a poker table, his head cradled in his arms. Two miners with the dirt of the dig still in their boots and pants stood at the bar.

The apron behind the bar eyed Buckskin warily and looked quickly at the door behind the bar. Buckskin drew his Colt and used it to motion the bartender away from the door. He saw no one else in the saloon.

A few quick steps and he reached the door to the back room. The barkeep scowled but the Colt kept him silent. Buckskin listened at the door, heard nothing and eased the door open. One man lay on a cot in the corner of the room. No one else was there.

Buckskin closed the door, threw a bolt locking it and walked over to the sleeping man, who stirred but didn't wake up. Buckskin kicked the bottom of the canvas cot and the man groaned and sat up.

He was Miles Kelton.

Buckskin pushed the muzzle of the Colt upward into the soft flesh under Kelton's chin. His eyes went wide, then they calmed.

"You can't do it, Morgan, you're no killer."

"I've killed my share. One more won't make no difference to me. You ready?"

"No man is ready to die. Let's talk about this. There's a lot of money involved. I can make you rich. Why you so dead set on running this thing to ground?"

"Because you're hurting a lot of people. Because you've killed at least seven people that we know about. Because you're a no-good bastard who should be wiped off the face of the planet. That enough reasons?"

"Not for me. I can see that you get a million dollars over the next five years. That enough money for you? Two hundred thousand a year for five years. You can travel, have a dozen women at once, do anything and everything that you've always dreamed of doing and never have to worry about making a living again."

"How much cash you have on you?"

"Cash, none."

"Forget it. The Cripple Creek Vigilantes are meeting right now passing judgment on you. You're up for murder for the death of Larry Douglas, Earl Jode and Godfrey Rudolph. Not much doubt that you'll be convicted of at lest one of the killings. You'll be hung before sundown."

"You can't do that. I want a fair trial, in the Springs."

"No chance at all. We should be fair like you were fair to those men you killed?"

"I want a trial."

"You're having a trial."

The back door blasted open and a shotgun roared before Buckskin could move. He dropped to the floor realizing that the deadly pellets had missed him. He rolled and looked for the shooter. No one stood in the doorway in a small cloud of white smoke.

Kelton!

He looked where the man had been sitting.

Gone. Buckskin checked the room as he sprinted for the door. He flattened against the side, poked his head and jerked it back. A gun barked outside and a bullet slammed through the opening where the door had been.

Buckskin dropped to the floor, pushed his Colt around the door frame and fired three times, then he took a quick look. He saw two men running fast down the alley toward the near street.

He jumped up and chased them. He saw them ahead when they charged into the street. One man turned each way.

Buckskin followed the shorter of the two men. He figured the barkeep must have come around through the alley to warn Kelton. When he heard the talk inside, he tried with the shotgun, then covered Kelton as he ran. The barkeep was a foot taller than Kelton.

The smaller of the two men still ran down the middle of the street when Buckskin surged into Bennett Avenue. It was Kelton ahead. He turned and looked back, then ran between two stores. Buckskin followed. Two shots slammed toward him as he rounded the corner of the store. One round hit wood near his shoulder, the other sang overhead.

Kelton had stopped and waited. Now he turned and ran again. The man couldn't be in that good a shape, Buckskin figured. The route went down the street behind Bennett, then north a block and another and then west. There were fewer and fewer houses here.

Kelton cut sharply behind a small house with smoke coming from the chimney. Buckskin worked around the house carefully. He saw Kelton waiting for him around the next corner and put a round through the wooden work on the corner, bringing a yelp of pain from Kelton. By the time Buckskin got to that corner, the man was gone.

The screen door slammed and Buckskin ran that way. A woman stood there with a baby in her arms near the rear door. Kelton stood behind her, his arm around her throat pinning her to him as a shield. His cocked six-gun pressed against the side of the woman's head.

"Not another step or this woman and her brat dies, Morgan. I've had enough of you."

"Not near enough, Kelton. You shoot her and you lose your shield, then you die as slow as I can do it. Knees first, I think. Yep, I'll shoot you in both knees first, then mess up both shoulders with .45 slugs right through the shoulder joints. You might not be conscious by that time, but a bucket of water will bring you up screaming. Better let the woman go."

Kelton didn't respond. He backed up toward the screen door, opened it and kicked it wide, then pulled the woman and child into the darkness of the screened back porch. Buckskin darted to the side of the house and around the corner.

Damn! This complicated things. Couldn't let him hurt the woman or child. Buckskin showed himself past the corner for a second and darted back. A six-gun round splintered the board on the corner near where his head had been.

Front door? No, Kelton would think of that. Window? Maybe. He looked at the side of the house and saw two windows. The first one was locked with a thumb twist. The second double-hung window pushed upward silently. He crawled inside and moved without a sound through the bedroom to the door.

With infinite care he turned the knob and edged the door open. Through the crack he could see into the hallway. Nobody there. He moved down it silently toward sounds of voices. Beyond lay a living room that gave way in an arch to the kitchen.

Kelton stood in front of the woman. Her dress had been ripped to her waist and her breasts showed. Kelton said something and she started to slap him, but he squeezed her breasts until she screeched with pain.

Buckskin couldn't risk a shot. The woman almost covered the man now from his view. He waited.

"After I kill this damned spying Morgan, you and me gonna have us a time, pretty lady. Oh, yes, we are."

Kelton looked behind him, then out the kitchen door into the screened porch. "Where the hell is that guy?"

Buckskin wasn't far away, but wasn't in any position to help the woman. He wouldn't do anything that might harm her, or let Kelton hurt her or the little girl. He pressed against the wall just inside the hallway. He could hear the voices, but didn't dare lift up to look at them again. One clean shot was all he needed, but he had no idea how to get it. Maybe the kitchen door from ground level.

By the time he got to the kitchen door, no one remained in the kitchen. He slipped in and took quiet steps to the door leading into the small living room. The woman sat on a chair next to a table. Kelton stood next to her. Her small daughter played with a doll on the floor next to her.

"Where is he?" Kelton shouted. "I could be cutting you into little pieces. Where is he?"

Buckskin saw his chance. The woman held something in her lap, a sewing basket. She moved some cloth and picked up a pair of scissors, holding them like a dagger. Kelton turned sideways to check the front door. The woman sprang from the chair, ready to plunge the scissors into Kelton. He turned back and saw her in time to lunge to the side. The scissors stabbed down and missed his chest, but the sharp points dug into his left wrist and plunged all the way through.

Kelton screamed in pain and fury. He turned, dropped his six-gun and tugged at the scissors with his right hand. The woman stood there, blocking any shot Buckskin had. Then she laughed. She scooped up the six-gun, cocked it and fired into the floor.

Buckskin missed his chance at a shot as the woman bent down. Now she blocked him again.

"Get out," she ordered. "You come around here again I'll kill you." Kelton backed away, then turned and ran for the front door. Buckskin snapped a shot at him just past the woman, but missed, and the lawyer rushed out the front door.

Buckskin circled the house and found his target 40 yards ahead as Kelton sprinted down the hint of a street. They were past most of the houses now, on the way toward the Florissant road.

Where was he going? Buckskin settled into his familiar trot behind the man. Buckskin had never been a speedster when it came to running. In school the other boys had beat him at the short distances, but he could outlast them in mile and two-mile races. He'd get Kelton, he just didn't know where or how. Now Kelton was 50 yards ahead. Too far for a revolver shot.

They ran on. They left the last house behind. Kelton slowed and Buckskin's relentless pace closed the gap. Kelton turned more toward the road across a half mile of rough land. A number of gullies had been created by winter rains that couldn't soak in.

Kelton dropped down the side of a ravine and for a moment was out of sight. He didn't have the revolver now so he couldn't be much of a threat. Buckskin ran forward. Kelton looked back as he scrambled up the far side of the arroyo. He screeched in pain once when he fell on his left arm. Then he jumped up and hurried on across the flat land.

Another 20 yards ahead lay a second ravine. Buckskin watched Kelton hesitate, then plunge down it. Buckskin figured if he sprinted he might get to the near bank before Kelton could scratch his way up the far side.

He heard a scream. Buckskin ran to the edge of the gully and looked down. Kelton lay near the bottom on top of a large flat rock. He evidently had tripped and rolled down the 20-foot-deep cut.

The rock moved. Buckskin looked closer. The top of the rock slithered and crawled and rattled in a chaos of confusion.

Rattlesnakes.

Kelton screamed again. Buckskin saw a snake strike, venting its venom into the pink flesh of Kelton's arm. The rattling of the snakes increased, and now a dozen snakes struck Kelton in the face, the cheeks, the neck, bit through his clothing at arms and legs.

For a moment Buckskin thought of running down there and dragging Kelton away from the rock. Then Kelton's last scream of panic and fear and desperation ended in a choking sound as he passed out.

One rattlesnake bite was seldom fatal, Buckskin knew. Two or three were serious. Four could be fatal. And 20 or 30 could pump so much poison into the flesh that it could kill a grown man in minutes.

How many snakes on the rock? A hundred? More?

It was far too late to try to rescue Kelton.

Cripple Creek Songbird

Buckskin holstered his weapon and walked back toward town. To kill a rattlesnake, the best way is to cut off its head. Now the snakes had cut off the head of the Five Star conspiracy. Miles Kelton was either dead or would be in an hour at the most. Now all that remained were the two big mine owners who had participated in the scheme. They would have to see the light. Buckskin had just the idea to make them come into line.

Chapter Twenty-seven

It was just after seven o'clock that same evening when the mine owners met in the big office of Cluny Norman's at the All American mine. The four owners Buckskin had been meeting with were there as well as the two renegades, Uriah York of the Gold Hill mine and Quinn Forbes of the Poverty.

Cluny had met the men at the door and all were in a somber mood. He didn't shake hands with York or Forbes. They all sat in straight-backed chairs and looked at Cluny behind his desk.

"Thank you all for coming. We have some important business to take care of. I think you all know Buckskin Morgan. I'll turn the meeting over to him."

Buckskin stood and went to the front of the room beside the desk. He looked at each of the miners. Neither York or Forbes would meet his gaze.

"I have an announcement. Miles Kelton is dead."

Four of the men in the room erupted with surprise and questions. Forbes and Uriah sat there grim-faced, silent.

"What happened?" Cluny asked.

Buckskin held up his hands to quiet the men. "No, I didn't kill him. He fell into a gully out east of town. He landed on a flat rock that must have had a hundred rattlesnakes sunning themselves. I couldn't count the times he was bitten."

"You were chasing him?" York asked.

"Yes. He tried to kill me three times. It was my turn to take a shot at him, but he got away with the help of the barkeep at the Deep Shaft Saloon and ran out of town."

"Good," Langdon said. "Glad that bastard is dead. Now maybe things can get back to normal around here."

Quinn Forbes started to say something but stopped.

"The next thing I want to talk about is Five Star," Buckskin said. York and Forbes looked up quickly, frowns etching their faces.

"Yes, Mr. Forbes, yes, Mr. York. We know all about your conspiracy with Miles Kelton to take over as many mines in this area as possible. We know that the three of you conspired to attack and damage two mines owned by others. We know that you conspired in the death of one miner, Earl Jode. We are aware of your scheming and have brought you here tonight for a settlement. What do you have to say for yourselves?"

York turned and stared at the other men. "You can't prove a thing. Neither of us did anything illegal that you can prove. We'll face you in court anytime you want."

"This will never get to court, York. We'll handle this the same way that you did, on our own, with our own people. A few facts. We know that Larry Douglas was murdered by your group. We know that Earl Jode was killed by the Five Star. We know that your men burned and destroyed buildings and equipment at the Princess mine. We know that two of your men assaulted and tried to rob and destroy the office building of the First Find mine.

"If we wanted to we could put you both on trial for murder, which we probably should do. Instead we want some instant justice. You can fight us if you want to, but it will result in the total ruin of your mines and your fortunes. Abide by our judgments and penalties, or suffer total destruction. Which shall it be?"

Uriah York leaped to his feet and paced the room. "By God, you can't do this to us. We live in America. We're free to run our businesses. We're citizens. We don't have to knuckle under to a bunch of vigilantes like you."

"Mr. York," Buckskin said, his voice level and deadly. "You've had at least a silent hand in the deaths of three men. You've been caught. You conspired with others to defraud honest Americans out of their property. You've been caught. You have lost your right to demand much of anything."

Quinn Forbes looked at York. "Sit down and shut up, Uriah, until we hear their suggestions. He's dead right, we've been caught. Now we have to take our punishment."

"Go to hell, Forbes. I'm getting out of here." York started for the door. Buckskin drew his Colt and shot the man in the right thigh. The explosion of the round in the room sounded like a thunderclap and rendered them all unable to hear for half a minute.

York stumbled forward and fell on his face. He screeched in pain.

Buckskin was the first one to him. He rolled him over and used his kerchief to tie up the exit wound that bled like a throat-slit shoat. York glared at Buckskin.

"I'd guess you're the skunk who shot me in the back," York said.

"Guess all you want, York. It's about all you have left."

Buckskin helped the mine owner up and back to a chair. He stared at York and then Forbes. "Are you both ready to hear what you both will be required to do?"

"What happens if we don't do it?" York brayed.

"Then your mine will be destroyed, your mansion burned down, you and your family run out of town with a death threat on you if you're ever seen in this county again."

"Shut up, Uriah, and listen," Forbes said.

Buckskin looked at York, who shrugged.

"You two will pay the complete cost for restoring the Princess mine to its original condition. Work is being done, you will pay for it. An initial payment of twenty-five thousand dollars by each of you will be required before the end of the banking day tomorrow."

"What the hell!" Uriah thundered. Forbes hit him in the shoulder with his fist and the surprised mine owner didn't go on.

"You will return the property of Earl Jode to his widow and other members of his family, after having dug out a new shaft to the tunnels, and dug out the tunnels You will provide the workers and material to do the job, or pay for the cost of doing the job. You will each make a deposit of five thousand dollars in the Earl Jode mine account at the bank before the end of the business day tomorrow."

Buckskin stopped and looked at both mine owners. Forbes nodded. Uriah York scowled and turned red in the face. He gripped the sides of the chair with both hands.

Buckskin consulted a pad of paper and continued. "You both will contribute to a fund for the widow of the slain guard on the recent gold ore wagon shipment. The widow, Mrs. John Garlish, will be compensated twenty thousand dollars for her loss."

"We didn't have nothing to do with that," Forbes said. "That was Kelton's own little thievery."

"Hard to prove now. The twenty thousand will be deposited in the bank by tomorrow noon in the name of Mrs. John Garlish.

"Since we believe that Godfrey Rudolph was a

co-conspirator with you in Five Star, we will not penalize you. We understand that Mrs. Rudolph is in control of the mine. Miles Kelton's share in the mine will be torn up, rendered null and void."

Forbes sat there with his head hanging down. Uriah York had lost his anger and now slowly shook his head.

"All of these criminal charges will be detailed, written down with names and addresses of witnesses, dates given, and when the document is completed, each of your gentlemen will sign it as a confession."

"By God, no!" York thundered.

"Then you'll be on the next train out of town tomorrow and the Cripple Creek mine owners association will take over control of your mine to run for the benefit of its employees and the town of Cripple Creek."

"I hope you rot in hell, Morgan."

"You tried to put me there at least five times, remember? None of them worked. Now, will you sign the document or are you ready to travel right now without your family?"

"Bastard."

"It actually is easier than you think to go straight and not be a son of a bitch, York. You decide now. Sign or not sign?"

"I'll sign, Forbes said.

York growled and turned away from them. When he looked back there were tears in his eyes. He nodded. "I'll sign."

"Good, now we come to the secondary compensation. Cripple Creek needs a new schoolhouse.

Somewhere that the kids can get a good education. You two gentlemen will each anonymously donate twenty thousand dollars to the school district to build a new school. No one will know who supplied the cash."

"Why don't you just bleed us into bankruptcy while you're at it?" York wailed.

"Your mine will earn about three million dollars in profits before it runs dry, York. What are you complaining about? Oh, the confessions, signed by both of you and done in duplicate on a typewriter, will be kept in separate locked boxes of both Mr. Cluny and the district attorney in the Springs. They will be sealed and not opened unless requested by either Mr. Cluny or Mr. Purvis." Buckskin checked his list, then nodded.

"Now, I think that about takes care of my business."

Cluny looked at York. "Uriah, don't ever try this damned Five Star shit again. You do and I'll kill you myself. Let's just take care of our mining and let the others find their own gold. There's plenty for everyone here in Cripple Creek."

York and Forbes stood.

"Gentlemen, we'll all see the two of you right here tomorrow at noon," Buckskin said. "You can make the payments in cash, by bank draft, or by gold bullion, whichever you choose. Twelve o'clock sharp right here, or you better hire an army to protect yourselves and your property because I'll be coming after you."

"Like the way you burned down my storage shed," York snarled.

"You had a fire? How unfortunate. Accidents can happen."

The two mine owners walked out of the office, and Buckskin saw them to the office building door.

"Twelve sharp tomorrow," Buckskin said in one parting jab. Back inside the office, the five men worked for an hour writing down notes on the crimes the two mine owners had committed or been a party to.

"My secretary will type this up, and make three copies," Cluny said. "Then we'll get the men to sign the confessions. With two copies we'll be sure that they won't be lost." They shook hands all the way around and couldn't keep the grins off their faces.

"I'll get my mine back just the way she was, or maybe a little better," Victor Irwin of the Princess said.

Buckskin scowled. "Ties that up well, but what about the Lucky Lady mine?"

The other miners shot questioning looks at Buckskin. He explained the series of events that led to the two one-eighth shares he and Cluny each owned and the apex that surfaced on Buckskin's claim.

"Hell, that means you own the whole thing," Ira Langdon said. "You own anything they've taken out of it."

"Sounds good to me," Buckskin said. "The way I figure it, Cluny's one-eighth share should still be good. I'll jump that to an even half the mine, Cluny, if you'll take over and develop it."

Cluny ran fingers through his hair. "Got one

mine that's taking up my time." He frowned. "Guess I could assign a manager to it to get it rolling. Take some money."

"That's why you get half the mine, Cluny. You're the one who's putting up the cash. I don't have any." The men all laughed. "Seriously, Cluny. Wouldn't that be a fair deal all the way around?"

The mine owner rubbed his hand over his face, then looked out at Buckskin from one eye. "Seems as though it would work," Cluny said.

"Damn," Purvis said. "I was about to offer to take the deal if Cluny was dumb enough to pass it up."

Buckskin let out a sigh. "Well, now I do feel better. You draw up the papers and I'll sign them tomorrow. I've still got that little runaway girl to find."

"She can't be in Cripple Creek," Irwin said, "or you would have found her by now."

Buckskin waved and walked out of the mine office. He stepped from the lighted doorway in the dark quickly so he wouldn't make an easy target. He wasn't sure just how convinced those two miners were that the Five Star had been blasted apart.

Nobody shot, nobody challenged him on the dark walk back to Mrs. Johnson's boardinghouse.

It was early. Emily and Mae sat at the living room table playing cards. He walked in and they waved.

"I'll see your five matches and I'll raise you two buttons and a toothpick," Mae said. She hesitated. "That's two more matches if you want to call."

Emily frowned, checked her cards, pushed them

together and put them flat on the table. She dropped two kitchen matches into the pot. "I call."

Mae wailed. "Darn. Nothing. I have a jack high."

Emily giggled. "Beats me, I only have a ten high."

"This a closed game, or can anybody get in?" Buckskin asked.

"Good, fresh matches in the game," Emily said. "Get a handful out of that box over the stove in the kitchen."

After the second hand, Emily asked him. "How did the show down go with the mine owners?"

"Good. They caved in the way we figured they would. We have too much evidence against them."

"So that's about over."

"We wind it up tomorrow noon."

"Then you're leaving?" Emily asked.

"Tomorrow I'll be out of a job. I haven't found Harriet Braithwaite and her father gave me the deadline. I'll have to go back to Denver, I guess, and admit I'm stumped."

"Too bad," Mae said, looking at Emily. "It's your deal." They played another half hour. Then Mae said she had some reading to get done tonight. Buckskin looked at her.

"You said you'd watch round town for Harriet. Did you find out anything?"

Mae nodded. "Maybe, I'm not sure. This one girl said she had heard about you. She didn't come right out and say she was Harriet, but I had the feeling she could be. You know, just a hunch."

Buckskin watched her, more interested now.

"You really think this girl might be Harriet Braithwaite?"

"She's the right age, about the right size. I don't know what to tell you. She hinted around that she was thinking of going back home, but she didn't say Denver. She told me that tomorrow she was going to make up her mind. I think she'll tell me in the afternoon. I'm going to have an ice cream with her at the hotel."

Buckskin shuffled the cards. "That's a slight glimmer of hope. More than I've had in two weeks. I better hang around another day and see what happens after your ice cream."

Mae grinned, nodded at Buckskin and hurried into the kitchen and back to her room. They could hear the bolt on her door slide into place.

"What happened to the young swain tonight?"

"Gomer had to work late. Something about getting ready for an audit. That's why we were playing cards. She's pretty well gone on this young man. It sounds serious."

"She's just a child."

"She's eighteen, a woman who knows her mind, and a few men are not going to tell her what to do. The man who marries her should be a strong one."

Emily stood. "You tired of playing cards?"

"Yeah. I feel like celebrating."

"How about a very nice white wine?"

"Best we can do?"

"Yeah. After my husband was killed I drank up half the town before I got control of myself. Now I don't touch anything stronger than a good wine."

Cripple Creek Songbird

She brought the wine from the kitchen and they went to his bedroom. It was that much farther away from Mae and the room directly above was vacant.

Chapter Twenty-eight

Buckskin lay on his bed in his room with Emily folded against him. She sighed and stroked his face, then his hair.

"You are just so damn good. Buckskin, you're spoiling me for other men, you know that. You don't even care. For you there'll be another woman in another town."

Buckskin chuckled. "Poor put-upon Widow Johnson. A week after I'm gone, you'll be seducing another young boarder who will be thrilled to be taken to bed by a more experienced woman. You'll love it."

She sat up and stared down at him. Then she smiled. "Buckskin Lee Morgan, I guess you've got it about right. But it will never be this sweet, this satisfying. I never was done better by my husband. Did I tell you that?"

Buckskin sat up and caressed her full breasts, tweaking the nipples until she purred.

"See what I mean?" she said. "Most men want a quick pop and then they can't wait to get their pants on. They don't understand how a woman works. It ain't just the poking she likes, it's all the kisses and soft talking and caressing and feeling and wanting before she even gets her clothes off. It's the romance of the whole thing. Then the poking and afterwards more kissing and touching and loving. We're not animls who mate and grunt and run away. Got to be more to it than that."

She reached over and kissed him. He kissed her back, then again, and pushed his tongue into her mouth. Emily moaned softly and pressed against him. When the kiss ended she sighed again and looked at him. A tear seeped over her eyelid and ran down her cheek.

"Damn, I wish you weren't going. Chew on me a little. It really makes me hot when you chew on my titties."

Buckskin moved down and licked her breasts, then nibbled at her growing nipples. When she began to pant, he sucked a breast into his mouth and chewed tenderly on her pink flesh.

"Oh my Gawd, oh my Gawd, oh my Gawd, but that is wonderful. I wish you was inside me right now just fucking up a storm. Damn, but I want you again, Buckskin."

She fell back on the bed and he came away from her breasts. She spread her legs and lifted her knees. Buckskin shifted so he knelt between her knees.

"Hurry, damn you! Hurry, I'm burning up inside."

He was hard in an instant and probed gently, then drove into her moist center in one stoke.

"Oh, Mother of Heaven!" Emily shouted. Then she moaned and panted and her hips began to thrust upward hard meeting him. She gasped and relaxed for a moment. Then it seemed to Buckskin that she tightened every muscle in her body. Her hips pounded upward in a frantic rhythm and she shivered; then spasms ripped through her making her whole body vibrate with the strength of the climax. She wailed softly and pounded harder with her hips until the spasms trailed off and she sighed. Her eyes blinked open an instant later.

"Oh, I forgot about you." She humped at him again and this time he met her thrust for thrust until sweat beaded his forehead and their pelvic bones crashed together. It was longer this time before he felt the magic rush of raw sexual power as the fluids spurted deep inside him and shot downstream until he bellowed in a roar of satisfaction and drove hard at her six times before he finished and fell on top of her exahusted and spent.

Her arms came around him strapping him to her. "You'll never get away from me now," she whispered in his ear. He only half heard her as he panted for breath, gasping in all the oxygen he could to replenish his tired muscles.

Neither of them spoke for a while. Then she moved under him and he lifted away and sat on the bed. She came up beside him and caught his hand.

"Now, that was a good fuck, a wonderful love-making that I'll remember a long time." She looked at him and turned his face around to hers. "You'll be gone in two days, I'd bet on it. So we have tonight and maybe tomorrow night."

"You sound pretty sure. What if Mae's little friend is Harriet and I have a chase to find her, or if it takes a while to convince her to go back to her family?"

"Trust me. I know about these things."

He reached over and kissed her lips, a soft, gentle kiss that made her gasp.

"See what I mean?" she asked. "How many men would do that after they got fucked? One in a thousand maybe. You're the one."

"You keep talking like that and I might take you with me back to Denver."

"Again, there you go, being nice after getting fucked. Most men would have their pants on by now, pat my naked tits and be out the door."

"You're just feeling sad tonight. Maybe before morning I'll get you in a better mood."

"I hope so. Where did we put that wine bottle? We haven't even opened it yet."

Before midnight the bottle was empty and the pair slept soundly.

The next morning neither one woke up until ten o'clock. Mae sat in the kitchen grinning as

Emily staggered in and poured herself a cup of coffee.

"Never drink wine, little one," Emily said. "It leaves you dead for two days. I guess I missed breakfast."

"That you did," Mae said laughing. "But I managed quite well and you're welcome. Boy, are you a mess."

"Oh, damn. Thanks for your kind words. I've got to duck my head in a bucket of cold water for about an hour. Don't hold up lunch for me."

Emily started for the door, then stopped. "Have you decided about telling him?"

"Yes. Both of us will tell him this afternoon after Gomer gets off work."

"Good. Right thing to do. You'll never be sorry. Right now I'm going to work on this hang-down head of mine. Thanks again for doing breakfast for me."

Mae put down her coffee cup. "You have a good night?"

Emily worked up a wonderful smile and nodded. "Oh, yes, but one of the last with Buckskin. Marvelous. Except for that damn wine." She waved and walked with great care back to her bedroom.

Buckskin shaved in cold water in his room, put on a town shirt and pants and brown vest and his low-crown brown hat and made it to the twelve o'clock meeting at the All American mine office five minutes early. The four honest miners were there. Cluny gave Bucskskin a copy of the confession to read. He skimmed it quickly. Everything was there they had talked about.

"Now if they show up and if they'll sign . . ."

Just then the two other men walked in. Both wore suits and hats and looked anything but happy.

"Is this where the execution takes place?" Uriah York asked.

"No execution is planned, but we can arrange it if that's what you want," Buckskin said.

"Pay him no mind," Quinn Forbes said. "He's a big bear whose claws have been pulled and he's still mad but can't do anything about it. Now, where's that damned paper? I ain't gonna sign anything until I read it."

Copies of the confession were given to both men. They sat down and read. Forbes didn't say a word. Four times York roared in anger, but calmed down enough to finish reading it. When he finished, he threw the three typed pages down on Cluny's desk.

"You got a pen or do I sign the damned thing in blood?"

Cluny provided a steel-tipped pen and an ink-well. Both men signed the two copies of the confession.

"Now for the cash," Buckskin said.

The men reluctantly brought out envelopes with bank drafts in them. Buckskin looked at the drafts. They appeared to be in order. All were on Denver or Colorado Springs banks. He checked off the amounts against the list he had made. Then he looked up.

"The dollar amounts are right, gentlemen. The money will go to the people stipulated in your confessions. This money will help pay back some of the damage you've done in this town. However, no amount of money can bring back a life. In ancient times you would have had to sacrifice yourself or one of the members of your immediate family to compensate for the death of another person. Be glad we've progressed a little from those days.

"Remember, if any of these checks don't clear, and if you ever start up anything like the Five Star conspiracy again, I'll be on you like a dozen rattlesnakes."

The two castigated mine owners stood and left the room. Victor Irwin looked at the two checks Buckskin handed him.

"Fifty thousand dollars. Oh, yes! Now I can get that building up and everything back to normal. I'll repay you men who sent over workers. You figure out a bill for me. I'm not paying, Forbes and York are paying, so do it right. I better get to the bank so they can start clearing these checks. It turned out to be a fine day after all."

Cluny took the floor and held an envelope. "Buckskin, we know that we never could have put down the Five Star mess the way it happened if you hadn't been here. You did all the work. We were just in support. We figure that you saved each of us more than fifty thousand dollars we would have spent before we would have eventually put down the Five Star.

"Any way of looking at it, we owe you just one hell of a lot. So, we're making a token payment to you. Each of the four of us are kicking in a few bucks to show our appreciation." He handed Buckskin the envelope.

"Hey, I didn't sign you up as clients," Buckskin said. "I did this because Miles Kelton tried to have me killed. Made me damn mad. You men don't owe me a thing." He handed the envelope back to Cluny.

"Fine, we don't owe you a thing. What this is is a small reward for helping us out. And it's a gift from one friend to another and can't be refused or we would be so embarrassed that we might just jump off a cliff somewhere." He handed the envelope back to Buckskin.

"You're a hard man, Cluny." Buckskin unsealed the envelope and looked inside. There were four checks made out to him in the amount of $5,000 each: $20,000. He shook his head. "Just can't be."

"Can be, is and will remain that way," Victor Irwin said. "We all decided. It's yours and you damn well earned it. I'd be out of business or dead if it wasn't for you. By rights we should have made it ten thousand each. So enjoy."

The others voiced their approval and Buckskin lifted his brows and sat down. "Surprise," he said. "I really never expected anything like this."

"Good," Cluny said. "For once we surprised you."

They talked about their sweet victory, and

then the pull of business called. Irwin left and soon after that Nate and Ira left as well. Then Cluny took out a paper and showed it to Buckskin. It was a four-page contract between the two of them establishing a 50-50 partnership in the Lucky Lady Mine.

"It's all there the way we talked about. We're equal partners. I'm responsible for financing, developing and running the mine. We split the profits down the middle. Read it through."

Buckskin turned to the last page and signed both copies of the contract. Cluny had already signed them. Buckskin put a copy in his shirt pocket.

"Let's go out and take a look at our new mine," Cluny said. "I sent over a crew this morning. The ramrod over there is Charlie Carson. He's the mine manager. Right now he's got six men, which is about all that can work in that situation. As soon as we find out where that vein goes. the real work will begin."

"Any chance it'll turn and go straight down and get fat and rich?" Buckskin asked.

"A good chance. Several of the working mines in that area have a strata shift. I'd guess this one will do the same. If it's anything like another nearby mine, it could make you a rich man."

Buckskin lifted his brows. "Afraid I wouldn't know what to do with money. I'm a workingman."

"Me too," Cluny said. "One nice thing is that

you can learn to get used to having money.
Now, let's take a walk."

Ten minutes later at the Lucky Lady Mine,
work had finished on punching out the upthrust
to the surface. The miners were working on the
far end of the vein where it headed downhill.
Buckskin and Cluny went down the ladder and
looked at the section that had been boarded up.
The vein was starting to turn downward more
sharply.

Charlie Carson was a big man with a big grin.
He had shaken Buckskin's hand and the two
had hit it off at once.

"Look at the angle," Charlie said. "I'd bet in
another fifteen to twenty feet this vein will be
going straight down and expanding in size and
we can really start diging out some gold."

On the surface a new crew rolled up with
three wagons loaded with lumber. Cluny
pointed them at some stakes with red cloth on
the tops.

"Right over there, boys. See if you can get it
put up in three days."

He turned to Buckskin. "That's the office,
storeroom and guard shack until we get some
more buildings put up. Can't be sure where to
place things until we get the downturn on that
vein. That's where the main shaft will be, of
course."

Buckskin shook his head. "Looks like you
have things in gear here, Mr. Cluny Norman,
my partner. I won't have a worry. And I'd figure
that it will take at least six months before you

dig out enough gold to pay off all the expenses. You keep a good set of books on the cost factor here. Don't lend men from one mine to the other without getting the costs down against the Lucky Lady."

"Yep. Got a new set of books working this morning on the Lucky Lady. I like the looks of that vein down there. Could be that we'll be in the black within three months. Before you get away from here, I'll need a permanent address for you. A spot where I can send your profit checks."

Buckskin told him the address. Charlie wrote it down on a clipboard he carried.

"Another small matter I need to take care of," Buckskin said. "I'll see you before I leave town." He shook his head watching the new crew setting pier blocks, lining up the new building's foundation and laying down the beams. "You really get things moving, Cluny. Glad I picked a good partner."

Five minutes later, he swept into the Johnson boardinghouse. He went straight to his room and took out the picture of Harriet Braithwaite and studied it.

"I'll be damned," Buckskin said softly. It could be what he'd suspected on the walk back there. He took the picture and went into the living room, then to the kitchen, where the two women sat peeling potatoes. They said hello and he waved. He sat down opposite the girl and stared at the picture. Then he used his hands and framed the picture so he couldn't see the girl's blond hair. He studied just the face.

"I'll be damned," he said.

Emily smiled.

Mae giggled.

"I'll be double damned." He looked up at Emily. "You knew, didn't you?"

"Just the last two or three days. I promised I wouldn't tell."

"Harriet Braithwaite. Were you ever going to tell me?"

"Sure. I would have told you this afternoon, after I had that meeting with my imaginary friend."

"Oh, damn. I've been living here with you right under my long and unresponsive nose for, what, a week and a half or so, and I never noticed. Red hair. Niece from Kansas City. It all flowed so naturally and so reasonably that I never stopped to take a close look at 'Mae' here."

"Here at the boardinghouse isn't the first time you met me," Harriet said. "Remember the first day you came to town and you talked to Abe Alexander at his hardware and general store?"

"The young boy with brown hair?" Buckskin exploded. "That was you too? You disguised yourself as a boy to get a job and so I wouldn't recognize you. Sure as hell worked. Did Abe know?"

"No, he didn't have any idea," Harriet said. "When Aunt Emily here came in the store, I decided I should work for her. At least then I could be a girl again."

Buckskin poured himself a cup of coffee and sat back at the table. "This is turning out to be a pretty good day after all. Cluny Norman is an equal partner with me in my gold mine and he's going to develop it. Now I locate the elusive Miss Braithwaite. I'm glad you decided that you want to go home. Your folks are really worried about you."

"I hoped that they would worry a little, but I don't think they're all broken up. I've been living away from home most of the time for the last four years." She frowned. "But about going home. There is one major problem. I was hoping that you might be able to help me with it."

Chapter Twenty-nine

Buckskin Morgan stared at the young girl. "I don't understand, Harriet. How could you have a major problem? If it's money, that's no worry."

"It's not money, It's Gomer."

"The Gomer I know, the one who lives here?"

"Yes. I'm in love with him and we talked about getting married. Then I told him who I am and now he's starting to have second thoughts."

"Like he thinks your father might squash him and kick him into a Denver jail?"

Harriet Braithwaite nodded and her frown deepened. "That or much worse. He thinks my father is a monster and that anyone who has even kissed his little girl will get charged with rape and railroaded right into prison for twenty years. I keep telling him there won't be a problem.

"Yes, Mr. Morgan, I'm still a virgin. Nothing too serious happened those times on the front porch swing. I never let Gomer into my room. I'm not damaged goods, as you men love to say."

"Then what's the problem?"

"Convincing Gomer that I love him and want to marry him and that I want him to come to Denver with us tomorrow."

"Tomorrow? Yes, I can see that Gomer might think that was rushing things a little." Buckskin grinned. "Just how hard have you been pushing him? You know, you probably have a lot of the same traits that you think your father has. Like being a little on the bossy side, like wanting your own way, like not giving others enough room so they can make up their own minds."

"That's ridiculous. I'm easy to get along with, open-minded, and . . ." She stopped. "Oh, darn. That is just exactly what my father would say if I accused him of the same things." She wailed and threw her arms around Emily. "Am I really that bad?"

"Of course not, Harriet. Of course not. It's just the big bad male animal talking there."

Buckskin grinned and stood. "Get your hat, young lady. We're going calling."

"Where?"

"To the All American mine company."

"But he doesn't get off work until five o'clock."

"If he's going to go to Denver with us, it

doesn't matter much how long he works today, does it? I know his boss, it will be just fine. The three of us need to have a long talk."

Harriet stood and her delicate chin came out and she stared hard at Buckskin. "Mr. Morgan, are you trying to help me with Gomer or just trying to get me back to Denver?"

"If I don't help you with Gomer, then neither of you will be going back to Denver."

She grinned. "Good, let's go."

They found Gomer in a small office at the side of the big building that held the clerks and accountants. He was surprised to see Harriet.

"You talk to him a minute. I'll go see Cluny Norman and tell him what's going on."

When Buckskin came back, Gomer had a frown edging into his features. Harriet had her arms folded and sat in his chair in back of his desk.

"First sight?" Buckskin said. "Good, now let me explain a few things and ask a few questions. Gomer, what's your intentions toward this small and beautiful young lady?"

"Intentions? I want to marry her. I don't want to go to Denver and get smashed by her father."

"Daddy doesn't—" Buckskin held up his hand and stopped her.

"You want to marry the girl. Fine. Do you enjoy your work here?"

"Yes. It's fulfilling, exciting. I've worked up to be the head accountant."

"Are you afraid to try a new business, a new situation where there might be a hundred accountants instead of three or four?"

"Certainly not. I know my trade. I can do better at it than anyone."

"So you're afraid of Mr. Hercules Braithwaite?"

"Oh, yes, indeed. He's so rich and has so much power he could squash a little bug like me."

"Did it ever occur to you that he wouldn't do anything to hurt his daughter? Anything he might do to you would hurt her terribly, and drive her away from her family. He wouldn't risk that.

"With the same logic, he loves his daughter and wants to do everything that he can to make her happy. Now that you're in the picture, he'll want to keep you happy, so she will be happy. Is that too much happiness for you to deal with?"

Gomer stood there blinking. He started to say something, then stopped. "Oh, well, yes, I can see your point."

"Now, another thing. You're in a dead-end job here. You're as far as you can go. No more promotions. You could spend the next fifteen years as head accountant here. If you go to Denver, there's a guarantee that you'll get a good job as an accountant or a manager in one of the Braithwaite firms. There your future is as big and broad and wonderful as you want to make it.

"Consider this. Hercules Braithwaite has no sons. His only child is this small beautiful package here. If you marry her, there would be an extremely good chance that someday you could take over the whole Braithwaite empire."

Gomer Haskel's eyes went wide. Then he sat down quickly on the edge of the desk. Harriet grinned and stood and took his arm.

"Come on, Gomer. I'll help you pack," she said.

His eyes were glazed. He looked at Buckskin, who nodded.

"But I need to talk to Mr. Norman, to give him two weeks notice, to tell him how much I've enjoyed working for him."

Buckskin nodded. "All done, Gomer. I told Cluny Norman what was happening. He says he understands and wishes you well and he gave me this fifty-dollar bill to give you as a bonus for doing such good work. We're free to go."

Back at the boardinghouse, the four of them gathered in the kitchen. Supper was under way. Harriet finished peeling potatoes and Emily worked on getting the roast and vegetables just right. Gomer and Buckskin sat at the table sipping cinnamon-flavored coffee.

Gomer looked at his pocket watch. "Yes, it's much too late to be heading for Denver now. We'll stay here tonight and get the first stage for Florissant in the morning. It leaves at eight-fifteen so it can be there in time for the train."

"Yes, Gomer. That sounds like a good plan," Harriet said, her tone soft, her manner submissive.

Buckskin looked at Emily, who had let her

mouth drop open when she heard Harriet's reply. She winked at Buckskin.

Supper was a banquet that night, with the roast and four kinds of vegetables and mounds of mashed potatoes and good skillet beef gravy and thick slices of bread with fresh butter and strawberry jam.

When the other boarders left the table, the four remaining were still smiling.

That night Gomer and Harriet sat on opposite ends of the porch platform swing and made plans for the future.

Emily coaxed Buckskin into going to his room for one last night of lovemaking.

"No wine," he said, and Emily grinned.

The trip to Denver went on schedule. Buckskin had wired Hercules Braithwaite from Florissant that he had found Harriet, that she was safe, unharmed, in good spirits and delighted to be returning home. He figured the surprise of Gomer Haskel was better delivered in person.

From Colorado Springs to Denver they talked about the best way to spring the news on Mr. Braithwaite.

"Maybe I should stay outside until after the reunion and then come in," Gomer said.

"I should say not," Harriet said. "I want you by my side every second. We'll both go in and meet Father. I'll tell him who you are and that we're going to be married. Then we'll talk about what job you'll have with the company."

They looked at Buckskin. "Safety in numbers," he said. "I think the best approach will be for all three of us to go into his office or home, wherever he is, and take him on all at once."

A few minutes later Buckskin thought of a better plan. "There's a public telephone in the railroad station. I'm sure your father's office has one. I'll telephone him and ask him if we can meet him at your home. That will be a better place, more familiar for you, Harriet, softer, less formal."

"Oh, yes. I like that. Mother will be there too, and I think she'll be relieved when I tell her that Gomer and I are to be married."

When they arrived in Denver, the public telephone wasn't working. Buckskin persuaded one of the railroad people to let him use a railroad phone and soon he had Hercules himself on the line.

"Mr. Braithwaite. This is Buckskin Morgan. We're in town and Harriet said she wants to go straight home. We'll get a cab and should be there shortly. Could we meet you there?"

"Meet you there? Well, yes, I suppose. I can cancel that meeting, do it tomorrow. All right. I'll be home in an hour or so."

Mrs.Braithwaite had no idea that Harriet was coming home, and she broke down and cried tears of relief when they all walked into the house a short time later.

She hugged Harriet. Then her eyes went wide when she realized the long blond hair had been dyed and cut.

"Your beautiful hair . . ."

"Gone, Mother. But hair can grow back. It's been fun being a redhead for a while." She turned. "Mother, this is Gomer, Gomer Haskel. He's the man I'm going to marry. I met him in Cripple Creek and we're both very much in love and I want you to be on my side in this if Father has any objections."

Her mother frowned and glanced at Gomer and gave him a hint of a strained smile.

"Harriet, dear, could I talk to you for a moment."

"Mother, no, don't worry. I'm not pregnant and I haven't been sleeping with Gomer. I'm still a virgin."

Mrs. Braithwaite took a step backward as if someone had slapped her. "Harriet, really."

"Mother, I knew that's what you were going to ask me. So I told you. I'm not a child, Mother. I won't be shipped off to some silly girls school. I'm a grown woman and I've found the man I love and want to spend the rest of my life with him. Isn't that what you did?"

"Well, yes, dear . . ."

"I know, I know, a six-month courting and a six-month engagement. This is the modern world, Mother. We're almost into the twentieth century. Things move faster now. I want you to promise to be on my side if Father objects."

"Well, he does seem like a nice boy."

"Mrs. Braithwaite," Gomer said. "I'm twenty-two years old and a qualified head accountant. I've been earning my living since I was sixteen."

"Yes, that's nice." She looked at Buckskin.

"And you must be Mr. Morgan, who went to find Harriet. We thank you. Did you tell Hercules that you were coming here?"

"Telephoned him, ma'am. He said he'd be along shortly."

"That could be a while. Let's go into the sitting room and make ourselves comfortable. I'll have Tilly bring us some iced lemonade."

"Mother?"

"Yes, yes, all right. I agree that you don't need to go back to that school. If this is the man you have decided upon, then I see no reason to oppose you. Accountant. So he could work in one of the stores."

"At the main headquarters office, Mother. Gomer is a trained accountant and manager."

"Yes, dear."

Before the iced lemonade came, the front door banged open and Hercules Braithwaite marched into the room. He looked at Harriet, scowled and walked closer.

"What the hell happened to your hair?"

"I had it cut, Daddy. Don't you like this new look?"

"Not much. I like your hair long."

"It's been that way since I was five. I'm not a little girl any longer." She turned and motioned to Gomer, who jumped to his feet. "Father, I'd like you to meet Gomer Haskel. Gomer is from Denver originally and had been working in Cripple Creek. Gomer and I are going to get married."

"Are you . . ."

"No, Daddy, I'm not pregnant. I'm not even damaged goods, as you men love to say. I love Gomer and we're going to live here and in two months we'll announce our engagement."

"Oh." Hercules seemed to have lost his train of thought. The iced lemonade came and he took the first glass and sat down.

"Daddy, Gomer is a trained accountant and accountant manager. He worked for the biggest mine in Cripple Creek. I was talking with Mother about what position he could take over in your headquarters office."

"What? Accountant. Yes, always a need for the men with the figures. Yes, I expect we can find a good position for him. Homer, was it?"

"No sir, my name is Gomer, Gomer Haskel."

"Yes, Gomer. All right. We'll talk about your position tomorrow." He looked around until he saw Buckskin. "Morgan, you did it. You found our little girl." He blinked and then stood. "It seems you and I have some business to attend to, Morgan. Will you ladies excuse us for a moment?"

He moved out of the room at a fast march and Buckskin fell in behind him.

In the den, with the door closed, he questioned Buckskin about Gomer.

"Yes, sir," Buckskin told him. "What she said about him is true. I stayed at the same boardinghouse where Gomer did. Soft-spoken, intelligent, good man with figures. Should fit into your firm well."

"We'll see. Good work. Let's see, the agreement was for twenty dollars a day and expenses and ten thousand for her safe return. Would you call Harriet safely returned?"

"In much better shape emotionally then when she left home," Buckskin said.

"You've been gone, what, about fourteen days? Expenses?"

"A hundred and fifty dollars."

Braithwaite put down the figures, totaled them and wrote out a bank draft. He made a note of the amount, then handed the check to Buckskin. "I think you'll find that the right amount."

Buckskin didn't even look at it. He slid it in the pocket of his jacket and nodded. "I'll say good-bye to Harriet and be gone. That's a mighty fine young lady you have there. I hope you appreciate her."

Back in the sitting room, Buckskin said good-bye to Mrs. Braithwaite, then to Harriet. She jumped up and ran over and gave him a big hug, then a kiss on the cheek.

"Thanks just ever so much," she said "I'm pleased with how this is working out."

"So am I," Buckskin said.

He found the front door, skipped down the steps to the street and hailed a passing cab. No use walking now that he was rich. He had over $30,000. A fortune—and he also was half owner of a gold mine that could really make him rich.

That night Buckskin stayed in the best room at the fanciest hotel in Denver. He ate a ten-dollar dinner in the dining room and then went to the opera. He hated opera, but if he was going to be rich . . .

After the opera he went back to his regular hotel with its small, dingy room and looked through the mail that had been pushed through the slot in his door. Bills, and letters and an advertisement or two. A long envelope in pale pink lay next on the stack. He picked it up. Perfumed. Maybe a job. Never could tell. He put the perfumed letter on the small desk and fell into bed. Tomorrow he'd take a look at the letter. Tomorrow or the next day. For a short time he was going to take it easy and at least pretend that he was rich. Then it would be back to work on a new assignment. Idly he wondered where it would be. He looked at the perfumed letter again, shook his head and turned out the light.